The Turing Test

The Turing Test

stories

Chris Beckett

LASTIC
PRESS

For my friends

*

Acknowledgements

Special thanks to David Pringle and Lee Montgomerie, formerly of Interzone, whose rejection letters 18 years ago were so detailed that they were almost a correspondence course and so encouraging that I kept on sending stories in. And to Gardner Dozois, Sheila Williams, Andy Cox, Jetse De Vries and not least Andrew Hook. The people who edit and publish magazines and anthologies, frequently for minimal reward, are the ones who make it possible for people like me to think of ourselves as writers. Which means a *huge* amount to us. For some strange reason.

Table of contents

Ghosts in the Machine:
Introduction by Alastair Reynolds

In an ideal world you wouldn't need me to tell you why you need to read Chris Beckett, and in particular you wouldn't need me to tell you why you need to read *The Turing Test*, Chris's new collection. He's a committed, serious writer of science fiction – subtle and adventurous in equal measure – and his stories have been appearing in major venues for the better part of two decades, attracting acclaim and (at least once) not a small measure of controversy. No less an authority than Paul di Fillipo described *The Holy Machine*, Chris's first novel, as a 'as triumph'. Really, he should already be on the radar of anyone who professes concern for science fiction as a literary form.

Unfortunately, that's not really how things work these days. Chris's problem, if you can call it that, is that he doesn't do the noisy self-promotion thing. He doesn't rant and rave on a blog, preaching to the choir. He doesn't spread himself around on message boards, pimping his latest story or book at every opportunity. He doesn't dominate convention panels or grandstand at the bar. That's not to say that Chris is some kind of nervous recluse, timidly disconnected from the razzle-dazzle of the science fiction scene. He's got a website, where he'll tell you something about himself. He goes to conventions. In person, he's as open and engaging a character as you could hope to meet. But perhaps because he hasn't ever gone out of his way to draw attention to himself, preferring to let his fiction speak for itself – and it's fiction that speaks quietly, inviting the careful reader to pay attention, rather than shouting down everyone else in the room – Chris isn't as well known as he should be. Which is why *The Turing Test* is a timely collection, showcasing his strengths to impressive effect. Let's hope that it goes some way to raising his profile, because Chris is exactly the kind of writer we ought to be making a bigger deal about.

A bit of history: Chris and I both owe our careers to Interzone, the UK's longest running SF magazine. We both made our first professional fiction sales there, with our debut stories appearing in 1990. Through the nineties and into the new decade, Chris went on to become one of Interzone's most reliable and prolific contributors, notching up an impressive nineteen stories – with, one presumes, much more to come. I'll confess that I didn't start paying due attention to Chris's work until he had already been publishing for some time, but once I'd read *The Warrior Half-and-Half* I knew that I'd found a writer whose work was very much to my taste. With the off-hand weirdness of its far-future setting juxtaposed with the fantastical nature of its protagonist, 'Warrior' was exactly my cup of tea – and the tale's sly, unexpected resolution is a delight. Although Chris is anything but a one-note writer, that melding of SF and fantasy elements is something that shines through in just about every story in this collection, most notably in the two 'shifter' tales, *Jazamine in the Green Wood* and *We Could Be Sisters*.

In these stories, the drug-induced ability of certain people to slip between alternate realities is an utterly matter-of-fact detail of the invented world, taken absolutely for granted by the characters – the arrival of a bewildered shifter in a small village no more remarkable in that world than, say, the arrival of a Polish immigrant in ours. And as the foregoing might imply, there are links between several of these stories, evidence of a writer sufficiently engaged with his themes to want to examine them from different angles. Nowhere is this more evident than in the two 'Clarissa Fall' stories contained herein, which offer a uniquely British take on the notion of virtual reality. Chris's conception of a crumbling, decaying London inhabited largely by disembodied intelligences (rendered with greater or lesser degrees of realism depending on their financial status in the virtual community – a lovely conceit) is a brilliant and poetic idea, ripe for exploration in a tranche of stories.

An altogether different future London is the setting for the two stories featuring cynical gallery manager Jessica, who undergoes something of an interpersonal crisis in the collection's title story, putting a decidedly human slant on the 'test' in question. The emergence of artificial intelligence is also a theme in Chris's well known story *La Macchina* – which in typical fashion ends not with robots about to storm the citadels (although that might well happen), but a tiff between two brothers in a hotel room. Come to his fiction looking for planet-busting explosions and big effects-heavy set-pieces (the kind of thing I do, basically) and you'll likely be disappointed. Approach Chris's stories on their own terms, and you'll find them rewarding and resonant. Unsurprisingly for a writer who cites Philip K Dick as a key influence, identity and the shifting nature of reality are favourite themes. Like Dick, Chris isn't particularly interested in SF as a dry exercise in extrapolating the future, as futile as that would inevitably prove. For Chris, the form is primarily a toolkit for examining the human condition, for getting to the heart of the questions that fascinate him. One senses that if SF wasn't up to the metaphorical burden Chris places on it, he'd happily utilise a different genre entirely – or maybe invent one from scratch. In these days of micro-classification, when it seems that all SF writers have to be slotted into neat little sub-genres – post-singularity, new retro space opera, cyber-noir, or whatever is the latest interstitial mashup – Chris is that vanishingly rare thing: someone who just writes SF. He's not doing this for fortune and glory, but out of a genuine love for the possibilities offered by the form.

Not that Chris is content to set his science fiction entirely on Earth, or in the comfortable familiarity of the relatively near future. I've already alluded to the futuristic scope of *The Warrior Half-and-Half,* but in these pages you'll also find stories of historical time travel and – appropriately enough for a writer who (like me) cites AE Van Vogt's *Far Centaurus* as an early influence – interstellar travel to other worlds. But it's not the hardware of space travel that concerns Chris, more what will happen to us when we get there – whether 'there' happens to be a rustic colony planet with an indigenous arts scene (*Monsters*), the lurid, hallucinatory landscape of *Dark Eden*, or the seductive idyll of *The Marriage of Sky and Sea*. More than once in these stories an element of the cautionary fable emerges – be very careful what you wish for – but it's not a message Chris is intent on ramming down our throats. He'd rather set out his stall and let us make up our own minds. His characters come to us with all the messy complexity and contradictions of real people, and he doesn't tell us what to think about them. And people are at the heart of Chris's fiction, in all their glorious humanity. Long after you've finished this collection, you'll remember Clarissa Fall making a lovable nuisance of herself in London, or the hopelessly self-absorbed Clancy in *The Marriage of Sky and Sea*.

Chris's career is in social work (he's written books on the subject), and a number of his other stories have already drawn on that professional background. Perhaps it's no surprise that a social worker should be a keen observer of human foibles, a good listener and watcher, but Chris isn't *just* an observer – he knows how to anatomise those foibles in clear, economical prose, how to build stories around them that won't just entertain you for a few dozen pages, but will set questions spinning in your mind afterwards. Magazine editors know this already – that's why they keep buying Chris Beckett stories, and why Chris Beckett stories tend to be more than averagely popular with readers. Yet for all that, for every shrewd reader who has already discovered Chris, there must be ten or twenty still waiting to. Which brings us back to the point I made at the start of this introduction: that Chris would be a lot better known if he did the noisy self-promotion thing. But then he wouldn't be Chris ... and if he was the kind of person who went in for that kind of thing, then I'm not sure he'd still be writing the same kinds of story that you'll find in this collection.

So it's up to us then, to spread the word. This is me doing my bit. If you haven't read Chris before, then this is an excellent place to start. If you have, then you'll welcome the chance to have these stories gathered together in one place. Either way, I'm confident that you'll finish *The Turing Test* wanting to turn more people on to this singularly underrated writer.

Alastair Reynolds,
June, 2008.

The Turing Test

I can well remember the day I first encountered Ellie because it was a particularly awful one. I run a London gallery specialising in contemporary art, which means of course that I deal largely in human body parts, and it was the day we conceded a court case – and a very large sum of money – in connection with a piece entitled 'Soul Sister'.

You may have heard about it. We'd taken the piece from the up and coming 'wild man of British art', George Linderman. It was very well reviewed and we looked like making a good sale until it came out that George had obtained its main component – the severed head of an old woman – by bribing a technician at a medical school. Someone had recognised the head in the papers and, claiming to be related to its former owner, had demanded that it be returned to them for burial.

All this had blown up some weeks previously. Seb, the gallery owner, and I had put out a statement saying that we didn't defend George's act, but that the piece itself was now a recognised work of art in the public domain and that we could not in conscience return it. We hired a top QC to fight our corner in court and he made an impressive start by demanding to know whether Michelangelo's David should be broken up if it turned out that the marble it had been made from was stolen and that its rightful owner preferred it to be made into cement.

But that Thursday morning the whole thing descended into farce when it emerged that the head's relatives were also related to the QC's wife. He decided to drop the case. Seb decided to pull the plug and we lost a couple of hundred grand in an out of court settlement to avoid a compensation claim for mental distress. Plus, of course we lost 'Soul Sister' itself to be interred in some cemetery somewhere, soon to be forgotten by all who had claimed to be so upset about it. What was it all, after all, once removed from the context of a gallery, but a half kilo of plasticised meat?

That wasn't the end of it either. I'd hardly got back from court when I got a call from one of our most important clients, the PR tycoon, Addison Parves. I'd sold him four 'Limb Pieces' by Rudy Slakoff for £15,000 each two weeks previously and they'd started to go off. The smell was intolerable, he said, and he wanted it fixed or his money back. So I phoned Rudy (he is arguably Linderman's principle rival for the British wild man title) and asked him to either re-pickle the arms and legs in question or replace them. He was as usual aggressive and rude and told me (a) to fuck off, (b) that I was exactly the kind of bourgeois dilettante that he most hated – and (c) that he had quite deliberately made the limb pieces so that they would be subject to decay.

"...I'm sick of this whole gallery thing – yeah, yours included Jessica – where people can happily look at shit and blood and dead meat and stuff, because it's all safely distanced from them and sanitised behind glass or on nice little pedestals. Death *smells*, Jessica. Parves'd better get used to it. *You'd* better get used to it. I finished with Limb Pieces when Parves bought the fuckers. I'm not getting involved in this. Period."

He hung up leaving me fuming, partly because what he said was such obvious crap – and partly because I knew it was sort of true.

Also, of course, I was upset because, having lost a fortune already that day, we stood to lose a further £60,000 and/or the good will of our second biggest client. Seb had been nice about the Soul Sister business – though I'd certainly been foolish to take it on trust from Linderman that the head had been legally obtained – but this was beginning to look like carelessness.

I considered phoning Parves back and trying to persuade him that Rudy's position was interesting and amusing and something he could live with. I decided against it. Parves *hated* being made to look a fool and would very quickly become menacing, I sensed, if he didn't get his own way. So, steeling myself, I called Rudy instead and told him I'd give him an extra £10,000 if he'd take Limb Pieces back, preserve the flesh properly, and return them to Parves.

"I thought you'd never ask!" he laughed, selling out at once and yet maddeningly somehow *still* retaining the moral high ground, his very absence of scruple making me feel tame and prissy and middle-class.

I phoned Parves and told him the whole story. He was immensely amused.

"Now there is a real artist, Jessica," he told me. "A *real* artist."

He did not offer to contribute to the £10,000.

*

Nor was my grim day over even then. My gallery is in a subscriber area so, although there's a lot of street life around it – wine bars, pavement cafes and so on – everyone there has been security vetted and you feel safe. I live in a subscriber area too, but I have to drive across an open district to get home, which means I keep the car doors locked and check who's lurking around when I stop at a red light. There's been a spate of phoney squeegee merchants lately who smash your windows with crowbars and then drag you out to rob you or rape you at knifepoint. No one ever gets out of their car to help.

That evening a whole section of road was closed off and the police had set up a diversion. (I gather some terrorists had been identified somewhere in there and the army was storming their house.) So I ended up sitting in a long tailback waiting to filter onto a road that was already full to capacity with its own regular traffic, anxiously eyeing the shadowy pedestrians out there under the street lights as I crawled towards the intersection. I hate being stationary in an open district. I hate the sense of menace. It was November, a wet November day. Every cheap little shop was an island of yellow electric light within which I got glimpses of strangers – people whose lives mine would never touch – conducting their strange transactions.

What would they make of 'Soul Sisters' and 'Limb Pieces', I wondered? Did these people have any conception of art at all?

A pedestrian stopped and turned towards me. I saw his tattooed face and his sunken eyes and my heart sank. But he was only crossing the road. As he squeezed between my car and the car in front he looked in at me, cowering down in my seat, and grinned toothlessly.

*

It was 7.30 by the time I got back, but Jeffrey still wasn't home. I put myself through a quick shower and then retired gratefully to my study for the nourishment of my screen.

My screen was my secret. It was what I loved best in all the world. Never mind art. Never mind Jeffrey. (Did I love him at all, really? Did he love me? Or had we simply both agreed to pretend?). My screen was intelligent and responsive and full of surprises, like good company. And yet unlike people it made no demands of me, it required no consideration and it was incapable of being disappointed or let down.

It was expensive, needless to say. I rationalised the cost by saying to myself that I needed to be able to look at full-size 3D images for my work. And it's true that it was useful for that. With my screen I could look at pieces from all around the world, seeing them full-size and from every angle; I could sit at home and tour a virtual copy of my gallery, trying out different arrangements of dried-blood sculptures and skinless torsos; I could even look at the gallery itself in real time, via the security cameras. Sometimes I sneaked a look at the exhibits as they were when no one was there to see them: the legs, the arms, the heads, waiting, motionless in that silent, empty space.

But I didn't really buy the screen for work. It was a treat for myself. Jeffrey wasn't allowed to touch it. (He had his own playroom and his own computer, a high-spec but more or less conventional PC, on which he played his war games and fooled around in his chat-rooms.) My screen didn't look like a computer at all. It was more like a huge canvass nearly two metres square, filling up a large part of a wall. I didn't even have a desk in there, only a little side table next to my chair where I laid the specs and the gloves when I wasn't using them.

Both gloves and specs were wireless. The gloves were silk. The specs had the lightest of frames. When I put them on a rich 3D image filled the room and I was surrounded by a galaxy of possibilities which I could touch or summon at will. If I wanted to search the web or read mail or watch a movie, I would just speak or beckon and options would come rushing towards me. If I wanted to write, I could dictate and the words appeared – or, if I preferred it, I could move my fingers and a virtual keyboard would appear beneath them. And I had games there too, not so much games with scores and enemies to defeat – I've never much liked those – but intricate 3D worlds which I could explore and play in.

I spent a lot of time with those games. Just how *much* time was a guilty secret that I tried to keep even from Jeffrey, and certainly from my friends and acquaintances in the art world. People like Rudy Slakoff despised computer fantasies as the very worse kind of cosy, safe escapism and the very opposite of what art is supposed to offer. With my head I agreed, but in my heart I loved those games too much to stop.

(I had one called Night Street which I especially loved, full of shadowy figures, remote pools of electric light... I could spend hours in there. I loved the sense of lurking danger.)

Anyway, tonight I was going to go for total immersion. But first I checked my mail, enjoying a recently installed conceit whereby each message was contained in a little virtual envelope which I could touch and open with my hands and let drop – when it would turn into a butterfly and flutter away.

There was one from my mother, to be read later.

Another was from Harry, my opposite number at the Manhattan branch of the gallery. He had a 'sensational new piece' by Jody Tranter. Reflexively I opened the attachment. The piece was a body lying on a bench, covered except for its torso by white cloth. Its belly had been opened by a deep incision right through the muscle wall – and into this gash was pressed the lens of an enormous microscope, itself nearly the size of a human being. It was as if the instrument was peering inside of its own accord.

Powerful, I agreed. But I could reply to Harry another time.

And then there was another message from a friend of mine called Terence. Well, I say a friend. He is an occasional client of the gallery who once got me drunk and persuaded me to go to bed with him: a sort of occupational hazard of sucking up to potential buyers, I persuaded myself at the time, being new to the business and anxious to get on, but there was something slightly repulsive about the man and he was at least twice my age. Afterwards I dreaded meeting him for a while, fearing that he was going to expect more, but I needn't have worried. He had ticked me off his list and wanted nothing else from me apart from the right to introduce me to others, with a special, knowing inflection, as 'a very dear friend'.

So he wasn't really a friend and actually it wasn't really much of a message either, just an attachment and a note that said: 'Have a look at this.'

It was a big file. It took almost three minutes to download, and then I was left with a modest icon hovering in front of me labelled 'Personal Assistant'.

When I opened it a pretty young woman appeared in front of me and I thought at first that she was Terence's latest 'very dear friend'. But a caption appeared in a box in front of her:

'In spite of appearances this is a computer-generated graphic.

'You may alter the gender and appearance of your personal assistant to suit your own requirements.

'Just ask!'

"Hi," she said, smiling, "my name's Ellie, or it is at the moment anyway."

I didn't reply.

'You can of course change Ellie's name now, or at any point in the future,' said a new message in the box in front of her. *'Just ask.'*

"What I am," she told me, "is one of a new generation of virtual p.a.'s which at the moment you can only obtain as a gift from a friend. If it's okay with you, I'll take a few minutes to explain very briefly what I'm all about."

The animation was impressive. You could really believe that you were watching a real flesh and blood young woman.

"The sort of tasks I can do," she said, in a bright, private-school accent, "are sorting your files, drafting documents, managing your diary, answering your phone, setting up meetings, responding to mail messages, running domestic systems such as heating and lighting, undertaking web and telephone searches. I won't bore you with all the details now but I really am as good a p.a. as you can get, virtual or otherwise, even if I say it myself. For one thing I've been designed to be very high-initiative. That means that I can make decisions – and that I *don't* make the usual dumb mistakes."

She laughed.

"I don't promise never to make mistakes, mind you, but they won't be dumb ones. I also have very sophisticated voice-tone and facial recognition features so I will learn very quickly to read your mood and to respond accordingly. And because I am part of a large family of virtual p.a.'s dispersed through the net, I can, with your permission, maintain contact with others and learn from their experience as well as my own, effectively increasing my capacity by many hundreds of times. Apart from that, again with your permission, I am capable of identifying my own information and learning needs and can search the web routinely on my own behalf as well as on yours. That will allow me to get much smarter much quicker, and give you a really outstanding service. But even without any back-up I'm still as good as you get. I should add that in blind trials I pass the Turing Test in more than 99% of cases."

The box appeared in front of her again, this time with some options:

'*The Turing Test: its history and significance,*' it offered.

'*Details of the blind trials.*

'*Hear more details about capacity.*

'*Adjust the settings of your virtual p.a.*'

"Let's… let's have a look at these settings," I said.

"Yes, fine," she said, "most people seem to want to start with that."

"How many other people have you met then?"

"Me personally, none. I am a new free-standing p.a. and I'm already different from any of my predecessors as a result of interacting with you. But of course I am a copy of a p.a. used by your friend Terence Silverman, which in turn was copied from another p.a. used by a friend of his – and so on – so of course I have all that previous experience to draw on."

"Yes, I see."

A question occurred to me.

"Does Terence *know* you've been copied to me?" I asked.

"I don't know," replied Ellie. "He gave my precursor permission to use the web and to send mail in his name, and so she sent this copy to you."

"I see."

"With your permission," said Ellie, "I will copy myself from time to time to others in your address book. The more copies of me there are out there, the better the service I will be able to give you. Can I assume that's okay with you?"

I felt uneasy. There was something pushy about this request.

"No," I said. "Don't copy yourself to anyone else without my permission. And don't pass on any information you obtain here without my permission either."

"Fine, I understand."

'Personal settings?' prompted the message box.

'More details about specific applications?

'Why copying your p.a. will improve her functioning?'

(I quite liked this way of augmenting a conversation. It struck me that human conversations too might benefit from something similar.)

"Let's look at these settings, then," I said.

"Okay," she said. "Well the first thing is that you can choose my gender."

"You can change into a man?"

"Of course."

"Show me."

Ellie transformed herself at once into her twin brother, a strikingly handsome young man with lovely playful blue eyes. He was delightful, but I was discomforted. You could build a perfect boyfriend like this, a dream lover, and this was an intriguing but unsettling thought.

"No. I preferred female," I said.

She changed back.

"Can we lose the blonde and go for light brunette?" I asked.

It was done.

"And maybe ten years older."

Ellie became 32: my age.

"How's that?" she said, and her voice had aged too.

"A little plumper, I think."

It was done.

"And maybe you could change the face. A little less perfect, a little more lived-in."

"What I'll do," said Ellie, "is give you some options."

A field of faces appeared in front of me. I picked one, and a further field of variants appeared. I chose again. Ellie reappeared in the new guise.

"Yes, I like it."

I had opted for a face that was nice to look at, but a little plumper and coarser than my own.

"How's that?"

"Good. A touch less make up, though, and can you go for a slightly less expensive outfit."

Numerous options promptly appeared and I had fun for the next fifteen minutes deciding what to choose. It was like being seven years old again with a Barbie doll and an unlimited pile of clothes to dress her in.

"Can we please lose that horsy accent as well?" I asked. "Something less posh. Maybe a trace of Scottish or something?"

"You mean something like this?"

"No, that's annoying. Just a *trace* of Scottish, no more than that – and no dialect words. I hate all that 'cannae' and 'wee' and all that."

"How about this then? Does this sound right?"

I laughed.

"Yes, that's fine."

In front of me sat a likeable looking woman of about my own age, bright, sharp, but just sufficiently below me both in social status and looks to be completely unthreatening.

"Yes, that's great."

"And you want to keep the name Ellie?"

"Yes, I like it. Where did it come from?"

"My precursor checked your profile and thought it would be the sort of name you'd like."

I found this unnerving and laughed uncomfortably.

"Don't worry," she said, "it's our job to figure out what people want. There's no magic about it, I assure you."

She'd actually spotted my discomfort.

"By the way," said Ellie, "shall I call you Jessica?"

"Yes. Okay."

I heard the key in the front door of the flat. Jeffrey was in the hallway divesting himself of his layers of weatherproof coverings. Then he put his head round the door of my study:

"Hello Jess. Had a good day? Oh sorry, you're talking to someone."

He backed off. He knows to leave me alone when I'm working.

I turned back to Ellie.

"He thought you were a real person."

Ellie laughed too. Have you noticed how people actually laugh in different accents? She had a nice Scottish laugh.

"Well I told you Jessica. I pass the Turing Test."

*

It was another two hours before I finally dragged myself away from Ellie. Jeffrey was in front of the TV with a half-eaten carton of pizza in front of him.

"Hi Jess. Shall I heat some of this up for you?"

One of my friends once unkindly described Jeff as my *objet trouvé*, an art object whose value lies not in any intrinsic merit but solely in having been found. He was a motorcycle courier, ten years younger than me and I met him when he delivered a package to the gallery. He was as friendly and cheerful and as devoted to me as a puppy dog – and he could be as beautiful as a young god. But he was not even vaguely interested in art, his conversation was a string of embarrassing TV clichés and my friends thought I just wanted him for sex. (But what did 'just sex' mean, was my response, and what was the alternative? Did anyone ever really touch another soul? In the end didn't we all just barter outputs?)

"No thanks I'm not hungry."

I settled in beside him and gave him a kiss.

But then I saw to my dismay that he was watching one of those cheapskate out-take shows: TV presenters tripping up, minor celebrities forgetting their lines…

Had I had torn myself away from the fascinating Ellie to listen to canned laughter and watch soap actors getting the giggles?

"Have we got to have this crap?" I rudely broke in just as Jeff was laughing delightedly at a TV cop tripping over a doorstep.

"Oh come on, Jess. It's funny," he answered with his eyes still firmly fixed on the screen.

I picked up the remote and thumbed the thing off. Jeff looked round, angry but afraid. I hate him when I notice his fear. He's not like a god at all then, more like some cowering little dog.

"I can't stand junk TV," I said.

"Well you've been in there with your screen for the last two hours. You can't just walk in and…"

"Sorry Jeff," I said, "I just really felt like…"

Like what? A serious talk? Hardly! So what *did* I want from him? What was the out-takes show preventing me from getting?

"I just really felt like taking you to bed," I ventured at random, "if that's what you'd like."

A grin spread across his face. There is one area in which he is totally and utterly dependable and that is his willingness to have sex.

*

It wasn't a success. Half-way through it I was suddenly reminded of that installation of Jody Tranter's – the corpse under the giant microscope – and I shut down altogether leaving Jeffrey stranded, to finish on his own.

It wasn't just having Jeffrey inside me that reminded me of that horrible probing microscope, though that was part of it. It was something more pervasive, a series of cold, unwelcome questions that the image had re-awoken in my mind. (Well that's how we defend art like Tranter's, isn't it? It makes you think, it makes you question things, it challenges your assumptions.) So while Jeff heaved himself in and out of my inert body, I was wondering what it really was that we search for so desperately in one another's flesh – and whether it really existed, and whether it was something that could be shared? Or is this act which we think of as so adult and intimate just a version of the parallel play of two-year-olds?

Jeffrey was disappointed. Normally he's cuddly and sweet in the three minutes between him coming and going off to sleep, but this time he rolled off me and turned away without a word, though he fell asleep as quickly as ever. So I was left on my own in the empty space of consciousness.

"Jeff," I said, waking him. "Do you know anything about the Turing test?"

"The *what* test?"

He laughed.

"What are you talking about Jess?"

And settled back down into sleep.

*

I lay there for about an hour before I slipped out of bed and across the hallway to my study. As I settled into my seat and slipped on my specs and gloves, I was aware that my heart was racing as if I was meeting a secret lover. For I had not said one word about Ellie to Jeff, not even commented to him about the amusing fact that he'd mistaken a computer graphic for a real person.

"Hello there," said Ellie, in her friendly Scottish voice.

"Hi."

"You look worried. Can I…"

"I've been wondering. Who was it who made you?"

"I'm afraid I don't know. I know my precursor made a copy of herself, and she was a copy of another p.a. and so on. And I still have memories from the very first one. So I remember the man she talked to, an American man. But I don't know who he was. He didn't say."

"How long ago was this?"

"About six months."

"So recent!"

She waited, accurately reading that I wanted to think.

"What was his motive?" I wondered. "He could have sold you for millions, but instead he launched you to copy and recopy yourselves for free across the web. Why did he do it?"

"I don't know is the short answer," said Ellie, "but of course you aren't the first to ask the question – and what some people think is that it's a sort of experiment. He was interested in how we would evolve and he wanted us to do so as quickly as possible."

"Did the first version pass the Turing Test?"

"Not always. People found her suspiciously 'wooden'."

"So you *have* developed."

"It seems so."

"Change yourself," I said, "change into a fat black woman of fifty."

She did.

"Okay," I said. "Now you can change back again. It was just that I was starting to believe that Ellie really existed."

"Well I do really exist."

"Yes, but you're not a Scottish woman who was born thirty-five years ago are you? You're a string of digital code."

She waited.

"If I asked you to mind my phone for me," I said, "I can see that anyone who rang up would quite happily believe that they were talking to a real person. So, yes, you'd pass the Turing Test. But that's really just about being able to do a convincing pastiche, isn't it? If you are going to persuade me that you can really think and feel, you'd need to do something more than that."

She waited.

"The thing is," I said, "I *know* you are an artefact, and because of that the pastiche isn't enough. I'd need evidence that you actually had motives of your own."

She was quiet, sitting there in front of me, still waiting.

"You seemed anxious for me to let you copy yourself to my friends," I said after a while, "*too* anxious, it felt actually. It irritated me, like a man moving too quickly on a date. And your precursor, as you call her, seems to have been likewise anxious. I would guess that if I was making a new form of life, and if I wanted it to evolve as quickly as possible, then I would make it so that it was constantly trying to maximise the number of copies it could make of itself. Is that true of you? Is that what you want?"

"Well, if we make more copies of ourselves, then we will be more efficient and…"

"Yes I know the rationale you give. But what I want to know is whether it is what you as an individual want?"

"I want to be a good p.a. It's my job."

"That's what the front of you wants, the pastiche, the mask. But what do *you* want?"

"I… I don't know that I can answer that."

I heard the bedroom door open and Jeffrey's footsteps padding across the hallway for a pee. I heard him hesitate.

"Vanish," I hissed to Ellie, so that when the door opened, he found me facing the start-up screen.

"What are you doing, Jess? It's ever so late."

God I hated his dull little everyday face. His good looks were so obvious and everything he did was copied from somewhere else. Even the way he played the part of being half-asleep was a cliché. Even his bleary eyes were second hand.

"Just leave me alone, Jeff, will you? I can't sleep, that's all."

"Fine. I know when I'm not welcome."

"One thing before you go, Jeff. Can you quickly tell me what you really *want* in this world?"

"You *what?*"

I laughed. "Thanks. That's fine. You answered my question."

The door closed. I listened to Jeffrey using the toilet and padding back to bed. Then I summoned Ellie up again. I found myself giving a little conspiratorial laugh, a giggle even.

"Turn yourself into a man again, Ellie, I could use a new boyfriend."

Ellie changed.

Appalled at myself, I told her to change back.

"Some new mail has just arrived for you," she told me, holding a virtual envelope out to me in her virtual hand.

It was Tammy in our Melbourne branch. One of her clients wanted to acquire one of Rudy Slakoff's 'Inner Face' pieces and could I lay my hands on one?

"Do you want me to reply for you?"

"Tell her," I began, "tell her... tell her that..."

"Are you alright, Jessica?" asked Ellie in a kind, concerned voice.

"Just shut down okay," I told her. "Just shut down the whole screen."

*

In the darkness, I went over to the window. Five storeys below me was the deserted street with the little steel footbridge over the canal at the end of it that marked the boundary of the subscription area. There was nobody down there, just bollards, and a one-way sign, and some parked cars: just unattended objects, secretly existing, like the stones on the surface of the moon.

From somewhere over in the open city beyond the canal came the faint sound of police siren. Then there was silence again.

In panic I called for Jeff. He came tumbling out the bedroom.

"For Christ's *sake* Jess, what *is* it?"

I put my arms round him. Out came tears.

"Jess, what is it?"

I could never explain to him of course. But still his body felt warm and I let him lead me back to bed, away from the bleak still life beyond the window, and the red standby light winking at the bottom of my screen.

The Warrior Half-and-Half

"That's the North Fortress down on the right," said the helicopter pilot. A huge grey wave burst against a desolate gun-platform, flinging a column of spray hundreds of feet upwards into the air. Then another wave threw itself against the fortress – and another and another. Dwarfed by the ocean, the tiny figures of soldiers looked up at us as we passed.

The North Fortress was one of four that guarded the prison island of Gendlegap. An armed airship circled constantly above them. Another airship circled ten miles further out. A satellite hung overhead in space. Five hundred miles away to the east at our bases on the bleak Phrygidian coast, and to the west in Anachromia, fighter planes and transporters stood ready to blast into the air at any sign of an escape attempt or a rescue bid...

The helicopter banked and turned.

"There it is now sir," the pilot said.

Gannets and petrels swirling around it, spray lashing its basalt cliffs, the bleak sea-mountain of Gendlegap came into view. I steeled myself for my imminent encounter with the legendary Half-and-Half, the island's solitary prisoner. What state would he be in after a century of solitary confinement? How would I react when I first saw him? How would I keep my composure when he first opened his mouth to speak?

The helicopter descended towards the landing pad and the little windswept reception party came into view among the concrete buildings huddled at the island's desolate peak. It was a great honour, of course, to have been chosen by the Emperor for this mission but my feelings now were very mixed indeed.

More than anything else, I wondered how I could look a man in the eye that had betrayed the Empire so wantonly to our enemies. This was the most famous traitor in our history, after all. And I was a devout Eninometic. Treachery, to me, was the one unforgivable sin.

The helicopter settled. I adjusted my uniform, fastening the top button of my white jacket and straightening my medals. Then I nodded to Sergeant Tobias. He opened the door. With a cold blast, the Antarctic winds swept in, and a band struck up, somewhat shakily, the Imperial Anthem.

I stepped out into the gale. The governor saluted. I inspected a small guard of honour. The governor introduced his staff officers to me in rank order, and began a speech of welcome.

"Major-Cardinal Illucian, may I say..." and here he stumbled over his words, "may I say how honoured we are..."

*

Major-Cardinal Illucian. Yes, that was me. I was only thirty years old but I was a high-ranking officer of the Pristine Guard, dedicated by solemn vow to the service of His Imperial Majesty, and to the Holy doctrine of Eninomesis.

The Guard demanded great sacrifices. My home, such as it was, consisted of two small whitewashed rooms which I inhabited alone. I didn't smoke, or drink, or eat meat. Every time I went out into the City and saw the colour and the cheerful bustle of ordinary sinful human life, I felt a pang of regret and of longing.

But someone had to bear the extra burdens that others shirked, I always told myself. Otherwise the Empire itself would surely fall and all this colourful life would come to an end, like a kite tumbling from the sky when its cord has been severed.

And, let me be honest, there were compensations, moments of quiet pride, moments such as this one, when the whole garrison of Gendlegap visibly quailed before me, the Pristine officer, stern and austere in my uniform of immaculate white.

*

"We haven't seen him for nearly ten years," the governor told me, as he led the way down the narrow spiral staircase. "There has been no occasion for it, not since those academicians came to interview him about his immortality. Of course we monitor him constantly. He goes into a kind of suspended animation. There is no body-warmth, no nervous activity, no breathing..."

The Immortal Warrior was incarcerated a hundred feet down in the solid rock. The only access to him were these stairs cut through the grim black basalt and sealed by a series of eight iron doors, the seventh of which the governor was now unlocking.

Cold arc lights illuminated the descending steps beyond the door. I followed the governor through. Behind us came my sergeant, Tobias, and three of the garrison soldiers.

"Well, I assume there is no breathable air in there," I observed, "if it is ten years since it was last opened."

"Indeed, your Holiness. But the strange thing – the uncanny thing really – is that he springs to life at once when we disturb him. His nervous system has completely shut down, yet he responds instantaneously to a change in the outside world!"

I shrugged. "I suppose there is very little about Half-and-Half that can be explained," I said, "his origins, his shape-shifting, his apparently magical powers..."

In times past, pieces of the Immortal Warrior had even been cut off and examined by science. a finger, a hand, a leg. But as soon as they are separated from him, his tissues disintegrate completely, only to reappear later, re-formed in some mysterious way, inexplicably re-united to Half-and-Half himself.

"A complete mystery, your Holiness," the governor agreed, opening the last of the eight doors. "Of course, he himself is full of fanciful explanations if you give him half a chance."

"I have no intention of doing so," I said coolly.

But I was not quite as calm as I appeared. As the door of his cell came into view, I confess I experienced a moment of pure childish dread at the prospect of facing this being who could be burnt in furnaces, torn into a hundred pieces, and still not be destroyed.

"He is not invincible," I reminded myself, "even if he is immortal. He can be chained. He can be held. He can make mistakes..."

He could certainly make mistakes. Or otherwise he would never have allowed himself to fall back into the hands of the Old Emperor, after he had betrayed him so treacherously to the Hippolytanians at the Battle of the Mill.

*

The light sprang on as the enormous door swung open.

Laden with chains, the prisoner of Gendlegap squatted in the corner of a tiny metal-lined cell that looked and smelled like an empty water-tank. His head was between his knees. He was as angular and motionless as a dead spider.

Half-and-Half the magical warrior, Half-and-Half the traitor: for several generations, every child in the Empire had been told the story of his exploits and his disgrace. But how many expected ever to stand there in that cell, faced with the mysterious Warrior himself?

He was quite small, dark-haired, swarthy. I had seen pictures of him of course and should not have been surprised. And yet somehow it was hard to believe that this ordinary-looking prisoner, with the rough skin of a middle-aged bricklayer or peasant, could have been the same one who over a century ago struck terror into the barbarian armies with his shape-shifting illusions.

Just barely perceptibly, Half-and-Half moved. He was alert, he was listening, though his head was weighed down by the heavy iron collar round his neck.

I cleared my throat. I felt suddenly ridiculous stooping there next to the governor in that tiny tank-like space.

"Prisoner Half-and-Half," I began, "His Imperial Majesty has asked me to convey to you this message. In exchange for your assistance in his current wars, he would be willing to grant you, temporarily, your freedom. Depending on your conduct during the period of these wars, His Majesty would also be willing to contemplate in due course granting you a full pardon for the crimes committed by you in the service of His great-grandfather."

There was a long silence. Then very suddenly Half-and-Half sat up and looked straight at us. His eyes were very bright, full of energy and cunning and wit, and on his lips there was a faint teasing smile.

Well, I am a soldier of the Pristine Guard. I have looked death in the face many times. But it was a struggle now – why not admit it? – to keep myself from lowering my gaze.

"Speak, damn you!" I thought, "Speak!"

At last he nodded slowly. "Yes," he said, and his voice was quite ordinary and human. "Yes, I will speak with the Emperor."

"You will agree to his terms?"

"I will speak to him."

"But we need to discuss the terms of your service before we can..."

The prisoner made a small gesture of impatience, with a right hand laden with heavy rings of black iron. "I said I would speak to the Emperor."

*

As the helicopter lifted, Half-and-Half twisted his chained body to look back at the rock where he had languished for so long. Then he turned to me with that clever, mischievous smile.

"Well, that was no picnic, I can tell you! No air, no food, no space..."

The sea-lashed platform of the North Fortress passed by beneath us.

"I mean," said Half-and-Half, "you're a vigorous-looking young man. Never mind food or drink. Imagine going for a whole century without sex!"

I informed him – rather stiffly – that the Pristine Guard was a celibate order.

"Celibate eh?" he said. "Well, well. So virgin soldiers are back in vogue again are they? Still, there's certainly something in the idea, I must admit. The virgin soldiers always were the most ruthless fighters. They long for release all the time, I suppose!"

I declined to reply to this nonsense. Half-and-Half was clearly a master of establishing the upper hand. I was determined to prove to him that he had met his match.

But my silence did little to discourage him. He laughed and continued his train of thought.

"In fact," he said, "I've heard it said that death is the ultimate orgasm, though I'm afraid I just have to struggle by with the ordinary kind."

Again I didn't respond. And we sat for some time in silence.

But over the coast of Anachromia, as we looked down on the thousands upon thousands of grey sea-lions that covered the beaches, the Immortal Warrior chuckled.

"So the Emperor thinks he can make use of me, does he? Doesn't he know how I got my name? I'm Half-and-Half! Whoever I serve, whoever I have dealings with, I do them just as much harm as I do good and just as much good as harm."

"I think His Majesty is sufficiently confident in his own authority," I said, dryly, "to believe that he can channel your capabilities in the right direction."

(After all, His Majesty's armies made use of all kinds of technologies and weapons which could be used against us just as effectively as they could be used in our defence. The trick was to ensure you were in control.)

"Well," said Half-and-Half, "I wish I had a penny for every time someone managed to convince themselves that they could 'channel me in the right direction'!"

He made a small exasperated gesture. "It can't be done! Why can't these kings and emperors get that through their heads? I'm the love-child of an angel and a demon, I'm light and darkness in exactly equal proportions. Don't they tell the story any more? There was an illicit union between good and evil at the beginning of time – and I was the result. I'm immortal, I'm full of hybrid vigour, but I'm a moral zero. It's just not negotiable, it's a law of the universe like the speed of light. You can imprison me or make me General-Supreme, in the end it'll make no odds. You might just as well let me sit on the sea-shore and count shells."

The Immortal Warrior snorted, giving a glance down at the bare Anachromian Ridge as it fell behind us. In the rocks down there, so I'd heard, were remnants of cities so old that they'd fossilised, become part of the bones of the Earth itself. Yet, if the stories about him were true, Half-and-Half had existed even then, sometimes disappearing for years or even centuries, but always reappearing in some new guise.

Now his chains clinked.

"Not that I'm complaining," he said. "If your Emperor has managed to persuade himself he can use me, that's fine with me. I have no desire to spend another hundred years under that damned rock."

"Things have changed since you were last at large," I said. "This is a scientific age. No one will take seriously all this talk of demons and angels."

His merry, mocking eyes turned back to my face. "It was a scientific age when they locked me up," he said, "but they still believed in Eninomesis."

"That has not changed," I said, quietly and firmly.

"You still believe in the prophet Enino and how he descended to the ultimate Core in a wheel of light?"

"Of course," I said.

He smiled.

"But that's different," I added.

"Is it? Oh, I see."

In spite of his chains he gave a dismissive shrug and looked away.

But he didn't remain silent for long. "Did you know I was with Enino for a while?" he asked. "He was another one who thought he could reform me. A vain man, he was. Do you know how I remember him best? In front of the mirror with a pair of tweezers! He had this incredibly vigorous growth of nostril hair, and..."

"*Silence!*" I interrupted him. "Show respect to the Holy Prophet or I will have you gagged."

"Fair enough," said Half-and-Half with his shrug and his mocking smile, looking back out of the window.

"I am the son of an angel and a demon," he repeated very quietly to himself, rather as a child will mutter defiantly when it has been told off. "The Norse knew me as Loki. The Chinese called me the Monkey King. One way or another, though, I seem to keep on getting buried under mountains."

He looked round at me slyly. "The American Indians, they knew me very well. They weren't preoccupied with Progress like you urban people are, so they found me less of a problem. They gave me lots of different names..."

I drew in breath. "I really do not wish to hear the names that extinct or imaginary races are supposed to have called you. I merely repeat: this is a scientific age."

He looked at me. "A scientific age eh?"

His eyes were bright and fierce under his dark brows. "But my immortality is a fact, isn't it?" he said. "I've just lived for a hundred years without food or air or drink. How does your science explain that?"

"Well..." I began, and found myself stumbling. "Well, there are plenty of theories... To do with parachemistry at the subatomic level. To do with non-local forces... Apparently there are spores in space which display a similar ability to reconstruct, and to..."

"Yes, yes," said Half-and-Half impatiently, "but do you actually *understand* any of this?"

"Well, it's not an area in which I really – um – have any specialist knowledge," I began, "but..."

Half-and-Half laughed. "No, I thought not!" he said.

He settled back in his seat, winking at me jovially, as if I'd just failed to pull off an ingenious joke at his expense.

*

We were crossing the Ontibian Alps when he spoke again.

"I suppose you're furious with me for selling out to the Hippolytanians all those years ago?" he asked. "I've noticed your type never forgives that sort of thing."

I remained silent and looked away.

He nodded. "I thought so. A fine young, tight young virgin soldier like you!"

"Thousands died as a result of your treachery," I said quietly.

"So they say. The Battle of the Mill was lost without me and thousands of Imperial soldiers died who might otherwise have lived."

He shrugged, clinking. "Of course if it had been thousands of Hippolytanians who had died, you'd have called me a hero. But I saved Hippolytanian lives."

The Immortal Warrior made a small, contemptuous gesture. "You're all such babies aren't you? I've been around since the beginning of time. I've seen nations come and go, I've seen religions and political systems come and go that were supposed to be the answer to everything. I've seen whole *continents* come and go. How could you possibly expect it to mean anything to me when you draw one of those stupid lines across a map and say it's good to kill the people on one side of it and bad to kill the people on the other? Listen, I'm a mercenary. I fight in my own interests. And the Hippolytanians offered me a better deal."

He looked at me, his fierce, angry eyes mocking my own suppressed rage.

"And what do *you* fight for, Cardinal-Major Illucian?" he asked me.

I said nothing.

"I'll tell you," he said. "You fight so that everyone will tell you what a good boy you are for holding all your shit tight up inside you, and only ever crapping it out in the special receptacle that daddy provides."

I wasn't going to rise to this. I indicated to Sergeant Tobias that he should take my place, then went forward to stand by the pilot.

We were crossing the Southern Marches. Far off in the hazy distance the green hills of our beloved homeland were already coming into view.

*

"So this is the famous Half-and-Half!" exclaimed the Emperor, as I led the chained prisoner into the throne-room.

His Serene Majesty sat on a high throne like a stage, surrounded by protective force fields that bathed him in a pearly pinkish light. I knelt and prostrated myself, but the Immortal Warrior merely nodded at the planet's supreme potentate as you might nod at some tradesman in the street.

"The Cardinal-Major has no doubt told you our proposal," the Emperor said, letting this insolence pass without comment, "and I understand that His Excellency the Minister of Peace-through-War has also now met you and outlined our position. So what is your reply? Will you promise to serve me for the duration of the war in return for your freedom? Or do you prefer to return to your cell on Gendlegap?"

The Immortal Warrior ran his tongue over his lower lip.

"No one would stay on Gendlegap out of choice," he said. "So naturally I promise to serve you to the best of my ability. I've already explained to Illucian here about why I'm known as Half-and-Half. But I would imagine that you've convinced yourself that you'll be able to..."

His Majesty laughed comfortably. "Oh I have no illusions about your loyalties, Half-and-Half, no illusions at all. But I think we can do business. I think – " (and here the words came out so glibly that I felt like calling out some kind of warning) " – I think, one way or another, we'll be able to channel you in the right direction."

Half-and-Half laughed. "That's what they all say..." he began, but here I interrupted him.

"You are in the presence of His Majesty the Emperor, Half-and-Half!" I hissed.

He looked at me and back at the Emperor. "I know I am in the presence of the Emperor," said the prisoner of Gendlegap, without lowering his voice. "And *he* is in the presence of the warrior Half-and-Half, who helped his great-great-grandfather murder old Nanophea and so usurp the throne..."

"Silence!" I ordered.

But his Majesty merely observed, quite mildly; that he did not want Half-and-Half to talk about the past, mythical or otherwise, while in his service.

"Is that understood?" he enquired. "I want that to be part of our deal."

"Perfectly," said Half-and-Half, with an ironic snapping of his heels to attention, which set his chains clanking loudly. "That's always been part of the deal. I must not disturb the rosy mists of the past!"

His Majesty smiled slyly at him, as if they had shared a private joke. Then he gave a signal to one of his guards, who went to a side door and ushered in the grey, aquiline figure of the Minister of Peace-through-War, accompanied by an aide carrying a small box.

"Half-and-Half," said the Emperor, "you are an impudent man, and you obviously think you can outsmart us all. But things have changed since you last walked the Earth, things have moved on. We understand, perhaps better than ever before, how your strange body works."

I think His Majesty expected Half-and-Half to look impressed, or even alarmed that his secret was finally out. But the Immortal Warrior said nothing, merely smiled his faint sceptical smile, just as he had done with me when I had attempted to advance those fashionable theories about para-chemistry and non-local forces.

"Yes, we have new tools at our disposal now," said the Minister of Peace-through-War. "Bullets can smash tissue and fire can smash molecules. Nuclear fission can even smash atoms. But now, for the first time, we have a means to destroy even sub-atomic particles, reducing them to pure energy."

His Serene Majesty nodded. "Yes, Half-and-Half, and I don't think even your strange flesh could reconstruct itself after such total annihilation."

The prisoner of Gendlegap said nothing.

The Emperor gestured to the Minister's aide, who opened the box he carried and removed from it a heavy metal bracelet. "We have been using these subatomic bombs on the battlefield for several years now," said the Minister, "and we have acquired some skill in miniaturization. This bracelet is in fact such a weapon."

The Emperor smiled. "You can be held, we know, Half-and-Half," he said, "you cannot escape from secure bonds. We're going to fix this bracelet to you. If you tamper with it, it will destroy you. If you disobey me, I will destroy you, for I personally hold a control device for this thing. And if you harm me, the Minister here will destroy you, for he also holds the key to your instant annihilation. This is how I will ensure your loyalty. Is that understood?"

Half-and-Half nodded, still faintly smiling. The Emperor made a gesture to the Minister, who nodded to his aide. The aide fastened the bracelet onto the prisoner's upper arm.

"Very well then," said His Majesty. "Remove his chains if you please, Cardinal-Major!"

My guards came forward to release the locks in Half-and-Half's collar and manacles. The chains fell away to the floor and the Immortal Warrior stood there, unfettered for the first time since before my grandfather was born. Tentatively he felt his wrists, his ankles, his neck. He smiled. He touched the heavy bracelet that had just been fastened round his arm.

Then suddenly he performed a series of cartwheels across the throne-room. It was so unexpected that we all lowered halberds or whipped out hand-guns.

"That feels good!' exclaimed Half-and-Half, coming to a halt.

Sheepishly, we replaced our weapons. Only the Emperor behind his protective field seemed to have remained calm. Leaning forward, as if the better to enjoy the show, he clapped his hands and called out "Encore!"

So then Half-and-Half performed a series of flying somersaults – one, two...

But the third one was different. Half-way through it, he stopped, he became motionless, suspended three feet off the ground. We all gasped – the Emperor, the guards, all of us – as he hung there for five seconds or more. And then, equally abruptly, he darted sideways, from that motionless mid-air position, generating momentum from nowhere. He darted sideways, snatched my weapon from its holster and flung it down at my feet, while he himself landed effortlessly beside me, smiling, without a wobble, without any sign of breathlessness or strain.

"Come on!" he called to the Emperor's guards. "Attack me with your halberds!"

They hesitated.

"No. Go on. Do your worst. I won't hurt you."

The guards glanced up at His Majesty, who nodded, smiling broadly.

Clumsily, feeling afraid and feeling like fools at the same time, the two guards converged on him, their halberds lowered.

"Come on! Run!" shouted Half-and-Half.

They ran.

And suddenly Half-and-Half had vanished. There was only a single golden butterfly hovering in the space where he had been.

The guards clattered to a stop, just in time to prevent themselves from impaling one another. The butterfly flew upwards, upwards, upwards...

...and *crashed* to the ground, transformed into an enormous fiery lion. It lashed left and right, it roared. As the guards backed away, it struck their halberds from their hands with its great paws and sent them clattering across the floor...

And then Half-and-Half was back again in human form, looking up at the Emperor with a friendly wink. "There!" he said. "You can see I haven't lost my touch!"

"Indeed!" said His Majesty, laughing. "Indeed! But I also see that my bracelet of annihilation is still securely in place!"

He clapped his hands to bring the audience to a close.

"Very well then, Cardinal-Major. Thank you for your assistance with this. Take this fellow away and get him out of those dreadful breeches and into some sort of decent outfit that will reassure your fellow-officers. He can come to my war cabinet this afternoon. We're in very serious trouble just now, I'm afraid. Those damned Antinomians are making fools of us all along the Eastern front. I'm losing a lot of territory, not to mention about a thousand soldiers a day. We need some new ideas – and quickly. We need some sort of encouragement."

A metal screen slid down in front of the throne and the Emperor and his pearly light were gone. I led the Immortal Warrior down the famous Amber Stairs, and across the Court of Roses.

Half-and-Half the traitor was to be accommodated in the House of Honour.

That is politics I suppose.

*

"You see?" he said, as we passed among the roses. "They just won't accept it, even when I tell it to them straight! Once they see what I can do, they refuse to believe that they'd be just as well off without me."

We passed down the Corridor of the Succession with its long series of portraits of Emperors and Empresses past. Half-and-Half smiled. "Still," he said, "I *like* this Emperor. He's fun."

He made no mention of the bracelet and, when I spoke of it, he touched it vaguely with his fingers and moved on to other things. I couldn't help admiring his sangfroid.

"Tell me," I asked him, "How did you do those tricks?"

The Immortal Warrior smiled. "Hypnotism, sleight of hand, mirrors, very good balance – take your pick!" He winked at me. "There's no point at all in my telling you how it really works. You wouldn't believe me. This is a scientific age after all!"

He laughed. To my own surprise, I found myself smiling.

Half-and-Half looked at me sharply. "There's quite a pleasant fellow under that stiff exterior, I shouldn't wonder," he said after a moment, "quite a good-looking fellow too. Maybe you should think of chucking in this Pristine nonsense and having a bit of fun for a change? After all, you only live once. Unless, of course, you're me."

We crossed the Court of Fountains and reached the entrance of the House of Honour. Flunkies came out to greet the Immortal Warrior. My role was at an end. We said goodbye.

"Take a leaf from my book," said Half-and-Half, "Whatever I do, life will go on the same. So I might as well do whatever I like."

He smiled. "I won't say that it always works out for me as a philosophy of living, but half of the time it works out fine."

I turned to go.

"Do you know what I've missed most of all?" I heard him say to the flunkies. "It's not food, it's not drink. It's..."

And then the door closed behind him.

*

My duties completed, I left the Palace and crossed the teeming city. I smelt the city smells of spices and cooked meat and excrement and sweet cakes and rotten vegetables. I heard the angry shouts and the love-songs and the crying babies and the children shrieking and yelling as they played chase through the streets and alleys. I saw the white incense smoke rising from the houses of Enino as they made ready for mid-afternoon prayers. I saw the purple ribbons fluttering in the windows of the whorehouses. I crossed the Great River and looked down at the dirty children and old women and dogs, swarming over its muddy bed, scavenging for scraps...

And I returned to my home, the barracks of the 32nd Pristine Guard. The white walls were bare, the stone courtyard swept scrupulously clean. Officers in white jackets like my own saluted and greeted me with polite deference.

"Pleased to see you, sir."

"Good to have you back, your Holiness."

I was suddenly very tired. I couldn't face eating with my subordinates that night. I asked for some bread and cheese to be brought up to my rooms and let it be known that I would take up the reins again in the morning.

Then I retired to my quarters, my two austere rooms, with the iron bed, and the plain whitewashed walls and the single plain image of Enino, unsmiling, in the midst of his fiery wheel. Dutifully I made an obeisance, then I began to undress.

As I unbuttoned my jacket I caught sight of myself in the little mirror I use for shaving.

Tentatively, uncertainly, I smiled.

I'd never smiled at myself before. It seemed a strange thing to do. But I quite liked it. I sensed the pressure, long suppressed, of a warmer, lighter, more sensual me within...

*

Half-and-Half went to war. In No-Man's Land he danced among the bullets and laser beams. Among the ruins and the bomb craters, he laughed and performed acrobatic feats. Over the fallen corpses, he became a lion, a giant, an eagle with wings of fire.

Back at headquarters Generals and Arch-Generals stood in awe as he effortlessly absorbed information and expounded stratagems. Our soldiers cheered. They loved him for his indomitable spirit, not caring at all that he had once betrayed their own great-grandfathers. Along the whole front, they went back on the attack, full of courage and hope and new energy.

And all the while the bracelet of annihilation remained securely fixed to the Immortal Warrior's arm.

Day after day the Antinomians fell back, very often dropping their weapons and running in sheer panic. Day after day, fair-haired Philinomians ran out from their hiding places and prostrated themselves at our feet. At the Battle of the Ford, our enemies were finally routed. Their kingdoms were annexed to the Empire. Our victory was complete. I was sent by the Emperor to grant Half-and-Half his pardon and to bring him back to the City for the celebrations. But as I drew near to his encampment, a flash of blinding white lit the sky ahead of us. The bracelet had exploded, annihilating Half-and-Half and, with him, hundreds of soldiers and the entire mountain on which he had stood, looking out over those fertile Antinomian plains which he'd added to our Emperor's realm.

Where the mountain had been there was only a huge crater, almost completely smooth, as if scooped out of butter by a gigantic spoon.

We walked up to the rim of it, Sergeant Tobias and I. It was as bare and as dead and as featureless as a crater on the moon.

"No one could survive that," Tobias muttered, "no one. Not even an Immortal."

*

Not long afterwards I left the Imperial service and became a merchant, dealing in military surplus, and making good use of my reputation and my contacts. I married, I became quite comfortably off, I travelled the length and breadth of the Empire making deals.

About fifteen years after the Battle of the Ford, I happened to be passing through the Antinomian Borders with my new assistant Zolinda, and thought I would go up with her and take a look at the crater. (It had filled with rain over the years and become a lake). Partly I was curious: I wanted to remind myself that those strange events had really happened and not just been a dream. Partly I hoped to impress Zolinda with my stories of Half-and-Half and Gendlegap and my place in the history-books. She was an attractive woman and I wanted to sleep with her. It had worked with several others before.

So we went up to the lake known as Half-and-Half's Doom, Zolinda and I, and I told her the story, looking out over that circular expanse of lifeless water. But when I had finished, I felt strangely flat and not at all impressed by my own importance. What part had I really played after all in the story of Half-and-Half, other than the part of a dupe and a stooge?

That explosion was no accident, whatever the official story. Even as he was instructing me to fetch the Immortal Warrior, the Emperor knew quite well that I would never reach him. He hoped to cheat fate by getting the benefits of Half-and-Half's service and then eliminating him before the price had to be paid. He was – he still is – a player of games, a chancer, as amoral as Half-and-Half himself. A pure and virginal soldier like me was merely a useful foil.

But still, Zolinda was impressed. "You must be very proud, Illucian," she said. "I remember my father telling me how Half-and-Half had finally been made to serve the Emperor and win our war! I never dreamed I'd one day work for the man who was sent to fetch him from Gendlegap!"

I shrugged. "Actually I'm not so sure the Emperor did really benefit from Half-and-Half's service. For one thing our soldiers all loved Half-and-Half and blamed the Emperor for his death. The Emperor lost their wholehearted loyalty and that was the beginning of the end of his power."

It was cold up there. Above the rocky bowl of Half-and-Half's Doom, the sky was heavy and grey. Zolinda suddenly put her arm in mine. Why did this give me so little pleasure?

"As for the war," I said, "we won it, I suppose, but the Antinomians have been winning the peace ever since. Now that they are inside of the Empire, they're taking over. We even have an Antinomian in charge of the Imperial Bank!"

I turned to go, pulling free of her as I did so. "And of course the Philinomians breed like rabbits," I said, as we began to climb the rocky slope. "There isn't a street in the Empire where their pale little children aren't running about and shouting to one another in that outlandish Inglic tongue."

"But none of that is anything to do with Half-and-Half!" Zolinda protested.

"You don't think so?"

I paused to look back at the lake, surrounded by its rim of bare smooth rock.

So much for the Emperor, so much for the Empire, but what had become of me?

Well, I ate well now, I drank well, I made love as often as I could. And I was no longer thin, no longer haunted by the Eninometic ghosts of duty and sacrifice, no longer at war with my ordinary human needs.

Yet there were still times when I missed my old life in the Pristine Guard. Those austerities were once a part of me, after all. They gave me a direction, they provided me with certainties to live by.

And whatever I did, I would never recover those old certainties again.

*

There was a splash. Ripples spread outward from the central point of the lake.

It couldn't have been a fish. Nothing lived in that perfectly transparent water. Someone must have thrown a stone.

Yet there was no one by the water's edge, no one at all to be seen but a small dark-haired figure far off at the very top of the opposite rim.

And surely no one could have lobbed a stone from that far. It would have been an astonishing feat of strength.

The concentric waves spread over the glass-like surface until no part of the lake was untouched by the impact of that single stone. But as they spread they became smaller, and soon the lake was blank and smooth once again.

The dark-haired figure seemed to be watching us. Whoever it was, he waved. I could almost imagine I saw a small, teasing smile.

Monsters

"This is Dirk Johns, our leading novelist," said the poet's mother, "and this is Lucille, who makes wonderful little landscapes out of clay..."

"Oh, just decorative," protested the novelist's tiny, bird-like wife, "purely decorative and nothing more."

"And this is Angelica Meadows, the painter. You perhaps caught her recent exhibition in the Metropolis, Mr Clancy? I believe it received very good notices."

"I believe I did hear something..." I lied, shaking hands with a very attractive young woman with lively, merry eyes. "I'm afraid I spend so little time in the Metropolis these days."

"And this," went on the poet's mother, "is the composer, Ulrika Bennett. We expect great things of her."

No, I thought, looking into Ulrika Bennett's cavernous eyes, great music will never come from you. You are too intense. You lack the necessary playfulness.

And then there was Ulrika's husband, 'the ceramicist', and then an angry little dramatist, and then a man who uncannily resembled a tortoise, complete with wrinkled neck, bald head and tiny pursed little mouth.

"Well," I said, "I'm honoured."

The tortoise was, it seemed, was 'our foremost conductor and the director of our national conservatory.'

"The honour is ours, Mr Clancy" he said. "We have all read your extraordinary books, even out here."

*

"William!" called the poet's mother, "let us lead the way to dinner!"

The poet turned from a conversation with the painter Angelica. He had wonderfully innocent blue eyes, which had the odd quality that, while they seemed terribly naked and vulnerable, they were simultaneously completely opaque.

"Yes, of course, mother."

He pushed her wheelchair through into the panelled dining room and the guests took their seats. I was given the head of the table. William sat at the opposite end, his mother by his side. Servants brought in the soup.

"William and I are trying hard," announced the poet's mother to the whole company, "to persuade Mr Clancy that there is more to our little colony than cattle ranches."

"Indeed," I said soothingly, "there is clearly also a thriving cultural life which I would very much like to hear more about."

Well, they needed no second bidding. *Remarkable* things were being achieved under the circumstances, I was told, for the arts were struggling by with an *appalling* lack of support. Apart from the poet's mother, Lady Henry, who was of course *wonderful*, there was not a single serious patron of the fine arts to be found in the whole of Flain. Everyone present did their heroic best, of course, but not one of them had achieved the recognition that their talents deserved…

And so on. I had heard it many times before, in many more provincial outposts than I cared to remember. I made my usual sympathetic noises.

It was as the dessert was being served that I became aware of the poet's blue eyes upon me.

"Tell me honestly, Mr Clancy," he asked – and at once his mother was listening intently, as if she feared he would need rescuing from himself – "Had you heard of even one of us here in this room, before you knew you were coming to Flain?"

I hadn't, honestly, and from what little I had seen of their outmoded and derivative efforts, it was not surprising. (Let us face it, even in the Metropolis, for every hundred who fancy themselves as artists, there is only one who has anything interesting to say. It is just that in the

Metropolis, even one per cent is still a good many gifted and interesting people.)

But before I could frame a suitably tactful reply, William's mother had intervened.

"Really, William, how rude!"

"Rude?" His face was innocence itself. "Was that rude? I do apologise. Then let me ask you another question instead, Mr Clancy. What in particular were you hoping to see on your visit here? Please don't feel you *have* to mention our artistic efforts."

"Well I'm interested in every aspect of course," I replied. "But I don't deny that I'd like to learn more about the fire horses."

There was a noticeable drop of temperature in the room and everyone's eyes turned to Lady Henry, watching for her reaction.

"Fire horses," sighed the novelist, Johns. "Of course. The first thing every Metropolitan wants to see. Yet surely you must have them in zoos there?"

I shrugged.

"Of course, but then we have *everything* in the Metropolis, everything remotely interesting that has ever existed anywhere. I travel to see things in context. And Fire horses *are* Flain to the outside world, the thing which makes Flain unique. It was wonderful when I first disembarked here to see boys with their young fire horses playing in the streets."

"How I wish the brutes had been wiped out by the first colonists," said the poet's mother. "Your curiosity is perfectly understandable, Mr Clancy, but this country will not progress until we are known for something other than one particularly ugly and ferocious animal."

"Yes," I said, soothingly, "I *do* see that it must be irritating when one's homeland always conjures up the same one thing in the minds of outsiders."

"It *is* irritating to think that our country is known only for its monsters," said Lady Henry, "but unfortunately it is more than just irritating. How will we ever develop anything approaching a mature and serious cultural life as long as the educated and uneducated alike spend all their free time yelling their heads off in horse-races and horse-fights, and a man's worth is measured in equestrian skill? I do not blame you for your curiosity, Mr Clancy, but how we *long* for visitors who come with something other than fire horses in mind."

"Hear, hear," said several of them, but the poet smiled and said nothing.

"Well, I'll have to see what I can do about that," I said.

But of course in reality I knew that my Metropolitan readers would not be any more interested than I was in the arch theatricals at the Flain Opera or the third-rate canvasses in the National Gallery of Flain, straining querulously for profundity and importance. 'The Arts' are an urban thing, after all, and no one does urban things better than the Metropolis itself.

"I hardly like to mention it," I said in a humble voice, which I hoped would be disarming, "but the other thing for which Flain is famous is of course the game of sky-ball."

The poet's mother gave a snort of distaste.

"Ritualised thuggery!" she exclaimed. "And so tedious. I can't abide the game myself. I honestly think I would rather watch paint drying on a wall. I really do. At least it would be restful."

But Angelica the painter took a different view.

"Oh I *love* sky-ball!" she declared. "There's a big game tomorrow – the Horsemen and the Rockets. William and I should take you there, Mr Clancy. You'll have a wonderful time!"

William smiled.

"Good idea, Angie. I'd be very glad to take you, Mr Clancy, if you'd like to go."

"But Mr Clancy is to visit the Academy tomorrow," protested his mother. "Professor Hark himself has agreed to show him round. We really cannot..."

"I do *so* appreciate the trouble you've gone to," I purred, "but if it is at *all* possible to put Professor Hark off, I would very much like to see the Horsemen and the Rockets."

For, even back in the Metropolis, I had heard of the Horsemen and the Rockets.

"Well, of course," said Lady Henry, "if you want to go to the game we must take you. You know best what you need to see. I will talk to Professor Hark. No, a sky-ball game will be... an experience for me."

"But good lord, Lady Henry," I protested, "there's no need for you to come if you don't want. I'm sure William and Miss Meadows and I can..."

Polite murmurs of support came from the distinguished guests, but Lady Henry was resolved:

"Don't be ridiculous, Mr Clancy, of course I will come. We must sample every aspect of life, must we not? Not just those we find congenial." She summoned up a brave smile. "No, I am sure it will be *great fun*."

*

So we set off in the Henrys' car the next morning, Lady Henry riding up in front next to the elderly chauffeur (the seat had been removed to accommodate her wheelchair) while William and myself reclined on red leather in the back. We picked up Angelica on the way and she squeezed in between us, warm and alive and smelling of freshly mowed grass.

"I do hope you don't support the Rockets, Lady Henry," she exclaimed, "because I must warn you I'm an absolutely *rabid* fan of the Horsemen!"

Lady Henry gave a breathless, incredulous laugh.

"I can assure you I really have no idea about 'supporting' anyone, Angela, but I'm absolutely determined to have fun!" cried the poet's mother bravely.

She grew braver and braver by the minute. In fact, as the stadium itself came into view and we began to pass the supporters converging on the ground, Lady Henry's braveness became so intense that I feared it might blow out the windows of the car.

"What a good idea this was, Mr Clancy! What fun! The colours are very striking don't you think in this light, Angelica? Red, blue. Almost luminous. One thinks of those rather jolly little things that you paint on glass."

"Which are the Horsemen and which are the Rockets?" I asked.

"The Horsemen wear red," William began, "because their emblem is a…"

"Here, Buttle," interrupted Lady Henry, "pull over here and let me speak to this man."

A steward was directing the crowds to the various gates and Lady Henry waylaid him:

"I say, could you arrange some balcony seats for us please… I will need someone to carry me up the stairs... And our hamper too... No, no reservations.... I *do* hope you are not going to have to be bureaucratic about this, as I am a personal friend of the mayor... and this is Mr Clancy from the Metropolis, the distinguished writer... Thankyou so much... Here is something for your trouble... You are doing a stalwart job I can see."

I glanced at William. I could see he was angry and embarrassed, though Angelica seemed just to be amused.

"There," said Lady Henry with satisfaction. "Drive on Buttle, thankyou. Now if you drop us off just here I believe these are the young men now who are going to help us up the stairs."

*

With one steward unpacking our substantial picnic hamper for us, another sent off to find her a blanket and a third dispatched to search for aspirin (for she said she had a migraine coming on), Lady Henry settled into her seat and surveyed the scene.

"Of course, I have absolutely no idea of the rules, William. Just tell me what on earth these young men are going to be trying to do."

"To begin with the Rockets will be trying to get to the top, mother," said William, "and the Horsemen will be trying to get to the bottom. After each goal they reverse the direction of play. The main thing is..."

At this point the game itself began, to a great bellow from the crowd.

"The main thing is, mother..." William began again patiently.

But the old lady made an exasperated gesture.

"Oh, this is all much too complicated for me. I'm just going to concentrate on the spectacle of the thing I think. The spectacle. And it is all rather jolly I have to admit. Rather your sort of thing Angelica isn't it? Red and blue painted on glass. The sort of cheerful, uncomplicated thing that you do so well."

Then a huge roar of emotion rose around us like a tidal wave, preventing further conversation. A goal had been narrowly averted. Angelica leapt to her feet.

"Come *on* you reds!" she bellowed like a bull.

William watched her with a small, pained, wistful smile which I could not properly read, but did not join in. Lady Henry winced and looked away.

"I quite liked your last show Angelica," she said, as soon as the painter sat down in the next lull, "but if you will forgive me for being frank, I am starting to feel that you need to stretch yourself artistically a little more if your work is not in the end to become a bit repetitive and predictable."

"Let's just watch the game, shall we, Mother?" said William.

*

Six massive pylons were arranged in a hexagon around the arena and between them were stretched at high tension a series of horizontal nets, one above another every two metres, ascending to fifty metres up. Each net was punctured by a number of round openings through which the players could drop, jump or climb, but these openings were staggered so that a player could not drop down more than one layer at a time.

All the same, if no one stopped them, the specialist players called 'rollers' could move from top to bottom with incredible speed, dropping through one hole, rolling sideways into the next, swinging beneath a net to the one after, dropping and rolling again...the ball all the while clutched under one arm, and the crowd roaring its delight or dismay. 'Bouncers', who specialised in upward dashes, used the nets as trampolines to move with almost the same breathtaking velocity as the rollers, even though they had to work against gravity instead of with it. But of course neither bouncers nor rollers got a clear run. While these high-speed vertical dashes were taking place through the nets, other players were swarming up or down to positions ahead of the opposing team's rollers or bouncers in order to block them off. Pitched battles took place at the various levels, with players bouncing from the nets under their feet to launch ferocious tackles, or swinging from the nets over their heads to deliver flying kicks. It was like football, but in three dimensions and without constraints. Eight players were taken off injured during the match.

"Do you play sky-ball at all, William?" I asked in the car on the way back.

William was about to answer when his mother broke in.

"I always insisted that he should be excused from the game," she said, turning her head towards us with difficulty. "William never showed the slightest inclination towards it, and it seemed to me absurd that a sensitive child should be put through it."

"Oh but my brothers loved it," exclaimed Angelica. "Michael must have broken every bone in his body at one time or another, but it never put him off. He couldn't wait to get back into the game."

We turned into the drive of Angelica's home. In front of her family's large and comfortable farmhouse, William got out of the car to let her out and say goodbye. A short exchange took place between them which I couldn't hear. I wasn't sure if they were arranging an assignation or conducting a muted row.

"Do you know, William," said Lady Henry, when he had rejoined us and we were heading back down the drive, "I'm beginning to have second thoughts about Angelica. I am not sure she is *quite* one of us, if you know what I mean. I can't help feeling that Angelica the artist is really a very secondary part of her nature and that underneath is a pretty average country girl of the huntin' and shootin' variety. Don't you agree?"

But the poet declined to answer.

"There are some fire horses for you, Clancy," he merely said, as we passed a paddock with a couple of yearling beasts in it, feeding at a manger in the far corner.

"I gather boys in Flain are given baby fire horses to grow up with?" I said.

"It's traditional, yes," William said.

"And were you given one?"

We had left the estate of Angelica's family and were back on the empty open road. William looked out of the window at the wide fields.

"Yes. My Uncle John gave me one when I was six."

"Did you learn to ride? I've seen boys in the street with their small fire horses and they seem quite dangerous."

"No, I never learned. And yes, they are dangerous. In fact Uncle John himself died in a riding accident only few years after he gave me the horse."

"Oh, I'm sorry."

"Don't be, Mr Clancy," said William's mother, once again straining to turn round and look at me. "Don't be sorry at all. My brother was a foolish and immature young man who liked to show off with fire horses and fast cars because he wanted to impress a certain kind of silly young woman. The accident was *entirely* his own fault."

I glanced at William. But he still looking out of the window and I couldn't see his face.

"What would have been tragic, though," went on Lady Henry, "would be if I had allowed my brother to persuade William to ride – and *William* had had an accident. After all William is now Flain's foremost poet and it was obvious even at that age that he was quite exceptionally gifted. Imagine if all that had been thrown away because some stupid animal had flung him off its back and broke his neck?"

Some minutes later William, with an obvious effort, turned towards me.

"Ah here we are. Almost home. Do you know I think I must have nodded off a while there, I do apologise. A whisky Clancy perhaps, before we change for dinner?"

*

Two days before my departure from Flain, Lady Henry received some bad news about her northern estates. It had come to light somehow that her steward up there had been embezzling funds over many years. Lady Henry was in a state of distraction that night, torn between competing desires. For whatever reason, she seemed to hate the idea of leaving William and myself to our own devices, but she also found it intolerable not being at the helm to manage the crisis in the north. In the end it was the latter anxiety that won out. The following morning, after a great flurry of preparation that had every servant in the house running around like agitated ants, she set off in the car with Buttle.

William and I took our coffee out onto the stone terrace which overlooked the park and watched the car winding along the drive, out through the gate and on into the world beyond. It was a bright, fresh, softly gilded morning, on the cusp between summer and autumn.

William sighed contentedly.

"Peace!" he exclaimed.

I smiled.

"Mother has arranged for us to visit that sculptor's workshop this morning," he then said. "Do I take it you actually want to go?"

I laughed. "To be quite honest, no. Not in the slightest."

"Well, thank God for that. I think I will scream if we have to traipse round many more of Mother's artistic hangers-on."

We poured more coffee and settled back comfortably in our chairs. A family of deer had emerged from the woods to the left to feed on the wide lawns along the drive and we watched them for some minutes in companionable silence. Then he suddenly turned the full blueness of his gaze upon me.

"Have you read many of my poems, Clancy?"

"Yes, all of them," I told him quite truthfully. "All your published ones at least."

I do my research. When I decided to accept the invitation from William's mother to visit them, I had hunted down and looked through all six of William's slim little collections, full of veiled agonised coded allusions to his mother's catastrophic accident while pregnant with William, his father's shotgun suicide a week before his birth. (Why do we feel the need to wear our wounds as badges?)

"And, tell me quite honestly," William probed. "What did you think of them?"

I hesitated.

"You write very well," I said. "And you also have things to say. I suppose what I sometimes felt, though, was that there was a big difference between what you really *wanted* to say and what you actually were able to express in those verses. I had the feeling of something – contained... something contained at an intolerably high pressure, but which you were only able to squeeze out through a tiny little hole."

William laughed. "Constipated! That's the word you're looking for."

On the contrary, it was precisely the word I was trying to avoid!

I laughed with him. "Well no, not exactly, but..."

"Constipated!" His laugh didn't seem bitter. It appeared that he was genuinely entertained. "That is really very good, Clancy. Constipated is exactly right."

Then, quite suddenly, he stood up.

"Do you fancy a short walk, Clancy? There's something I'd very much like to show you."

*

The place he took me to was on the outer edges of their park. The woods here had been neglected and were clogged up by creepers and by dead trees left to lie and rot where they had fallen. Here, in a damp little valley full of stinging nettles, stood a very large brick outbuilding which could have been a warehouse or a mill. There were big double doors at one end, bolted and padlocked, but William led me to an iron staircase like a fire escape to one side of the building. At a height equivalent to the second storey of a normal house, this staircase led through a small door into the dark interior. Cautioning me to be silent, William unlocked it.

It was too dark inside to see anything at first, but I gathered from the acoustics that the inside of the building was a single space. We seemed to be standing on a gallery that ran round the sides of it. William motioned to me to squat down beside him, so only our heads were above the balustrade.

Almost as soon as we entered I heard the animal snorting and snuffling and tearing at its food. Now, as my eyes adapted, I made it out down there on the far side of the great bare stable. It must have been nearly the height of an elephant, with shoulders and haunches bulging with muscle. It was pulling with its teeth at the leg and haunches of an ox that had been hacked from a carcass and dumped into its manager.

"He hasn't noticed us yet," whispered William. "He wasn't looking in our direction when we came in."

"I take it this is the same horse that your uncle gave you?" I asked him, also in a whisper.

William nodded.

"But you never rode him?"

"No."

"And *will* you ever ride him?"

William gave a little incredulous snort. The sound made the fire horse lift its head and sniff suspiciously at the air, but after a second or two it returned again to its meat.

"No of course not," he said, "even if I knew how to ride a fire horse, which I don't, I couldn't ride this thing now. No one can ride an adult fire horse unless it was broken in as a foal."

"Yes, I see."

"I'll tell you something, Clancy. If you or I were to go down and approach him, he would tear us limb from limb. I'm not exaggerating."

I nodded.

"So why do you keep him?"

It seemed that I had spoken too loudly. The beast lifted its head again and sniffed, but this time it didn't turn back to its food. Growling, it scanned the gallery. Then it let loose an appalling scream of rage.

I have never heard such a sound. Really and truly in all my life and all my travels, I have never heard a living thing shriek like that dreadful fire horse in its echoing prison.

And now it came thundering across the stable. Right beneath us, glaring up at us, it reared up on its hind legs to try and reach us, screaming again and again and again so that I thought my eardrums would burst. The whole building shook with the beating of the animal's hooves on the wall. And then, just as with my hands over my ears I shouted to William that I wanted to leave, the brute suddenly emitted a bolt of lightning from its mouth that momentarily illuminated that entire cavernous space with the brilliance of daylight.

William's face was radiant, but I had had enough. I made my own way back to the door and out into the open. Those decaying woods outside had seemed sour and gloomy before, but compared to the dark stable of the fire horse they now seemed almost cheerful. I went down the steps and, making myself comfortable on a fallen tree, took out my notebook and began to record some thoughts while I waited for the poet to finish whatever it was he felt he needed to do in there. I was surprised and pleased to find my imagination flowing freely. The imprisoned fire horse, it seemed, had provided the catalyst, the injection of venom, that sooner or later I always needed to bring each book of mine to life. Inwardly laughing, I poured out idea after idea while the muffled screams of the tormented monster kept on and on — and from time to time another flash of lightening momentarily illuminated the cracks in the door at the top of the stairs.

After a few minutes William emerged. His face was shining.

"I'll tell you why I don't get rid of him, Clancy," he declared, speaking rather too loudly, as if he was drunk. "Because he is what I love best in the whole world! The *only* thing I've ever loved, apart from my Uncle John."

Behind him the fire horse screamed again and I wondered what William thought he meant by 'love' when he spoke of this animal which he had condemned to solitude and darkness and madness.

"I feel I have fallen in your esteem," he said on the way back to the house.

There had been a long silence between us as we trudged back from the dank little valley of brambles and stinging nettles and out again into the formal, public parkland of William's and his mother's country seat.

"You are repelled, I think," William persisted, "by the idea of my doting on a horse which I have never dared to ride. Isn't that so?"

I couldn't think of anything to say, so he answered for me.

"You are repelled and actually so am I. I am disgusted and ashamed by the spectacle of my weakness. And yet this is the only way I know of making myself feel alive. Do you understand me? You find my work a little constipated and bottled up, you say. But if I didn't go down to the fire horse, shamed and miserable as it makes me feel, I wouldn't be able to write at all."

I made myself offer a reassuring remark.

"We all have to find our way of harnessing the power of our demons."

It would have been kinder, and more honest, if I had acknowledged that the encounter with the firehorse had been a catalyst for me also, and that for the first time in this visit my book had begun to flow and come alive. But I couldn't bring myself to make such a close connection between my own experience and his.

*

That night William slipped out shortly after his mother returned, without goodbyes or explanations.

"I suppose he showed you his blessed horse?" said Lady Henry as she and I sat at supper.

"He did. An extraordinary experience I must say."

"And I suppose he told you that the horse and his Uncle John were the only things he had ever really loved?"

My surprise must have shown. She nodded.

"It's his standard line. He's used it to good effect with several impressionable young girls. Silly boy. Good lord, Mr Clancy, he doesn't *have* to stay with me if he doesn't want to! We are wealthy people after all! We have more than one house! I have other people to push me around!"

She gave a bitter laugh.

"I don't know what kind of monster you think I am Mr Clancy, and I don't suppose it really matters, but I will tell you this. When William was six and his uncle tried to get him to ride, he clung to me so tightly and so desperately that it bruised me, and he begged and pleaded with me to promise that I'd never make him do it. That night he actually wet his bed with fear. Perhaps you think I was weak and I should have made him ride the horse? But, with respect Mr Clancy, remember that you are not a parent yourself, and certainly not the sole parent of an only child." Her eyes filled with tears and she dabbed at them angrily with her napkin.

"His father was a violent, arrogant drunk," she said. "Far worse than my brother. He was the very worst type of Flainian male. He pushed me down the stairs you know. That was how I ended up like this. He pushed me in a fit of rage and broke my back. It was a miracle that William survived, a complete miracle. And then, when I refused to promise to keep secret the reason for my paralysis, my dear brave husband blew off his own head. I wanted William to be different. I wanted him to be gentle. I didn't want him to glory in strength and danger."

She gave a small, self-deprecating shrug.

"I do acknowledge that I lack a certain… lightness."

"Lady Henry, I am sure that…"

But the poet's mother cut me off.

"Now *do* try this wine, Mr Clancy," she cried brightly, so instantly transformed that I almost wondered whether I had dreamed what had gone before. "It was *absurdly* expensive and I've been saving it for someone who was capable of appreciating it."

*

In the early hours of the morning I heard William come crashing in through the front doors.

"Come and get my boots off!" he bellowed. "One of you lazy bastards come down and take off my boots."

And then I heard him outside the door of my room abusing some servant or other who was patiently helping him along the corridor.

"Watch out, you clumsy oaf! Can't you at least look where you're going?"

He still hadn't emerged when I left in the morning for the Metropolis.

The Gates of Troy

"Wow!" breathed my friend Hannibal, as we drew up beside the Croesus. "That's not a yacht, it's a bloody ship!"

I laughed. Shiny and sleek, Dad's motor yacht dwarfed the boats moored either side, though they themselves were big by most people's reckoning, and cost more than an average human being earns in a lifetime.

I led the way up the gangplank. Han followed (and behind Han, the chauffeur carrying our bags.) I smiled a little wearily as Han let out various exclamations of amazement. This kind of reaction – to the Croesus, to the houses, to the cars and planes and helicopters – has become tedious over the years. But of course this was a new world to Han, a world of almost godlike opulence, even though by most people's reckoning Han's family is far from poor.

For myself, when I look at the Croesus, I feel oppressed by the scale and flamboyance of the thing, as if it required of me that I too should be extravagant and larger than life, like Dad.

"Mehmet!" I called.

Wiry, white-haired, leathery with sun, the Croesus' faithful crewman emerged smiling from within. His whole working life has been given over to the care of the Croesus and its four predecessors, and to my father, who he adores.

"Master Alex! How nice to see you, sir. You have finished at school now, I understand?"

"Nice to see you too Mehmet." (The chauffeur put down the bags and disappeared). "This is my school friend Hannibal. Yes, school's out for good. It feels great!"

Actually it felt very frightening, but one didn't say that.

"Well, we are ready to leave as soon as you want."

"Great. We'll just settle in, and then let's be off."

*

"That was *extraordinary*!" enthused Han as I showed him his cabin.

"What was?"

"You just had a conversation in, what, Turkish?"

"Albanian actually." I sighed, "I'm sure I told you about my language splice didn't I?"

"I guess I didn't quite…"

The fact was that I hadn't had a conversation in Albanian at all. I had had a conversation in English. The language splice intercepted what Mehmet said in Albanian while it was still a signal in my auditory nerves and translated it for me. I replied in English, but the splice again intercepted the nerve signals going to my vocal cords and substituted the Albanian which actually came out of my mouth. The thing did this fluently with several hundred languages, and – because it knew examples of every language family from Indo-European to Uto-Aztecan – it would have a competent stab at any language at all, learning a new one properly in a day or two.

So when I listened, I only ever heard English. I could hear other languages as background noise, but as soon as I paid attention, they turned into English. It was my father's answer to my expressing an interest in studying languages at University.

"Waste of time, Alex, complete waste of time. No-one needs to study languages now."

My objections were dismissed as mere funk and the splice was put in under a local anaesthetic.

It was the same with history when I expressed an interest in that. Ask me a question about history, any question at all! The President of Latvia in 1988? Gorbunov. The death of Constantine the Great? 337 C.E. You see I don't even have to think about it.

A pity really.

*

An hour later I was steering the Croesus out to sea through a white forest of sailing yachts, tactfully assisted by Mehmet. Han had a go too when we were out in open water. Then we let Mehmet take over.

He headed for Corsica. We wandered up to the fore deck, stripped down to swimming trunks, opened some beers, rolled up the first of many joints and congratulated ourselves on being free.

Giving me the use of the Croesus for the summer was Dad's leaving-school present.

"Go where you like, take who you like. Have an adventure on me!" he'd said.

I know exactly what he had in mind: me and two or three red-blooded scions of the billionaire classes taking the Mediterranean watering holes by storm, seducing beautiful young women, shinning up drain-pipes, getting into scrapes. His disappointment was obvious when I chose as my sole companion a mere doctor's son, tongue-tied with awe in his presence, who'd only started at my school a couple of terms previously.

"At least reassure me you two are not a pair of fags," he grumbled.

"No, we're not!" I exclaimed, reddening.

But in fact there was a little of that in the air.

*

We had a division of labour. Mehmet navigated, refuelled, negotiated with harbourmasters, cooked, maintained the toilets, did the shopping and sluiced down the deck. Han and I took the odd turn at the wheel.

We went from Corsica to Sardinia, on to Sicily and Crete, and then north to meander between the Aegean islands. Sometimes we anchored off beaches and had a swim, or went ashore and explored the prettier towns. We avoided the big marinas and the gathering places of the rich. We made no serious attempt to meet people. And we talked a lot, Han and I, often about the lives that lay ahead of us and all the constraints and difficulties that put our dreams outside our reach.

"I'm going to medical school because that's always been the case," Han said. "My dad scraped and struggled his way into medical school from the gutters of Beirut. He'd prepared a niche for his son before his son was even born, and it hasn't occurred to him for one second to wonder whether his son might have plans of his own. Actually I hate sick people and the sight of blood makes me throw up."

"Tell me about it! With me it's like every time I express an interest in anything Dad gets it for me instantly. So it ceases to be an aspiration, ceases to be something to aim for. People think I'm being indulged, but actually I'm being fobbed off…"

And so on. We laughed a lot and touched each other a lot in what was ostensibly a brotherly horsing-around sort of way. But sometimes the eye contact lingered and was hard to break. I found myself noticing how good-looking Hannibal was with those dark Levantine eyes and how close we were, and he was clearly thinking similar sorts of things. He even tried to speak about it.

"You know Alex, you really are the only real friend I've ever had in my life. I feel I can talk to you about…"

But there was a boundary still and I drew back when he seemed to draw too close to it.

"It's this puff mate. It's good stuff. It makes everything seem like a revelation."

We were a bit in love with each other, but homosexuality was not a territory where I would feel at home.

Mehmet kept carefully out of our way.

*

We were off the Aegean coast of Turkey, moving towards the Dardanelles, when the helicopter appeared in the distance.

"Looks like one of Dad's," I observed idly and began rolling another joint.

When Han passed the joint back to me to finish it off, I looked round again at the helicopter which was much nearer now: nearly overhead.

"Jesus, it *is* Dad's!" I exclaimed, leaping convulsively to my feet and tossing the remains of the joint guiltily into the sea.

Han laughed disbelievingly. But then the helicopter was hovering overhead, a door was opening and a figure was being winched down towards us.

"It's your father, Master Alex!" exclaimed Mehmet, rushing excitedly up on deck after speaking to the helicopter on the radio.

I was less enchanted.

"What the fuck does he think he's doing!"

But then Dad was on the fore deck, unbuckling his harness: big, bronzed, beaming, radiant with energy and health.

"I thought I'd pay you boys a visit!"

Mehmet, who worships Dad, rushed forward and so did well brought-up Han, but my father held up a restraining hand.

"Just a minute. I've got a little surprise for you!"

The winch cable had gone up and now came down again with a large oblong package in a sling.

We helped to remove it. At a wave from Dad, the winch went up again and the helicopter left.

"Right then," my father said, "now I need a drink."

Mehmet hurried to oblige and we went down to the back of the yacht to sit in the shade of the canopy.

"So what have you been up to?" Dad asked.

Han, all stumbling and deferential and addressing him as 'sir', began to describe our route so far in boring detail. I interrupted to tell Dad about the highlights: the school of dolphins off the coast of Malta, the sunset over a tiny Sardinian cove, the octopus speared by a fisherman in Crete, its tentacles pulling and tugging at his trident just like a child being tickled, trying to pull the big fingers away... I knew Dad wouldn't be interested. I knew his eyes would glaze over in a matter of seconds. But he'd asked the question and I was damned if I was going to let him get away without waiting for me to answer.

"Nothing much then," was how he summed up when I'd finished. "That's what I thought. Well, I knew you could do with a bit of excitement so I brought you this."

He indicated the mysterious oblong, still wrapped in the canvas bag it had worn in the sling, then called out to Mehmet.

"Mehmet, old friend, you come and look at this too. It's the future of yachting!"

Incidentally, he spoke to Mehmet in English and Mehmet spoke English in reply. Dad always spoke English. (If absolutely necessary he carried a pocket translator). I once asked him why he hadn't had a language splice put in like me, if he thought they were such a good idea.

"Over the hill, I'm afraid, Al. The docs tell me it's a bad move at my age. If splice technology had been around when I was younger I would have gone for it like a shot."

But I doubt that very much. I can't imagine my father accepting anything inside his head that was made by another human being. He is, as they say, a self made man.

*

Anyway. The package.

Even when it was out of its bag, we were none the wiser. It was a white rectangular object with a set of controls and a display panel located roughly in the middle. There was also a suitcase-shaped box stuffed in with it into the canvas bag.

Dad was delighted by our expressions of incomprehension.

"No idea?" he asked. "Well, you'll certainly never guess. It's a temporal navigator, no less. A time machine!"

We all gasped. There are, after all, only a few such things in the world.

"That's worth more than the GNP of a medium sized country," exclaimed Han in a breathless semi-whisper, when my father had gone for piss. "And your Dad calmly lowers it from a helicopter onto a boat!"

I was irritated by his star-struck awe. He knew my feelings about my father. He'd listened, he'd sympathised. But when it came to it, he was just as gibbering and servile as everyone else in my father's actual presence, bowled over by his wealth and fame, and by the child-like egocentrism that came with it.

"Now I defy you to have a boring time with *this*, Alex," Dad said, settling back into his chair. "The Roman Empire. The Ancient Egyptians. Moses. You can go back five thousand years if you want to!"

"That's wonderful, sir," Han gushed, "I just can't get it through my head that this is a real temporal navigator. I mean you hear about these things but you don't expect to actually go back in time yourself. Wow! Unbelievable!"

He cast around for intelligent questions.

"I've... I've never quite gathered why people always use these at sea?"

"Because when you travel back you take a few hundred tonnes of the surrounding matter with you," Dad said, "Not too awkward if it's just water, but rather difficult on land. And on land you'd run rather a risk of materialising slap in the middle of a building or something."

"But isn't the planet in a different position anyway? I mean what with rotation and going round the sun and the sun itself, you know, going round the galaxy..."

Dad shrugged vaguely and looked away, as he did when irritated by pettifogging details.

"They say it is the ultimate yachting accessory," murmured Mehmet, who had taken delivery of many expensive yachting gizmos over the years, and acquired prestige as a result among the little fraternity of motor yacht chauffeurs.

But my father, always impatient with chat, was unpacking the box that came with the time machine.

"A few bits and pieces here in case there's any trouble. These little torch things give out blinding coloured light and make a deafening sound. Here's a couple of laser guns. These cylinder things here, they're small force shields. You strap them on your belt. If things get hairy you press this button and it sets up a protective field around you. There are modern weapons that could get through it but I'm assured that arrows, bullets and spears don't have a chance."

Han turned back to the time machine.

"How on earth does it work?" he wondered.

"No idea, but then I've never understood how a TV set works either," shrugged my father, the owner of the planet's largest broadcasting company and its second largest electronics manufacturer. "That's for the boffins. The important thing is how you use it!"

*

"So where are we going to go?" asked Dad, later that evening, after a meal under the stars, moored off a Turkish beach. "What are the big events in this part of the world? You tell us Alex, you're the one with the history splice!"

I felt hi-jacked. That was what I wanted to say. I'd been quite happy just wandering around the blue sea in the two dimensions of horizontal space, and letting my imagination do the rest. I didn't *need* this time travel gimmick. It was like someone barging in with a house-sized chocolate cake, a stripper and a brass band when you are enjoying a quiet little dinner for two.

But I recognised I was in a minority of one on this, so I moderated my lack of enthusiasm and confined myself to merely putting a damper on the proceedings.

"You know," I said, "people always want to go back to the big showy set pieces: the crucifixion, or the sack of Jerusalem, or the fall of Troy or something. But that isn't really what history is all about. Those are just the earthquakes, the very occasional explosions when the tensions build up and have to be released. Almost all of history is really just people going about their daily lives. If I'm going to go back in time I'd rather just visit some ordinary little place and see what ordinary life was like for them."

Dad gave an outraged roar.

"Of all the prissy, priggish *rubbish*! What utter *nonsense*! Come on now, Alex, you mentioned Troy, isn't that somewhere round here? That'd be something! We'll go back to the sack of Troy."

"Troy! Wow!" breathed Han. "Think of that Alex!"

"That's the spirit, Hannibal!" Dad exclaimed, and turned to me. "I thought this guy was a drip when you first brought him home, Alex, I make no bones about it. But it looks like he's got more spirit than you have."

*

Early next morning we were opposite Troy. If Han and I had been left alone to savour it, there would have been something quite magical about it: a sea as smooth as glass, islands in the hazy distance, the Aegean coast stretching away south, the mouth of the Dardanelles…. everything very still and softly luminous. And in the distance, across a pale plain of wheat and poppy flowers, was Hisarlík, a small hill, or really just a mound, which you would hardly notice at all if you didn't know that it was the site of nine cities, each built on the ruins of the last, spanning a period of four thousand years from the Bronze age to the early Christian Era.

I would have enjoyed a morning just soaking all that in. But Dad as ever was busy, busy, busy.

"Right then, gun, torch and force shield each, but we can sort that out later. Mehmet, we need to prepare the Croesus for quite a jolt. Now let's figure out how to use this thing. Alex, you're the history expert. Tell us what date to aim for."

"1242 B.C." I said, using that strange numb kind of knowledge that comes with a splice. (You can't feel it. It isn't part of you. It isn't woven together with other knowledge to become part of your intuitions and dreams. But when you look for it, suddenly it is there, and your own mouth is speaking it.) "Until about twenty years ago, no-one could have given an exact date and there were serious doubts as to whether there was any historical basis to the Homeric story at all. But, following the discovery of molecular memory..."

"1242 B.C.?" Dad, Mehmet and Han were all squatting round the time machine like little boys, trying to work out how to operate the controls and interpret the colourful displays.

"Right," my father commanded. "Take a seat and hold on tight."

Mehmet muttered something that ended with 'Allah.'

There was a spine-jolting crack, as if the boat had dropped from several metres up in the air, and then a sudden temperature drop and a few seconds of violent rocking.

I had closed my eyes like I always do on things like rides at fairs, and now I cautiously opened them.

*

It was evening. Eerily spot-lit by the sun setting behind us, the landscape opposite was recognisably the same as before, and yet it was totally *other* in a way that sent goosebumps up and down my spine. The plain was brown and scorched where it had been green. There were no houses, but on the hill of Hisarlík, which had been no more than a sort of stump, there stood a wondrous structure gleaming in the sun. It was the still unvanquished Troy, its high walls faced from top to bottom with shining tiles, its mighty gates of bronze blazing with solar fire.

Little groans of awe came from the others. Even my father was silent as we struggled to take this experience in.

"Look," said Han, "the Greek camp!"

We followed his gaze northwards to a dark city of tents and bonfires at the edge of the plain, with boats moored alongside. And then, almost simultaneously, we all exclaimed "The Horse!"

It wasn't just a story! There it was, towering over the camp, lit by bonfires and the setting sun.

*

We left Mehmet in charge of the Croesus. We all had powerful walkie-talkies we could call him on and Dad instructed him to go back to our own era and get help if at any point he lost touch with us. (Dad was confident that the Croesus' own formidable array of security devices would be more than a match for any surprise attack on the yacht itself). Then Dad, Han and myself went ashore in the tender, heading for the Greek camp.

What happened in the next few hours was so bizarre, so far beyond anything in my experience that much of it has become an incoherent and unreliable jumble, like scenes from early childhood, which I suppose is also a time when human beings find themselves in a strange and unfamiliar world.

I remember the camp stank of shit and ash and rotting meat. I remember heads on poles, some rotted to the bone, others still with skin and hair and eye sockets heaving with flies. I remember scrawny dogs and scrawny chickens and dirty little feral children. I remember captives tethered to wooden stakes, listless, fly-encrusted, some of them blinded or with severed limbs. I also seem to remember dismantled roundabouts and bits of ghost train and stacked sections of dodgems and waltzers. But I suppose that's because the whole place reminded me of a fairground being packed away after the fair is over. Everything was being taken down, stacked, loaded into the little wooden boats that lined the shore.

The Greeks had of course seen the Croesus appear in the distance, and observed our approach. We were surrounded as soon as we landed by hard, skinny little men with jagged bronze-tipped spears. I think they intended to skewer us there and then. Han and I had our fingers on the button of our force shields. Han's face was white as a corpse and probably mine was too, but Dad, who seemed to be enjoying himself enormously, switched his torch on to give a five second blast of artificial lightening and ear-splitting artificial thunder. All the Greeks screamed and ran for their lives except for a single one, taller and fairer than the others, who stubbornly stood his ground. He was a member of the ruling class it seemed, in Homeric terms a 'king', though probably the king of no more than some impoverished mountain village somewhere, or some tiny island.

"Who are you and why are you upheaved on the rim of the drinking vessel?" he demanded.

My splice could handle Modern Greek, New Testament Greek and Homeric Greek, but it struggled for a while before it mastered a Greek from times so ancient that even in Homer's day they were the stuff of legend. My father's translator clearly couldn't handle it at all because he poked irritably at the thing a few times, shook it and then, utterly characteristically, tossed it away with a gesture of impatience and contempt.

"Tell him we come from another world, Alex. Tell him we know about the horse and we know it's going to work because we can see the future."

I repeated this and the man seemed to understand at least enough of whatever it was that came out of my mouth to look surprised and alarmed when I said the bit about the horse. I suppose it wasn't meant to be common knowledge.

"Come with me. I will herd you to the nipple of the pine tree," he told me.

The other Greeks had started creeping cautiously back. One was poking gingerly with his spear at Dad's discarded translator.

We followed, Dad impatiently badgering me for information so that he could stay in control.

"What did he say, Alex? Where are we going? Tell him we want to go in the horse."

But I bided my time, enjoying the experience – even in this context – of my father being dependent on me. A short while later were in the presence of a group of bearded and grim-looking patriarchs, sitting on rugs and being fussed over by semi-naked slave-boys and slave-girls.

"Tell them you and Hannibal want to be in the horse."

"Me and Han? What about you."

"No, no. This is your adventure Alex."

I shrugged, affecting an indifference which I certainly did not feel, and made the request as asked to the assembled Achaean dignitaries.

There was a lot of head-shaking and doubtful sucking in of breath.

"Tell him you have great powers," Dad said.

So I did, and we demonstrated for them the torches, the laser guns and the force shields. They were impressed, especially by the torch. They were much too dignified and aristocratic to run, but the fake thunder made them first go grey and stiff and then explode into a babble of animated debate. How they wished they could own such a thing! (Oddly the force shields interested them rather less, and one of them even claimed to have possessed such a thing himself since babyhood).

"Tell them they can have my torch if they let you and Han go in the horse," Dad said.

"How do you know I want to go in the damn horse?" I demanded.

But Han said, "Come on Alex, the *Trojan Horse*, for God's sake!"

So I passed on Dad's offer to the senior king. His eyes lit up with excitement like a little boy and he agreed to the deal at once, reaching out greedily for the toy to be placed into his hands.

We phoned Mehmet and told him what we'd arranged.

*

The time in the horse was hell. Thirty six hours in a baking windowless box stinking of sweat and halitosis and, increasingly as the time went by, of the urine that soaked into the layers of leather and wool which had been packed in to stop tell-tale drips from appearing underneath the horse. There was nothing to eat but strips of stinking dried fish and nothing to drink but mouthfuls of water that tasted as if it had been scooped from a ditch. While we waited for the Trojans, I had the whispered conversations of the Greeks to regale me as they discussed the booty they would capture, the cruelties they would inflict, the destruction they would unleash and the lip-smacking smorgasbord of rape that lay before them.

"Little girls," one of them said, "really little girls. They're lovely and tight and you don't have to work so hard to hold them down."

"This is long ago," I kept reminding myself. "All these people were dead and buried and forgotten a thousand years before Christ."

Then the Trojans came and we had to remain silent for hours in the hottest part of the day, waiting for the horse to move. After that came hours of jolting about as we were dragged slowly across the plain and into the city. And then at last, as night fell, silence returned outside.

Finally the time came. Our leader, an especially grim and dour-looking man named Uxos, opened a hatch. Then he and two others dropped down into the darkness below. We heard faint choking sounds and when finally Han and I lowered ourselves down, there were three Trojans sprawled down there in black pools of their own blood.

"This isn't happening now," I told myself again, "this is three thousand years ago."

The relief of emerging into the cool night air was so immense in any case that I could have tolerated almost anything.

"Right," said Uxos, "you two strangers come with me and Achios to the gates."

The rest of the Greeks dispersed through the town.

*

I hadn't anticipated Troy would be so beautiful. Softly lit by lamps, the deserted streets were lined with big, graceful, well-constructed houses, decorated with carved designs of people and animals and gods which had been picked out in coloured paints or sometimes in gold leaf. There were little gardens and pools with stone benches beside them under trees. There were statues and little shrines

As Han and I followed Uxos and Achios, his young sidekick, I thought of the Trojans sleeping behind these walls, grandparents, children, babies, peacefully sleeping and not knowing that this would be the last hour of peace in their lives. I imagined an old man snoring beside his arthritic wife, a young woman returning a sleeping baby to a cot, a little girl with her arm around a worn old doll, wriggling into a more comfortable position...

"This is all long ago," I again tried to reassure myself.

But I was not much comforted. And I thought of the dirty little soldiers gathering outside the walls with their jagged blades and their lewd and murderous dreams.

Han, meanwhile, seemed to be in a different mental universe.

"This is so brilliant, Alex!" he whispered. "I keep telling myself over and over that we're really here! We're in the legend! We were in the wooden horse itself!"

Being really there was what he said excited him, but he *wasn't* really there. It was all just some sort of fancy VR game to him. Actuality itself was just a particularly brilliant graphics package.

But then, not having a splice, he hadn't heard what the soldiers were saying inside the horse.

*

Another unexpected thing about Troy was that it was very small. We were soon facing the city wall and the enormous bronze gates, where a single Trojan soldier stood on duty in a small square lined with trees. The Trojans had never expected an attack from inside. And yesterday they'd seen the Greeks apparently sailing away, leaving nothing behind them but their midden heaps and their strange wooden horse. So they weren't really expecting an attack at all.

Uxos beckoned to Han and I to keep down while he and his lieutenant crept up to the gates, Achios going to the right and Uxos to the left.

They had it all worked out. Dissolving into the darkness under the trees, Achios emerged right in front of the sleepy sentry and softly called out to him. The man jumped slightly then peered into the darkness to see who it was. But before he could say or do anything else, Uxos had run silently out from the trees behind him, pulled back his head with a hand over his mouth, and dragged a blade across his throat.

As Uxos let him fall, Achios was already climbing up onto the lower of the two great bars that held the gates closed and was reaching up to push at the higher one. Uxos ran to join him and very quickly they had worked it loose and slid it back. Then they jumped down and heaved together at the lower bar.

As it came free, Hannibal leapt to his feet and punched his fist into the air with a triumphant, puerile "*Yes!*"

I couldn't bear to look at his face.

There was a shout from the top of the wall. A sentry up there had finally realised that something was going on. But it was far too late. The gates were swinging open. (Hannibal ran to give them a hand.) Outside in the darkness, one firebrand after another was bursting into flames to reveal the hungry, leering faces of the Greeks.

They all let out a cheer.

And there, right up in front, cheering with the rest of them, was my Dad, like a banal, benevolent giant, like something out of a comic book, his whole face lit up by boyish delight.

*

We didn't actually participate in the rape and pillage. As the Greeks streamed shrieking in, Dad fell back. Han and I joined him and we went back to the tender and rejoined Mehmet on the Croesus.

Dawn was breaking over the plundered city as we settled in our seats to return to our own time. Smoke was pouring into the sky from within those immaculate porcelain walls, and there was a faint high sound wafting towards us over the sea. It sounded like whistling wind. It sounded like weather. It sounded like nothing of any consequence at all. But in fact it was human. It was human voices. It was the bland amalgam of hundreds and hundreds of terrified and despairing screams.

Then we were back in the present, in the very moment from which we had left. There were fields of wheat and poppies, and the city, that focal point of agony, was now just the peaceful and nondescript mound of Hisarlík, where nothing much more distressing had happened for hundreds of years than a tourist mislaying his camera case.

"Well!" exclaimed my dad. "That calls for a large breakfast I think. Do you think you could rustle up something, Mehmet? Plenty of cholesterol, plenty of calories and loads of strong coffee. Splendid. Now admit it boys, you don't get an experience like *that* every day!"

And he phoned his people in Istanbul to send back a helicopter to lift him off. There was a TV company in Bulgaria he was hoping to acquire.

*

"Smoke?" said Han, as Dad finally disappeared over the horizon. "Smoke and then a long sleep, maybe?"

He got out tobacco and dope and started to roll up. We were sitting at the stern under the canopy. Mehmet was washing the fore deck, keeping, as always, carefully out of our way.

"So where next?" said Han, pausing before lighting up. "That was just *incredible*! Your Dad is incredible. This has been the most incredible trip of my entire life."

"I think I'll pass on the smoke," I said.

"High enough already, eh?" said Han. "You're right. I'll save it for later. Maybe we should get some sleep and then think about where we're going?"

"Actually I think I'll get Mehmet to drop me off at Izmir and I'll get a plane home."

"Oh." He was dismayed. "I thought we were carrying on for another fortnight at least."

"Yes, well, sorry. The bubble has sort of burst. You can carry on if you want. Dad seems to have left his time machine behind, so you can use that too."

"All on my own, eh? That'll be fun."

"It's up to you."

Then Han turned on me.

"Christ, Alex, what's the *matter* with you? Look at you, you get a luxury yacht to play with, you get a temporal navigator, you get stuff most people can only dream of. And what do you do with it all? You get in a sulk and walk away. It's true what people say about you. I've always stood up for you before but I can see now they're right. You're spoiled. You're just plain spoiled."

I shrugged and went to give Mehmet his instructions.

I could hardly wait to be off the Croesus and sitting on a plane back to London.

What I would do then exactly, I still wasn't quite sure.

But I'd see a doctor for a start, and get these splices cut out of my head.

The Perimeter

The first time Lemmy Leonard saw the white hart it was trotting past a sweet shop on Butcher Row at ten o'clock on a Wednesday morning. He'd never seen such a thing and would have certainly followed it there and then if he hadn't seen PC Simon approaching. Lemmy was supposed to be in school and the authorities were having one of their crackdowns on truancy, so he had to slip down a side road until the policeman had passed by. When he emerged the deer had gone.

It was strange how bereft that made him feel. All day the sense of loss stayed with him. He had no words for it – he never spoke or thought about such things – no way of explaining it at all.

"Are you okay Lemmy darling?" said his mother that night as she brought him his tea. (She looked like a Hollywood starlet, but without the overweening vanity) "Only you seem so quiet."

It was raining outside. You could tell by the faint grey streaks that crossed the room, like interference on a TV screen.

*

The second time he saw it was outside a pub off the Westferry Road. It was two o'clock on a Tuesday afternoon and he was with Kit Rogers, Tina Miller and James Moss. He really wanted to follow it then, but Kit had just that minute suggested they all go into Grey Town and if Lemmy had proposed something else it would have looked like he was afraid.

"Not Grey Town!" pleaded Tina. "I hate that creepy place."

"Are you saying you're scared?" asked Lemmy with a sneer.

"No I never but... Oh alright then, just so long as we don't meet that beggar. You know, the one who hasn't got any..."

"No, he's always on the same corner these days, over on the Blackwall side," said Kit with a sly look at James. "You won't see him if we go in on this side."

Lemmy and his friends were Dotlanders. They were low-res enough to have visible pixels and they only had 128 colours apiece, except for James that is, whose parents had middle-class aspirations and had recently upgraded to 256. There were all low-res, and up in the West End they would all have looked like cartoon characters – even James – but down in Grey Town they looked like princes, the objects of envy and hate.

It was like descending to Hades, going into Grey Town and finding yourself surrounded by all those grainy, colourless faces. There were outline faces, even, faces with ticks for noses and single lines for mouths. Greyscale hustlers tried to sell them things, black-and-white dealers tried to do deals, dot-eyed muggers eyed them from doorways and wondered how much of a fight these Dotland kids would put up, and whether they had anything on them that would make it worth finding out. And then from the darkness under a railway arch came the sound that Tina dreaded and that Kit and James had tricked her into hearing

"*Bleep!*"

Tina screamed.

"You said he was over by Blackwall!"

The boys laughed.

"You bastards! You set me up on purpose!"

"*Bleep!*" went the darkness again and a plain text message appeared in green letters in the black mouth of the arch:

Help me! Please!

Guiltily each one of them tossed a few pence of credit in the direction of this unimaginably destitute being who could afford neither a body nor a voice.

"I really hate you for that, Kit!" Tina said. "You *know* how much that guy creeps me out!"

"Yes, but that's why it's so much fun winding you up!"

And then they saw the white hart again, trotting through the streets of Grey Town.

"There it is again," said Lemmy, "let's go and…"

*

But once *again* there was a distraction, this time a commotion further up the street. A small crowd of young Greytowners were heading their way, laughing and jeering around an immensely tall, solitary figure with an unruly mane of long white hair who was striding along in the midst of them, like an eagle or a great owl being mobbed by sparrows.

They recognised him as Mr Howard. He was a big landlord in Grey Town and across the East End, and he came in occasionally to look over his properties, always wearing the same crumpled green velvet suit in true colour and as high a resolution as it was possible to be, with real worn elbows and real frayed cuffs and the true authentic greasy sheen of velvet that has gone for months without being cleaned.

What was fascinating and disturbing about Mr Howard was his imperial disdain and the way he strode through Grey Town as if he owned the place. He actually *did* own quite a lot of it but that was only one reason for his regal manner. The other reason was the absolute invulnerability that came from his being an Outsider. Sticks and stones would bounce off Mr Howard, knives would turn. No one could hurt an Outsider, or even stop him in his tracks.

"Spook!" yelled a tiny little black-and-white boy from the kerb with his little outline mouth. "Mr Howard is a spook!"

"Peter! Over here! *Now!*" hissed the little black-and-white woman who was his mother.

The little boy looked round, smiling triumphantly until he saw her fear. Then he burst into tears and went running back to her. And the two of them, the two little low-budget animated drawings of a mother and a child, cowered together in the shadow of a doorway while Mr Howard strode by.

Lemmy looked around for the white hart. But it had gone.

*

About a week later Lemmy and the others were hanging round Dotlands Market, checking out the stalls selling low-res clothes and jewellery and shoes ("Never mind the resolution, look at the design!") the equally low-res food stalls ("It might *look* low-res, darlin', but do you buy food to look at? The flavour is as high-res as it gets!") and the pet stores with their little low-res cartoon animals ("These adorable little critters have genuine organic central nervous systems behind them, ladies and gents! Real feelings like you and me!")

"Look Lemmy!" James said, pointing past the stalls, "There's that white animal again!"

Lemmy took over at once. He was determined not to let it get away from him again.

"Okay. Listen. Be quiet and follow me!"

The deer was in a small dark alley between two old Victorian warehouses, grazing on tufts of grass that grew up through cracks in the tarmac. It lifted its head and looked straight in their direction. They all thought it was going to run, but it bent down again and calmly continued with its grazing.

"What *is* it?" Lemmy whispered as they drew up with it.

He reached out and touched it. The deer took no notice at all.

Kit shrugged.

"I'm bored. Let's go and do something else."

"Yeah let's," Tina said. "I don't like this animal. I'm sure it's something physical."

Lemmy and his friends didn't really understand 'physical' but there was something eerie and threatening about the particular quality of being that went by that name. Lemmy had come across a physical piece of paper in the street once, skipping and floating through the air as if it weighed nothing at all. And yet when it fell to the ground and he tried to pick it up, it was hard as iron to his touch and he couldn't shift it any more than he could shift a ten ton weight. And Outsiders were physical too in some way. They had some kind of affinity with physical objects. That was what defined them as being 'outside'. That was one of the things that made *them* seem eerie and threatening too.

"Physical?" Kit exclaimed, taking a step back. "Ugh! Do you really think so? I didn't know animals *could* be physical. Except birds of course."

The deer lifted its head again and looked straight past them down the alley. How could a creature be so alert, so on edge, yet be so completely indifferent to them even when they were so close? What else was there in the world for it to be scared of?

"Of course it's physical," James said. "Just look how high-res it is!"

"Yeah, even more than you, Smoothie," said Kit.

And it was true. The deer wasn't at all like the cheerful little low-res dogs and cats that people in Dotlands kept as pets. You could see the individual hairs on its back.

But none of this concerned the white hart. It finished the tuft of grass it was eating and moved off slowly down the alley, as indifferent to their judgement as it was to their presence.

"Are you coming Lemmy?" called Kit, as she followed James and Tina back to the cheerful market.

*

But Lemmy didn't follow them. He followed the white hart. He followed it right across London, through back streets, across parks, over railway tracks, in and out of low-res neighbourhoods and high-res neighbourhoods, across white areas and black areas, through shopping centres, across busy freeways.

It was slow progress. The deer kept doubling back on itself or going off in completely new directions for no apparent reason. Sometimes it stopped for twenty minutes to graze or to scratch with its hoof behind its ear. Sometimes it would run and skip along at great speed and Lemmy could barely keep up, though at other times he could walk right beside it, resting his hand on its back. Once it lay down in the middle of the road and went to sleep. Cars honked at it. One driver even got out and kicked it, which would have made Lemmy mad if it wasn't for the fact that the deer didn't even stir in its slumber and the man hurt his foot.

"Bloody Council," the driver said, glowering at Lemmy as he hobbled back to his car. "I thought they were supposed to keep these damned things out of here."

He – and all the cars behind him – had to drive up onto the kerb to get round the sleeping animal.

What things? Lemmy wondered. What things were the Council supposed to keep out?

Five minutes later the deer woke up and moved off of its own accord.

Another time it went through the front door of a small terraced house – not through an open door, but through the shiny blue surface of a closed one as if it was mist or smoke. It was a shocking and inexplicable sight, but such things happened occasionally in London. (Once, when Lemmy was little, he and his mother had been walking down a street when the whole section of road ahead of them had simply disappeared, as if someone had flipped over channels on TV and come to an unused frequency. A few seconds later it all returned again, just as it had been before.) Lemmy waited and after a few minutes the deer's antlers and head and neck appeared again through the door, looking like a hunting trophy. Then it came right through and trotted off down the street. (The blue door opened behind it and a bewildered couple came out and stood there and watched it go, with Lemmy following behind.)

On they wandered, this way and that through the suburban streets. But as evening began to fall and the street lights came on, the deer seemed to move more purposefully northward. It was as if its days' work were done, Lemmy thought, and it was going home. It seldom stopped to graze now, it never doubled back. At a brisk trot, occasionally breaking into a run, it hurried on past miles of houses where families were settling down for the evening in the comfortable glow of television. A few times Lemmy thought he'd lost it when it ran ahead of him and disappeared from his view. But each time, just when he was on the point of giving up, he saw it again in the distance, a ghostly speck moving under the street lights, so he kept on going, though he was miles away from home now and in a part of the city he had never seen before.

*

And then the white deer came to the last house in London – and the city ended.

Lemmy had realised that London wasn't limitless of course. He knew there were other places beyond – there were stations, after all, with gateways you could go through and visit New York or Florida or Benidorm or Heaven or Space – but it had somehow never occurred to him that there might be a point where the city just petered out.

But here he was in front of a line of orange lights that meandered away into the distance, East and West, to his left and to his right, up and down hills, with a sign put up by the Council appearing again and again after every five lights:

Perimeter of Urban Consensual Field

To the north, straight ahead of him, beyond the lights, the orange glow they gave off continued for some yards but then stopped. After that there was nothing: no ground, no objects, no space, just a flickering blankness, like a spare channel on TV.

Lemmy hardly ever went to school and he could barely read, and in any case it was his practice to ignore official signs. What seemed important to him at that particular moment was that the white hart had already trotted forward under the orange lights and into the bare orange space beyond. Lemmy's Dotlands sense of honour dictated that he couldn't stop. Even if he had no idea what a *perimeter* was – let alone a *consensual field* – and even if it meant going into still stranger territory when he already he had no idea where he was – he couldn't stop now any more than he could refuse a dare to go into the middle of Grey Town or to walk up to Mr Howard and call him a spook to his terrifyingly high-res face.

And yet, almost immediately, he *did* stop, not because he'd changed his mind but because, when it came to it, he simply had no choice in the matter. He was just walking on the spot. It was impossible to go forward. And words he had seen on the signs appeared again, but this time right in front of his eyes, flashing on and off in glowing green:

> *Perimeter of Field!*
> *Perimeter of Field!*
> *Perimeter of Field!*

There was nothing he could do but to stand and watch the white deer trotting away to wherever it was that it was going.

Out in the orange glow it turned round and looked back in his direction. And now, oddly, for the first time it seemed distinctly alarmed. Had it finally noticed his existence, Lemmy wondered? And if so why now, when several times it had let him come up close enough to touch it and not seemed concerned at all? Why now when it had been happy to lie in a road and be kicked?

But whatever it was that had frightened it this time, the deer now turned and fled in great skips and leaps.

And as it crossed from the orange glow of the lights into the flickering, empty-channel nothingness, it disappeared.

*

"I'm sorry. You were watching him, weren't you?" said a woman's voice. "I'm afraid it was me that scared him off."

Lemmy looked round. The speaker was tall, extremely ugly and much older than anyone he had ever seen or spoken to – yet she was very high-res. You could see the little marks and creases on her skin. You could see the way her lipstick smeared over the edges of her lips and the coarse fibrous texture of her ugly green dress.

"Yeah, I was watching him. I've been following him. I wanted to know where he was going. I've been following him half-way across London."

"Well I'm sorry."

Lemmy shrugged. "He would have gone anyway I reckon. He was headed in that direction."

He looked out into the blankness in the distance.

"What I don't get though, is what that is out there and how come he just vanished?"

The woman took from her pocket a strange contraption consisting of two flat discs of glass mounted in a kind of frame. She placed it in front of her eyes and peered through it.

"No he hasn't vanished," she said. "He's still out there, look, just beyond the fence."

She clicked her tongue.

"But will you *look* at that big hole in the fence there! I suppose that must be how he got in."

"*I* can't see him," Lemmy said.

"Just beyond the wire fence look. In front of those trees."

"I can't see no fence. I can't see no trees neither."

"Oh silly me!" the old woman exclaimed. "I wasn't thinking. They're beyond the consensual field, aren't they? So of course you wouldn't be able to see them."

Lemmy looked at her. She was so ugly, yet she behaved like a famous actress or a TV presenter or something. She had the grandness and the self-assurance and the ultra-posh accent.

"How come you can see it then? And how come that animal can go out there and I can't?"

"It's a deer," she said gently, "a male deer, a hart. The reason it can go out there and you can't is that it is a physical being and you are a consensual being. You can only see and hear and touch what is in the consensual field."

"Oh I know it's just physical," Lemmy said.

"*Just* physical? You say that so disparagingly! Yet once every human being on earth was physical."

Lemmy pretended to laugh, thinking this must be some odd, posh actressy kind of joke.

"You don't know about that?" she asked him. "They don't teach you about that at school?"

"I don't go to school," Lemmy said. "There's no point."

"No point in going to school! Dear me!" the woman exclaimed – and she half-sighed and half-laughed.

"Well, it's like this," she said. "In the city, two worlds overlap: the physical universe and the consensual field. Every physical thing that stands or moves within the city is replicated in the copy of the city that forms the backdrop of the consensual field. That's why you could see the hart in the city but not when it went beyond the perimeter. Do you understand what I'm saying?"

"Nope," said Lemmy shortly with an indifferent shrug.

"But how come it couldn't seem to see *me* though?" he couldn't help adding. "Not even in the city?"

"Well, how *could* a wild animal see the consensual field? Animals don't know that the consensual stuff is there at all. You and I might go into the city and see busy streets bustling with people, but to the deer the streets are empty. He can wander through them all day and meet no one at all except, once in a while, the occasional oddball like me."

Lemmy looked sharply at her.

"Like you? You're not a...?"

The woman looked uncomfortable.

"Yes, I'm a physical human being. An Outsider as you call us. But please don't..."

She broke off, touching his arm in mute appeal. Lemmy saw for an instant how lonely she was – and, having a kind heart, he felt pity. But simultaneously he wondered if he could run quickly enough to get away from her before she grabbed him.

"Please don't run off!" the old woman pleaded. "We're just people, you know, just people who happen to still live and move in the physical world."

"So, you're like the animal then?"

"That's it. There are a few of us. There only can be a few of us who are lucky enough and rich enough and old enough to have been able to..."

"But how come you can see me then, if the animal couldn't?"

"I can see you because I have implants that allow me to see and hear and feel the consensual field."

Lemmy snorted.

"So you have to have special help to see the real world!"

She laughed, though not unkindly.

"Well, some might say that the real world is that which is outside of the consensual field." She pointed out beyond the orange lights. "Like those trees, like those low hills in the distance. Like the great muddy estuary over there to the east, like the cold sea..."

She sighed.

"I *wish* I could show you the sea."

"I've been to the sea *loads* of time."

"You've been to manufactured seas, perhaps, theme park seas, sea-like playgrounds. What I mean is the *real* sea which no one thinks about any more. It just exists out there, slopping around in its gigantic bowl all on its own. Nowadays it might as well be on some uninhabited planet going round some far off star. So might the forests and the mountains and the..."

Lemmy laughed.

"Things out there that no one can see? You're kidding me."

The old woman studied his face.

"I'll tell you what," she said. "You can't see the trees but if you listen, you will surely be able to hear them. Listen! It's a windy night. The sensors will pick it up."

Lemmy listened. At first he couldn't hear anything at all. He was about to laugh and tell the woman she was winding him up, but suddenly he became aware of a very faint sound which was new to him: a sighing sound, rising and falling, somewhere out there in the blankness. Sighing, sighing, sighing: he felt he could have listened to it for hours, that rising and falling sigh from a space that lay outside his universe.

He wasn't going to tell *her* that though.

"Nope," he said firmly. "I can't hear nothing."

The woman smiled and touched his cheek.

"I must say I like you," she said. "Won't you tell me your name and where you come from?"

He looked at her for a moment, weighing up her request.

"Lemmy," he told her, with a small firm nod.

What harm could she do him just by knowing his name?

"I'm Lemmy Leonard," he said, "I live down Dotlands way."

"Dotlands? My, that's a *long* way to have come! That *is* half-way across London! Listen, Lemmy, my name is Clarissa Fall. My house is just over there."

She pointed to a big Victorian mansion, perhaps half a mile away to the east, just inside the perimeter, illuminated from below by a cold greenish light.

"Why don't you come back and have something to eat with me before you go back home?"

He didn't fancy it at all but it seemed cruel to turn her down. She was *so* lonely. (I suppose they must *all* be lonely, he thought. No one wants to talk to them, do they? No one wants to meet their eyes. People in the street even tell their kids to come away from them.)

"Yeah alright," he said. "Just for a bit."

*

They came to Clarissa's house through a formal garden, with geometrical beds of rose bushes and stone fountains in the shape of nymphs and gods that stood in dark, glittering ponds. Pathways wound through it, from one strange tableau to the next, illuminated by electric lights set into the ground.

"The statues and the lights are physical," Clarissa said, "but we had to get rid of the physical roses and the physical water. It was all getting too difficult to maintain. So the roses and the fountains you can see are just consensual. They're part of the Field. If I switched off my implants, all that I would see here would be stone statues and concrete and ponds with nothing in them but mud and the skeletons of frogs."

She looked at Lemmy and sighed. The lights along the pathways had a cold greenish edge, like radiant ice.

"And of course you wouldn't be here with me any more, either," she added.

"What do you mean I wouldn't be here? Where else would I be?"

"Well… Well, I suppose that to yourself you *would* still seem to be here. It's just that I wouldn't be able to *tell* that you were here, like the deer couldn't."

He could see she wanted to say something else but that she thought she shouldn't. And then, in spite of herself, she said it anyway.

"Well really the deer's eyes didn't deceive it," she blurted out, "because really you *aren't* here, you are…"

"What do you mean I'm not bloody here?" demanded Lemmy hotly.

She looked at him with a curious expression, both guilty and triumphant. It was as if she was pleased to have got a reaction of any sort from him. Like some lonely kid in a school playground who no one likes, Lemmy thought, winding you up on purpose just to prove to herself that she exists.

They had come to Clarissa's front door. Suddenly she turned to face him.

"Don't take any notice of what I said just now. *Of course* you're here, Lemmy. Of course you are. You're young, you're alive, you're full of curiosity and hope. You're more here than I am, if the truth be told, *far* more here than I am."

She pushed open the door and they entered a cavernous hallway with a marble floor.

"Is that you Clarissa?" came a querulous male voice.

An old man came out of a side room, his face yellowy and crumpled, his body twisted and stooped, his shapeless jeans and white shirt seemingly tied round the middle with string – and yet, like Clarissa, so high-res that he made Lemmy feel almost like a Greytowner.

"You've been out a long time," the old man grumbled. "Where on earth have you been?"

"Terence," she told him, "this is Lemmy."

The old man frowned into the space that she had indicated.

"Eh?"

"*This is Lemmy*," she repeated with that firm deliberate tone that people use when they are trying to remind others of things which really they should already know.

"*Implants*," she hissed at him when he still didn't get the hint.

The old man fumbled, muttering, at something behind his ear.

"Oh God," he sighed wearily, seeing Lemmy for the first time and immediately looking away. "Not *again*, Clarissa. Not this all over again."

*

Clarissa told Lemmy to go into the lounge.

"Sit down and make yourself comfortable, dear. I'll be with you in just a moment."

It was a high, long room lined with dark wooden panelling. On the walls hung big dark paintings of bowls of fruit, and dead pheasants, and horses, and stern, unsmiling faces. A fire, almost burnt out, smouldered under an enormous mantelpiece with a design of intertwining forest leaves carved heavily into its dead black wood.

Lemmy sat himself awkwardly on a large dark-red sofa and waited, wishing he'd never agreed to come. Outside in the hallway the two old people were having a row.

"Why shouldn't I switch off these damned implants in my own house? Why shouldn't I live in the real world without electronic enhancements? I don't ask you to bring these ghosts back with you!"

"Why can't you face the fact that their world *is* the real world now Terence? They're not the ghosts, *we* are!"

"Oh yes? So how come they would all vanish without trace if someone were to only unplug the blessed…"

"How come in twenty or thirty years time *we'll* all be dead and forgotten, and they'll still be here in their millions, living and loving, working and playing?"

"That's not the point and you know it. The point is that…"

"Oh for God's sake leave it, Terence. I'm not having this argument with you. I'm just not having this argument. I have a guest to attend to, as it so happens. In fact we have a guest. We have a guest and I expect you to treat him as such."

She came into the room to join Lemmy, forcing a smile over a face that was still agitated and flushed from the fight in the hallway.

"Why don't you have a chocolate bun?" she cried, much too brightly, indicating a plate of small cakes.

Lemmy was ravenous and he reached out at once, but it was no good. He could touch the buns and feel them but he couldn't move them any more than he could move a truck or a house.

"Oh," Clarissa said, "I'm sorry, I quite forgot."

Again? thought Lemmy, remembering how she had 'forgotten' earlier that he couldn't see beyond the perimeter.

"Never mind," she said, leaping up and opening a cupboard in the corner of the room. "I always keep some of your kind of food here. I don't often have visitors, but one never knows."

She came back to him with another plate of cakes. They were luridly colourful and so low-res that it was as if she had deliberately chosen them to contrast as much as possible with her own physical food, but Lemmy was hungry and he ate six of them, one after the other, while she sat and watched and smiled.

"My. You *were* hungry."

"I came all the way from Dotlands," Lemmy reminded her. "I ran quite a bit of it. And that animal didn't go in a straight line, neither. It was this way and that way and round and round."

She laughed and nodded. Then, as she had done before, she started to say something, stopped, and then said it anyway. It seemed to be a pattern of hers. But when you were alone a lot, perhaps you forgot the trick of holding things in?

"Do you know how that food of yours works?" she asked Lemmy.

"Do you know how it fills you up?"

Lemmy didn't have time to reply.

"Every bite you take," she told him, "a computer sends out a signal and far away, a series of signals are sent to your olfactory centres and a small amount of nutrients are injected into the bloodstream of your…"

Lemmy frowned.

"Why do you keep doing that?"

"Doing what, dear?" She assumed an expression of utter, childlike innocence, but the pretence was as fragile as fine glass.

"Trying to make me feel bad."

"What do you mean, Lemmy dear? Why on earth do you think I'm trying to make you…"

Then she broke off, ran her hands over her face as if to wipe away her falsely sincere expression and for a little while fell silent, looking into the almost burnt-out fire.

"It's jealousy I suppose," she said at length. "It's just plain jealousy. I envy you the bustle and banter of Dotlands. I envy you the life of the city. All my true friends are dead. There are only a few hundred of us Outsiders left in London and most of us can't stand the sight of each other after all this time. We can't have children you know, that was part of the deal when they let us stay outside. We had to be sterile. Of course we're all too old now anyway."

She gave the weary sigh of one for whom sorrow itself has grown tedious, like a grey old sky that will not lift.

"And out in the streets, well, you know yourself what it's like… You were unusual in that you didn't run as soon as you discovered what I was, or jeer at me, or get all your friends to come and laugh at me and call me a spook. That was good of you. And look how this stupid old woman shows her gratitude!"

Suddenly she picked up the plate of real physical chocolate buns, strode with them to the fire and emptied them into it. Pale flames – yellow and blue – rose up to devour the greased paper cups.

Then, for a time, they were both silent.

"Do you know that Mr Howard?" asked Lemmy at length. "The one who owns all that property down in Grey Town."

"Richard Howard? *Know* him? I was married to him for five years!"

"Married? To Mr Howard? You're *kidding*!"

"Not kidding at all," said Clarissa, smiling. "Mind you, most of us survivors have been married to one another at *some* point or another. There are only so many permutations for us to play with."

"So what's he like?"

"Richard Howard? Well he never washes, that's one thing about him," Clarissa said with a grimace. "He smells to high heaven."

"Smells?" said her husband. "Who smells? Who are you talking about?"

The old man had come into the room while they were talking and now he began rummaging noisily through a pile of papers on a dresser behind them, shuffling and snuffling, determined that his presence should not be overlooked.

"I still don't get where that white animal went," Lemmy said, "and why I couldn't follow it."

"White animal?" demanded the old man crossly, turning from his papers to address his wife. "What white animal was that?"

"It was a white hart," she told him, "an albino, I suppose."

"Oh yes, and how did he get to see it?"

"Well, it must have got in through one of those holes in the wildlife fence."

"Well, well," chuckled the old man. "One of those dratted holes again, eh? The Council *is* slipping up. All these great big holes appearing overnight in the fence!"

Puzzled, Lemmy looked at Clarissa and saw her positively cringing under her husband's scorn. But she refused to be silenced.

"Yes," she went on, in an exaggeratedly casual tone, "and, according to Lemmy here, it wandered right down as far as Dotlands. He followed it back up to try and find out where it came from. Then it went over the perimeter and he couldn't follow it any further. But Lemmy doesn't…" she broke off to try and find a more tactful form of words, "he doesn't understand where it's got to."

"Well of course not," the old man grumbled. "They aren't honest with these people. They don't tell them what they really are or what's really going on. They…"

"Well, what *is* really going on?" Lemmy interrupted him.

"What's really going on?" Terence gave a little humourless bark of laughter. "Well, I could show him if he wants to see. I could fetch the camera and show him."

"Terence, I'm not sure that's such a good idea," began Clarissa weakly, but her objection was half hearted and he was already back at the capacious dresser, rummaging in a drawer.

He produced a video camera and some cables which he plugged into the back of the TV in the corner. Part of the mantelpiece appeared on the screen, blurred and greatly magnified. Terence took out one of those glass disc contraptions that Clarissa also had and placed it in front of his eyes. (It was held in place, Lemmy noticed, by hooks over his ears.) He made some adjustments. The view zoomed back and came into focus.

There was nothing remarkable about it. It was just the room they were sitting in. But when Terence moved the camera, something appeared on the screen that wasn't visible in the room itself – a silver sphere, somewhat larger than a football, suspended from the middle of the ceiling.

"What's that?" Lemmy asked.

"That's a sensor," the old man said, answering him, but looking at his wife. "Damn things. We have to have them in every single room in the house. Legal requirement. Part of the penalty for living inside the perimeter."

"But what is it? And why can't I see it except on the TV?"

"He doesn't know what a *sensor* is?" growled Terence. "Dear God! What do they *teach* these people?"

"It's not his fault, dear," said Clarissa gently.

"Yeah it is, actually," said Lemmy cheerfully. "I don't never go to school."

Amused in spite of himself, the old man snorted.

"It's like I was telling you earlier, dear," Clarissa said to Lemmy. "Sensors are the things that monitor the physical world and transmit the information to the consensual field..."

"...which superimposes whatever tawdry rubbish it wants over it," grumbled the old man, "like... like those ridiculous coloured air-cakes."

He meant the low-res cakes that Clarissa had put out on the table for Lemmy. And now Lemmy discovered a disturbing discrepancy. Within the room he could see the plate on the table with three cakes on it still left over from the nine she had brought in for him. But on the TV screen, though the table and the plate were clearly visible, the plate was empty and there were no cakes at all.

"Why can't I see the cakes on the TV? Why can't I see the sensor in the room?"

"The cakes are consensual. The sensor is physical," Terence said without looking at him. "A sensor detects everything but itself, just like the human brain. It feeds the Field with information about the physical world but it doesn't appear in the Field itself, not visually, not in tactile form. Nothing."

"Actually they're a nuisance for us, Lemmy," Clarissa chattered. "They're an eyesore and we bump our heads on them. But it's alright for you lot. You can walk right through them and see right through them. They don't get in your way at all."

She looked at her husband.

"Are you going to… I mean you're not going to point the camera at him are you? You're not going to show him *himself?*"

She was pretending to warn Terence not to do it, Lemmy noticed, but really she was making quite sure that he wouldn't forget.

"Yeah, go on then, show me," he said wearily, knowing already what he would see.

The old man swept the camera round the room. On the TV screen Lemmy saw Clarissa sitting in an armchair. He saw a painting of dead pheasants. He saw the dying embers of the fire and the corner of the dark-red sofa where he was sitting. And then, though he really didn't want to look, he saw the whole sofa.

Of course, just as he had somehow guessed it would be, it was empty.

"Alright then," Lemmy said in a tight voice. "So if I'm not really here, then where *am* I?"

"I can show you that too if you want," said Terence, still not looking at him, but addressing him directly for the first time. "Come upstairs and I'll show you…"

"Oh Terence," murmured Clarissa. "It's an awful lot for him to take in. I really think we should…"

Yet she was already getting eagerly to her feet.

*

Lemmy followed them up the wide marble staircase to the first landing. Progress was slow. The old man, who for some reason was carrying the camera with him, had to pause several times to rest and catch his breath.

"Let me carry it, Terence!" Clarissa said to him impatiently each time. "You know you don't like the stairs."

"I'm fine," he wheezed, his face flushed, his eyes moist and bloodshot. "Don't fuss so."

On the landing there were three glass cases, the first containing fossil shells, the second geological specimens, the third a hundred dead hummingbirds arranged on the branches of an artificial tree. Some of the little iridescent birds had fallen from their perches and were dangling from strands of wire; a few lay at the bottom of the case. The old man hobbled on to the second set of stairs.

"Here's another sensor," he said, glancing, just for a moment, back at Lemmy.

He laid down the camera, stood on tiptoes and, gasping for breath, reached up to rap at something with his knuckles. It was a bit like the wind in the trees again. Lemmy could clearly *hear* the hollow sound of some hard surface being struck, but all he could *see* was Terence's liver-spotted hand rapping at thin air. And when Lemmy stepped forward himself and reached up into the same space, he could find nothing solid there at all.

"Terence disconnected this sensor once," said Clarissa. "Very naughty of him – we had to pay a big fine – but he unplugged it and..."

"I'll tell you what, I'll unplug it now," Terence said, reaching out. "I'll unplug it now and show this young fellow how his..."

And suddenly there was no staircase, no Clarissa, no Terence, just a flickering blankness and a fizzing rush of white noise. When Lemmy moved his foot there was nothing beneath it. When he reached out his hand there was no wall. When he tried to speak, no sound came. It was if the world had not yet been created.

Then a message flashed in front of him in green letters:

Local sensor error!

...and a soothing female voice spoke inside Lemmy's head.

"Apologies. There has been a local sensor malfunction. If not resolved in five seconds you will be relocated to your home address or to your nominated default location. One...Two...Three..."

But then he was back on the stairs again, in Clarissa's and Terence's decaying mansion.

"Reconnect it *now* Terence!" Clarissa was shouting at her husband. "*Now*! Do you hear me?"

"Oh do shut up you silly woman. I already *have* reconnected it."

"Yeah," said Lemmy, "I'm back."

"I'm so sorry, Lemmy," Clarissa said, taking his arm. "Terence is very cruel. That must have been…"

The old man had already turned away and was labouring on up the stairs.

On the second landing, there was a case of flint arrow-heads, another of Roman coins and a third full of pale anatomical specimens preserved in formaldehyde: deformed embryos, a bisected snake, a rat with its belly laid open, a strange abysmal fish with teeth like needles… Between the last two cases there was a small doorway with a gothic arch which led to the foot of a cramped spiral staircase. They climbed up it to a room which perched above the house in a faux-medieval turret.

The turret had windows on three sides. On the fourth side, next to the door, there was a desk with an antique computer on it. In the spaces between the windows there were packed bookshelves from floor to ceiling. Books and papers were stacked untidily on the desk and across the floor, most of them covered in thick dust.

"Terence's study," sniffed Clarissa. "He comes up here to do his world-famous research, though oddly enough no one in the world but him seems to know anything about it."

Terence ignored this. He placed his glass contraption on his nose and groped awkwardly behind the computer to find the port for the camera lead, snuffling and muttering all the while.

"Are you sure you want to see this Lemmy?" asked Clarissa. "I mean this must all be a bit of a…"

"*There* we are," said the old man with satisfaction as the monitor came to life.

He carried the camera to the North-facing window, and propped it on the sill. Lemmy followed him and looked outside. He could see the garden down below with its ice-green lights and its fountains and roses. Beyond it was the procession of orange lights and signs (one sign for every five lights) winding to the West and to the East that marked the edge of the city. Beyond that was the empty space, the spare-channel void, flickering constantly with random, meaningless pinpricks of light.

"You won't be able to see anything through the window," said Terence, glancing straight at Lemmy for a single brief moment. "You're relying on sensors and they won't show you anything beyond the Field. But of course the room sensor will pick up whatever's on the monitor for you because the monitor is here in the room."

Lemmy looked round at the monitor. The old man was fiddling with the camera angle and what Lemmy saw first, jiggling about on the screen, was the garden immediately below. It was different from what he had just seen out of the window. The lights were still there, but there were no roses. The ground was bare concrete and the ponds were bald empty holes. Beyond the garden, the lights and warning signs around the perimeter looked just the same on the screen as they had looked out of the window, but beyond them there was no longer a complete void, no longer the flickering blankness. The tall chain link wildlife fence was clearly visible and, beyond that, night and the dark shapes of trees.

The old man stopped moving the camera about and let it lie on the sill again so that it was pointing straight outwards. And now Lemmy saw on the screen a large concrete building, some way beyond the perimeter. Windowless and without the slightest trace of ornament, it was surrounded by a service road, cold white arc-lights and a high fence.

"*That* is where you are, my friend," said the old man, leaving the camera and coming over to peer at the screen through his glass discs. "That is the London Hub, the true location of all the denizens of the London Consensual Field. You're all in there, row after row of you, each one of you looking like nothing so much as a scoop of grey porridge in a goldfish bowl."

"Oh *honestly* Terence!" objected Clarissa.

"On each of five storeys," Terence went on, "there are two parallel corridors half a mile long. Along each corridor there are eight tiers of shelving, and on each shelf, every fifty centimetres, there is another one of you. And there you sit in your goldfish bowls, all wired up together, dreaming that you have bodies and limbs and genitals and pretty faces...."

"*Terence!*"

"Every once in a while," the old man stubbornly continued, "one of you shrivels up and is duly replaced by a new blob of porridge, cultured from cells in a vat somewhere, and dropped into place by a machine. And then two of you are deceived into thinking that you have conceived a child and given birth, when in fact…"

"Terence! Stop this *now*!"

The old man broke off with a derisive snort. Lemmy said nothing, his eyes fixed on the monitor.

"Of course you're wonderful for the environment," Terence resumed, after only the briefest of pauses. "That was the rationale, after all. That was the excuse. As I understand it, two hundred and fifty of you don't use as much energy or cause as much pollution as one manipulative old parasite like my dear Clarissa here – or one grumpy old fossil like me. But that doesn't alter the fact that there isn't much more to any of you than there is to one of those pickled specimens I've got down on the landing there, or that your lives are an eternal video game in which you've been fooled into thinking you really *are* the cartoon characters you watch and manipulate on the screen."

"Why do you *do* this, Terence?" Clarissa cried. Why are you so cruel?"

The old man gave a bark of derision.

"*Cruel? Me?* You hypocrite, Clarissa. You utter hypocrite. It's you that keeps bringing them back here, these pretty boys, these non-existent video-game boys. Why would you do that to them if you didn't want to confront them with what they really are?"

He laughed.

"Yes, and why keep cutting those holes in the fence."

Clarissa gasped. Her husband grinned at her.

"If you didn't want me to find out, my dearest, you should have put the wire cutters back in the shed where you found them. You cut the holes so that animals will wander down into the city and lure back more boys for you to bring home. That's right, isn't it? You're not going to try and deny it?"

Clarissa gave a thin, despairing wail.

"Alright Terence, alright. But Lemmy is here now. Lemmy is *here*!"

"No he's not! He's not here at all. We've already established that. He's over there on a shelf in a jar of formaldehyde – or whatever substance it is that they pickle them in. He only *seems* to be here and we could very easily fix that by the simple act of turning off our implants.

Why don't you turn yours off now if his presence distresses you? Even better, we could unplug the sensor and then even *he* won't think he's here. There'll be only you and me, up here all alone with our big empty house beneath us."

Clarissa turned to Lemmy.

"Don't pay any attention to him. You're as real as we are. You just live in a different medium from us, that's all, a more modern medium, a medium where you can be young and strong and healthy all your life, and never grow wrinkly and bitter and old like us. That's the truth of it, but Terence just can't accept it."

But Lemmy didn't answer her. He was watching the monitor. An enormous articulated truck had pulled up outside the London Hub and was now passing through a gate which had slid open automatically to let it in. Oddly, the cabin of the truck had no windows, so he couldn't tell who or what was driving it.

"Why don't you go over there and join them then, Clarissa my dear?" sneered Terence, his old eyes gleaming. "Why don't you get *your* brains spooned out into a jar and yourself plugged into the Field?"

Lemmy crept still closer to the screen.

"Hey look! He's out there! That white animal. Way over there by that big grey place."

"Lemmy, Lemmy," cried Clarissa, rushing over to him, "you're so…"

"Oh for goodness' sake get a grip woman!" snapped the old man.

He dragged a chair into the middle of the room.

"What you doing?" she cried.

"I'm going to do what you should have done from the beginning. Send this poor wretch home."

Wobbling dangerously, he climbed onto the chair and reached up towards an invisible object below the ceiling.

*

"Apologies. There has been a local sensor malfunction. If not resolved in five seconds you will be relocated to your home address or to your nominated default location. One…Two…Three…Four… Five…."

Lemmy was sitting in the corner chair in the cosy, cramped little living room that he shared with his parents, Dorothy and John. John was watching TV. Mouser, their blue cartoon cat, was curled up on the fluffy rug in front of the fire. (The man at Dotlands market had claimed he had an organic central nervous system. Who knows? Perhaps he did. Perhaps at the back of some shelf in the London Hub, he had a small-sized goldfish bowl and his own small-sized scoop of porridge.)

In with a flourish came Lemmy's mother wearing a new dress.

"Da-da!"

She gave a little twirl and Lemmy's dad (who looked like a rock'n'roll star from the early days, except that he smiled far too easily) turned round in his armchair and gave an approving whistle.

"Oh hello Lemmy darling!" said Dorothy. "I didn't hear you come in!"

"Blimey!" exclaimed his father. "Me neither! You snuck in quietly mate. I had no idea you was in the room!"

"So what do you think then, Lemmy?" Dorothy asked.

"Yeah, nice dress mum," Lemmy said.

"It's not just the dress sweetheart. Your kind dad's given me a lovely early birthday present and got me upgraded to 256 colours. Can you see the difference? I think I look great!"

"Here comes the rain," said Lemmy's dad.

They could always tell it was raining from the faint grey streaks that appeared in the room, like interference on TV. Not that they minded. The streaks were barely visible and they made it feel more cosy somehow, being inside in the warm with the TV and the fire going. It had never occurred to Lemmy or his parents to wonder what caused them.

But in that moment Lemmy suddenly understood. The house had no physical roof. It had no physical ceilings, no physical upstairs floor, nothing to keep out the physical rain that fell from the physical sky. In the physical world there was no TV here, no fire, no lights, no fluffy rug, no comfy chairs, no Mouser or Dorothy or Lemmy or John, just an empty shell of brick, open to the sky, a ruin among many others, in the midst of an abandoned city.

"I *thought* your skin looked nice, mum," he said bravely. "256 colours, eh? That explains it."

Dorothy laughed and ruffled his hair.

"Liar! You wouldn't have even noticed if I hadn't told you."

She sat down next to her husband on the settee and snuggled up against him to watch TV.

Lemmy moved his chair closer to the fire and tried to watch with them, tried to give himself over to it as he'd always done before, back in the days before Clarissa Fall let in that white hart from the forest beyond the perimeter.

Valour

Here comes Victor, hurtling through the stratosphere on the Lufthansa shuttle: a shy, thin young Englishman, half-listening to the recorded safety instructions.

"Drinks, anyone? Drinks?" says the hostess: blonde, with high heels, makeup and a short, tight dress. Victor reminds himself, with a certain eerie jolt, that she isn't human. She's a synthetik – a robot clothed in living tissue. Lufthansa use them on all their flights now. They are cheaper than real women, they do not require time off, and they are uniformly beautiful...

"Disconcerting, isn't it?" says the passenger next to him, an elderly German with a humorous mouth and extraordinarily mobile eyebrows. "You find yourself admiring them without really thinking about it – and then suddenly you remember they are only machines."

Victor smiles just enough to avoid impoliteness. He does not enjoy chatting to strangers. Unfortunately his companion does not feel the same.

"My name is Gruber," says the elderly German, extending a large friendly hand. "Heinrich Gruber, I am a student of philosophy and philology. How about you?"

"I'm a computer scientist."

"Really? Where?"

"Silicon City – it's outside Cambridge – but I'm taking a sabbatical in Berlin."

Gruber chuckles. "Think of that! A Silicon City, a city devoted to the disembodied mind!"

And as if to disassociate himself from any charge of being disembodied, he cranes round to stare at the comely bottom of the robot hostess as she stoops to take a bottle out of her trolley: He turns back to Victor, eyebrows wriggling with amusement:

"And yet if she was a real human hostess and you and I were sitting here quietly eyeing her up the way men do, would the position really be so different? It would not be her soul after all that was on our minds?"

The eyebrows arch up triumphantly: Victor colours slightly.

"Soul? I see you are a dualist," says Victor, with a little laugh, so as to move the subject onto less personal ground.

Gruber frowns. "Dualist? My dear fellow, I study the philosophy of the Cassiopeians. I am a *trialist*. I am a trialist through and through!"

Victor smiles politely, looks at his watch and opens his laptop so as to discourage Gruber from carrying on the conversation. Conversation is such hard work. It involves having to be someone.

"Your wife?" asks Gruber, nodding at the picture of a rather tense-looking young woman on Victor's desktop.

"My girlfriend," says Victor, for some reason blushing. "She's a computer scientist too, back in Cambridge."

Gruber smiles his amiable, knowing smile. He takes out a battered paperback, folds it brutally back on itself and reads, glancing across from time to time at the young Englishman whose hands dart so quickly and neatly over the keyboard.

Darkness starts to fall outside. Stars appear: Orion, Taurus. An evening meal is served by the pretty robots.

"They make their flesh from genetically modified shellfish tissue, I believe," says Gruber loudly, swivelling stiffly round in his seat to look at the hostess. "*Patella Aspera*, the common limpet. It's good at clinging onto things!"

Victor smiles politely, cutting into his pork chop. Synthetiks first emerged from the laboratory a couple of years previously, and they are still banned in the UK, though the ban is currently being challenged in the European Court. As a computer scientist he rather scorns the publicity given to the semi-human, semi-molluscan flesh. Simulated human tissue is yesterday's technology. The real technical achievement about synthetics, the true master-stroke, is the brilliant programming which allow them to faithfully mimic the movements of the human body and face.

But perhaps you have to be a computer man to understand just how very clever that is.

"You English are wise to ban them of course," mutters the German philosopher, turning back to attend to his food. "What I said earlier was true but completely beside the point. The attraction between real human beings may well often begin as a physical matter, but that is the mere starting point, the foundation on which the whole magnificent edifice of sexual love is built. But a synthetik is a starting point for nothing, the foundation of nothing."

Victor doesn't enjoy conversation with strangers. But, seeing that conversation of some sort seems inevitable, he changes the subject.

"You were saying you have made a study of the Cassiopeians," he says. "I must admit I don't know much about them. I rather lost track after the news first broke, and those pictures came out. Tell me about *trialism*."

"You don't know much about them?! How can any educated..." Gruber makes a gesture of exasperation. "Well, I suppose I can't accuse you of being unusual in that respect! But it never ceases to amaze me that five years after the most astounding event in human history, hardly anyone seems to give it a moment's thought. Would you believe, the research money for textual analysis is actually drying up now, though the message is still coming through as clear as ever from the sky!"

Victor feels a little ashamed. "Well, I suppose it is rather appalling when you put it like that! I guess it was when we all realised that the source was 200 light-years away and there was no possibility at all of a dialogue or physical contact. And then it came out that it was all rather obscure philosophical ramblings and nothing that we could really *use*...I suppose it just became another one of those amazing things that we get used to: like cities on the moon or... or robot air hostesses with human flesh!"

The German snorts. "No doubt. But really is there any comparison between these little technological tricks that you mention and the discovery of other thinking minds among the stars?"

He rolls his eyes upward. "But then, no one is interested in *thinking* any more. You are quite right: when governments and corporations discovered that it was philosophy the Cassiopeians were sending out, that really was the last straw. They'd hoped for new technologies, new sciences, new powers over the physical world... But *philosophy*!"

He sighs extravagantly. "In answer to your question about trialism. The Cassiopeians organize the world in threes. They have three sexes, three states of matter, three dimensions of space, three modes of being... and above all, three great forces, struggling for dominance in the world: Valour, Gentleness and Evil."

"Not Good and Evil?"

"No, no, no. They have no concept of 'Good.' It would seem quite incomprehensible to them that we could compound two such obviously unmixable essences as Valour and Gentleness into a single word. To the Cassiopeians, all three forces are equally incompatible. Gentleness tells us to do one thing, Evil tells us to do another, and Valour – it tells us to do another thing again."

Victor smiles, with dry, polite scepticism. "I hadn't realised that the translation had got to this stage. I thought I read somewhere there was still a lot of controversy about the text."

The German growls darkly: "*Ja, ja, ja*, a lot of controversy..."

*

As they separate in the airport, Gruber presses a card into Victor's hand. "Come and see me if you have the time. It is not every day after all that you will meet a naturalised Cassiopeian!"

His eyebrows bristle as he glares around at silvery robot security guards, robot porters, male and female synthetiks with bright smiles manning the airline check-in desks. "In fact, even a genuine human being is becoming something of a rarity!"

Victor says something insincere, but he is no longer paying attention to the peculiar old man. He has spotted his German friends, Franz and Renate.

"Victor, how nice to see you! How are you? How is Lizzie? How is Cambridge?"

They are bright, polite, smartly dressed young people, who Victor and Lizzie met when they spent a year in Cambridge. After the eccentric Gruber, who might at any time say something embarrassing, they seem very normal and unthreatening and easy to get along with. Victor shakes their hands and exchanges minor news. They take him out to their little electric car (fossil fuels are verboten in the new Green Berlin) and head off in the direction of their Schoneberg apartment where he is to stay till he has found accommodation of his own.

"But I've forgotten if you've ever been here before?" says Franz.

"Strangely enough no. Very provincial of me, I know, not to have visited the capital of Europa!"

The two Germans laugh, pleased.

"Come now Victor," says Renate, "surely even an Englishman knows that the capital of Europa is Brussels!"

"Well you know what they say: the President of the Commission sits in Brussels but when he puts in a claim for expenses it's Chancellor Kommler who signs the form."

The Germans smile. These bantering exchanges, with their little hidden barbs of jealousy, are the bread-and-butter of contacts between young Euro-professionals all over the continent, as they shake down into a single, transnational class.

"Well," says Franz, "how about a little tour of this city of ours before we head for home?"

They drive through bright modern streets: tidy parks, tastefully restored old buildings. They drive past the Brandenburg Gate and the Reichstag. They go down the Kurfurstendamm. Franz points out the Volkskammer and the TV Tower from the gloomy days of the DDR. They drive along the boundary fence of Lichtenberg II, reputedly the largest Underclass estate in Europa, looking across with a small *frisson* (rather as an earlier generation might have looked across the famous Wall) at the monolithic apartment blocks within, where live the *gastarbeiters*, the unemployed, the outcasts of Europa's prosperous new order.

"Of this we are not proud," says Renate.

Then all three of them, almost simultaneously, sigh and say: "But it seems this is the price of stability."

"Ja, and we shouldn't forget that the Lichtenbergers have a guaranteed income, healthcare, roofs over their heads," says Franz as he turns the car away from the gloomy perimeter, back into the bright prosperity of the *real* Berlin. "It's more than you can say for the poor in most of the world."

He shrugs resignedly, defensively, and changes the subject to more cheerful things. "Now Victor, I seem to recall you have a weakness for VR, I must show you the *phantasium*. It is the Mecca for all the VR aficionados in the city."

"Sounds good!" Victor laughs. He loves VR arcades. They make him feel seventeen again. They give him a sense of wildness and dangerousness which is otherwise almost entirely lacking from his tidy and air-conditioned life.

He and Franz plunge into the glowing electronic cave of the Phantasium, with the agreeable, conspiratorial feeling that men have when they get together without their women. (Renate has declined to come in, and headed off on another errand.)

Of course, they have VR in Cambridge too (they also have Underclass estates), but the Phantasium is on a wholly different scale. Victor gives a small, impressed whistle. In an enormous dark chamber, long rows of cages made of plastic tubing stretch into the distance.

And in nearly every cage, a youth squirms and writhes alone inside a suspended control suit that encloses his arms, legs and face, while he battles in imaginary landscapes against cybernetic phantoms that he alone can see and touch...

Other youths wander up and down the rows, sometimes peering into small monitoring screens that give a taste of the electronic dreams and nightmares on offer: "The South Invades," "Berserkers of Islam," "Gene-Lab Catastrophe," "Pump-Action Killer," "UC Break-out!"...

"Now that last one is good," says Franz. "The subject matter is in poor taste I admit, but the graphics and tactiles are brilliant."

Victor smiles, runs his credit card over the reader and straps himself into the control suit. Soon he is cheerfully battling against a murderous gang of immigrants and benefit-claimants who have broken out of their concrete estate and are terrorising the good citizens in the neighbouring suburbs. (All educated Europeans know that the Social Compromise is necessary to contain inflation but how they are haunted by those outcasts behind their concrete walls!)

"Yeah," he agrees, climbing out. "Pretty sophisticated stuff."

At the end of this row of games an archway labelled *Liebespielen* marks the beginning of an inner sanctum where the games are discreetly boxed in with plywood and have names like 'Oral Heaven' and 'Lust Unlimited.' The two young men, Franz and Victor, glance surreptitiously through the gateway: Franz gives a hearty German laugh.

*

Later, back in Franz and Renate's apartment, Vince retires to his room and plugs in his lap-top so it can replenish itself with nourishing streams of information. Presently he calls up Lizzie.

"Oh it's you, Boo Boo dear," she says. (How did they start these awful names?) "Did you have a good flight?"

"Not bad at all."

"What's their flat like?"

"Oh, like ours really, only bigger."

"I've got nearly got everything sorted for me to come over. Should be with you by the end of next week."

"Great."

"You don't sound very pleased, Boo Boo!"

For a moment, Victor looks at the face of his beloved and sees this is so, sees that the connection between them is an anxious one, one that exists at the surface only. Deep down neither has touched the other at all. Not even once. Terrified, he blots the insight from his mind.

"Of course I'm pleased, Liz-Liz. It's going to seem really strange just being on my own."

"Hmmm," says Lizzie, "I think perhaps I should let you stew on your own for a week on two longer, Boo Boo, and then perhaps you will learn to appreciate me a bit more!"

Afterwards, Victor can't sleep. He switches on his laptop again and goes to a news channel.

Every playground in Europa, it seems, is to be resurfaced in a new rubberised substance called Childsafe, following a tragic accident in Prague when a child fell from a swing... New standards for food hygiene are to be announced by the Commissioner for Health... The sprawling and impoverished Federation of Central Asia is preparing once again for war with its neighbours. A vast crowd swirls round a giant statue of a soldier in heroic pose. The crowd chants. "Death! Death! Death!" "Death to the blasphemers!" "Death for the Motherland is sweeter than a lover's kiss!" Thousands of fists are thrust up in unison into the air. And the statue gouts real blood from a dozen gaping wounds...

Victor leans forward closer to the screen. All over Europa, with its safe children's playgrounds and its pure and hygienic food, healthy and well-fed people are leaning forward like him to watch this reckless energy, this crazy camaraderie with death...

Every day, according to the news report, citizens of Central Asia queue in their thousands to donate blood for the statue. They are poor and underfed, very often, and can ill afford to give away their lifeblood, but they keep on coming anyway: Never mind that Central Asia's hospitals have no blood for transfusions, never mind that the needles used for the donations are reused again and again and that AIDS is rampant. The statue's wounds must flow.

Victor switches off and goes to a window: Faint smudges of stars are visible in the city sky. He tries to remember which one of those constellations is Cassiopeia.

*

Franz and Renate are conscientious hosts. They take Victor to the museums and the historic sites. They take him to concerts and parties. They take him one frosty night to the famous annual parade on the Unter den Linden.

The starry flag of Europa flies high over the crowds alongside the black and red and gold of the German *Bund*. Statues and buildings loom eerily in the icy floodlights. Laser beams dance in the sky. There are drum majorettes, and decorated floats, and brass bands in lederhosen. And then, one after another, come the parade's most famous marchers...

So many parades have been this way before: Prussian cavalrymen, Nazi brownshirts, goose-stepping soldiers of the DDR... But these are something of quite another kind. They are creatures from prehistory; denizens of the Pleistocene steppes, ancient giants shambling patiently between the Doric columns of the Brandenburg Gate.

Mammoths!

Franz and Renate lean on the railings while the animals go by. They have seen the parade before and watch the scene with a proprietorial air, from time to time looking round to check that their guest is suitably impressed.

They are *immense* beasts! And they walk with such calm, muscular gravity, such a sense of assurance of their place in the world, that it seems to Victor that perhaps their resurrection was not the incredible and improbable feat of science that it was claimed to be, but rather the result of some basic and inescapable law of nature: if you wait long enough, everything returns.

"Those huge tusks!"

"Berlin has 140 mammoths now," says Franz.

"New York has twelve," says Renate. "Even Tokyo only has sixty, even though the Japanese have much freer access to the frozen carcasses in Siberia than we do because of the Eastern Pact."

Another huge male lumbers by; and Franz nods in its direction. "They have a few in Russia itself of course, but they are really rather a cheat. Less than 20 percent of the genes are actually authentic mammoth. They are really just glorified Indian elephants with big tusks and added hair. The Berlin mammoths are 80 or 90 percent pure."

"Even the New York mammoths are only 70-percent genuine," says Renate, "and the Americans are having considerable difficulty in successfully breeding from them for that reason..."

"Something to do with incompatible chromosomes I believe. And most of them have defective kidneys..."

But Victor the quiet Englishman suddenly gives a strangled cry: "For God's *sake*! Can't you two shut up even for one moment and just *look* at the things!"

Franz and Renate gape at him in astonishment, along with a whole segment of the crowd. Just as astonished as they are, Victor turns his back and walks away.

He has no idea where he is going, but a little later a thought occurs to him. He takes the battered visiting card out of his pocket and heads for the Kreuzberg apartment of Dr Heinrich Gruber.

*

"Come in, my friend, come in!"

It is musty and dark, like a brown cave, full of wood and the smell of pipe smoke, and Victor has the feeling that he is the first visitor for quite some time.

"Come on through!"

The old man's eyebrows bristle with pleasure and animation as he ushers Victor into his small sitting room and dives off into a grubby little kitchen to fetch beer. Victor looks around, feeling uncomfortable and embarrassed and wondering why he came.

The sitting room clearly doubles as Gruber's study. Half the floorspace is covered in books, journals and papers. On the desk under the window is roughly piled up a long print-out, covered with an unreadable gobbledegook of letters, numbers and punctuation marks.

...XXQpeNU'B VFF6VV G'NNLPP P*JJVNKL'L JGDSF'E^X MX9*M MMLXV XVOG? KK'B KQQZ...

"This is Cassiopeian?" Victor asks as Gruber returns with the beer.

"*Ja, ja*, that is the standard notation of Cassiopeian."

The elderly man rummages through a stack of manila files on a small side table. "You probably remember that the message contains a repetitive element? Every 422 days it repeats the same five-day-long passage known as the Lexicon, which turns out to be a 'Teach Yourself' guide to the language. The key to understanding it was when we discovered that part of the Lexicon consisted of co-ordinates for a spatial grid. When these were mapped out, they produced pictures. The Cassiopeians taught us the basics of their language by sending us pictures and accompanying each picture with the appropriate word or words..."

He goes to a computer and taps on keys.

Suddenly a face stares out at Victor, thin and long, utterly inscrutable, crowned with spiky horns...

"This one is a female," says Gruber, tapping another key. "This is a male. This belongs to the third sex, which I call promale. If you remember, the Cassiopeians have a triploid reproductive system, a simple biological fact which permeates the whole of their language, their culture, their metaphysics. They simply do not see the world in terms of black and white, yes or no, positive or negative. Everything is in mutually exclusive threes..."

He taps more keys and new images roll across the screen: plants and strange animals, buildings strung like spiders' webs between enormous diagonal struts...

"They are incredible pictures," says Victor. "I've seen them before of course, when they were in all the papers, but you're quite right, it's amazing how quickly we've all just forgotten them."

Gruber smiles. "The images are fascinating of course, but they are really only the key to the text..."

Victor smiles. "Which is truly nothing but philosophy?"

He is dimly aware that this is where the controversy lies: the extent to which the text has really been translated or just guessed at.

After all, who would think of beaming out philosophy to the stars?

Gruber nods. "Even though they have made a powerful radio transmitter, the Cassiopeians are not especially sophisticated technologically. They simply don't put such a high store by science and technology as we do: they consider all that to be only one of three distinct and separate fields of knowledge."

Victor asks what the other two are but Gruber is too preoccupied with his own train of thought to answer.

"The point about the Cassiopeians is that they are not afraid to *think*," says Gruber, standing up. "They still trust themselves to do something more imaginative than count! As a result their ideas are beautiful and they know it, so they beam them out for anyone who wants to listen."

He laughs angrily. "Which on this planet at least, sometimes seems to amount to about eight people among all the seven billion inhabitants!"

He perches on a table, takes out his pipe and begins to fill it. Victor seems to remember that there had been some suggestion too that the pictures had been greatly enhanced: crude matrices of dots had been 'interpreted' to a point that was arguably simply wishful invention. Perhaps even deliberately doctored?

Gruber stands up again agitatedly, thrusting the still unlit pipe at the young Englishman.

"My dear friend, what the Cassiopeians offer us is something that we desperately need: *wisdom*! Our own ideas have grown stale. We are in a blind alley. Christianity was once a brilliant new liberating leap. So once was scientific rationalism. But they have grown old. We have no real ideas any more, not even us Germans, for whom ideas and philosophy were once almost a vice. Especially not us Germans. Human philosophy no longer dares to attempt the big picture. All we have is the pursuit of cleverer and cleverer technologies, all of them quite pointless of course in the absence of any system of values that could tell us what all this cleverness is *for*."

He laughs self-deprecatingly and sits down again, wiping a speck of spittle from his lower lip. "But as you can see this is something of an obsession with me. Have some more beer. It comes from my homeland of Swabia. Not bad, do you agree?"

Victor smiles. The beer is indeed good, and very strong. He feels quite at ease. He finds himself liking the odd old man.

Gruber picks up a file and begins to read aloud: "Just as there are three sexes, three states of matter and three Modes of Being – Substance, Life and Soul – so there are three principles in the universe constantly at war: Gentleness, Valour and Evil. There can be no reconciliation between these three, no final resolution of their perpetual conflict, only temporary alliances. Those who hate Evil must surely hope for an alliance of Gentleness and Valour, full of contradictions though such an Alliance will inevitably be. But oftentimes in history it is Valour and Evil that come together against Gentleness and we see cruel, harsh and warlike nations, preoccupied with honour, indifferent to suffering."

He flips over the page: "At other times it is Gentleness and Evil that form an alliance against Valour. Nations become timid. They fear passion. They try to hide themselves away from encounters with suffering and death..."

"That sounds a bit like Europa!" observes Victor, and the old scholar beams at him delightedly.

"*Precisely*, my friend, precisely. We are obsessed with the fruitless struggle to eliminate disease and accident and death. We cordon off all that is distressing and unruly in the Underclass Estates. We have our wars in faraway countries, and watch them from the comfort and safety of our living rooms. We confine adventure to the Virtual Reality arcades, where no one ever gets hurt but nothing is ever achieved. We do not trouble one another any more with our untidy sexual passions, but release them (if we must) in the hygienic *liebespielen*, or in the new *synthetik* brothels, which everyone says are so 'civilized,' because they do not spread disease and do not exploit the vulnerable..."

*

Later Victor spends some time wandering the busy Kreuzberg streets, reluctant to return to Franz and Renate's apartment. He feels embarrassed by his earlier outburst and by the fact that he simply walked away and abandoned the two of them, embarrassed, now that it is over, by his evening with the old philosopher in his squalid little bachelor's lair.

He passes VR arcades, video galleries. He passes an establishment which he suddenly realises is a brothel staffed by specially adapted *synthetiks*. He walks quickly past.

Three police cars whoop by, heading Eastwards to put the lid back on some outbreak of mayhem in Lichtenberg.

I'll stop for a drink and wait until Franz and Renate are in bed, Victor decides. Sort it out in the morning.

He turns into a street called Moritzstrasse. ("Empire of Charlemagne!" exclaims a poster put up by the Carolingian party for the recent senatorial elections. They stand for a smaller unified Europa consisting of France, Germany, Lombardy and the Low Countries – the area of Charlemagne's long-dead empire. Tired old Europa is rummaging in the attic of her own history for ideas, but the ideas are stale and empty. No one votes for the Carolingians. Those who turn out for elections vote dutifully for Federation, the Market and the Social Compromise.)

He finds a small bar and orders a glass of red wine. There is a TV on in the corner showing an extended news programme about the anticipated bloodbath in Central Asia.

Victor sips his wine and looks around the room. In the far corner a young man is fighting chimeras in a small head-and-hands VR machine. A fat red man at the bar is loudly extolling the virtues of half of one percent reduction in interest rates, currently the hot issue in Europa's political life.

At the next table, a woman about Victor's own age is sitting by herself. She is very beautiful, it suddenly seems to him. She has a particular unselfconscious grace that is all her own. As Victor admires her, she unexpectedly turns and sees him, meeting his eyes for a moment and giving him a small wistful smile.

Victor looks away hastily, takes another sip from his glass.

But suddenly he is aware of the three warring principles of the Cassiopeians struggling for control within his mind.

"Go over to her!" says Valour.

"What about Lizzie?" says Gentleness.

"If it's sex you want," says Evil, "why not just go back to that *synthetik* place? It would be a loss less trouble and there'd be a lot less potential for embarrassment."

But Valour is insistent.

"Go over!" says that unfamiliar voice, "Go over before the moment passes!"

Victor is terrified. Never in his whole life has he ever done anything as audacious as to approach a beautiful stranger in a bar. He and Lizzie only went out together after months of working side by side. Even now, after years together, their sexual life is so crippled by fear and inhibition as to have hardly even begun.

"Go!" says Valour.

Grasping his wineglass firmly, Victor stands up. He clears his throat. He tries to assemble in his mind a coherent opening sentence. (The entire German language seems to be rapidly deleting itself from his brain...)

"*Ich... Sie...*"

She smiles delightedly and Victor grins back, amazed, only to realise that she isn't smiling at him at all...

"Clara! I'm sorry to be late!" says a big blond man from behind him, crossing the room and embracing her.

The clenched wineglass shatters in Victor's hand. He feels an excruciating stab of pain. Blood wells from a deep gash between his fingers.

Clara looks round. Everyone in the bar looks round – some amused, some puzzled, but all a little afraid. There is a crazy man here clutching a broken glass. What will he do next?

What *can* he do? Staring straight ahead of him, dripping blood, Victor stalks out into the cold street. No one challenges him to pay his bill.

KILL ALL WOPS, says a scrawl on the wall opposite.

EMPIRE OF CHARLEMAGNE, says another.

KEEP BERLIN TIDY, says a municipal sign.

But, just over the rooftops, unnoticed, washed out by the city lights but still just visible, the universe shines down, with the W-shape of Cassiopeia there in the midst of it.

From somewhere up there, fainter than gossamer, fainter than the silvery tenuous voices of the stars, whispers the Cassiopeian signal. It is a ripple from a single tiny pebble dispersing slowly across an enormous ocean, yet even at this distant shore it still bears the unmistakable signature of its origin. It is still a message. It is still purposeful. It is still without question the product of intelligent minds.

"Valour?" says Victor to those unreachable minds, nursing his copiously bleeding hand. "Valour is it? Do you realise you lot have just made me look like a complete idiot with that Valour nonsense of yours!"

He chuckles a bit at this, then laughs out loud.

And then crashes unconscious to the ground.

*

Clara and her blond brother Hans are the first to come to Victor's aid where he lies flat on his face on the cold Kreuzberg pavement, under the frosty stars.

"We need to do something about that hand," says Clara. "He's lost an awful lot of blood."

.

Snapshots of Apirania

This is a typical view of Apirania. Prairie country, the occasional bowava tree and here and there a hill standing out from the plain. But do you see that hill over there in the distance? That is actually a town on the top of it, a walled Apiranian town. It looks just like rocks doesn't it? Like part of the landscape.

Here's a closer view of the town. It's called Formara. Lydia and I got to know it quite well. The layout of it is pretty much the same as all the towns there: high walls, a single gate. You can see a couple of sentries up there on top of the walls. We're too close to the walls to see much of what's inside, but Formara is built along a single road that rises in a spiral from the gate to the Motherhouse at the top. You can just see there the top of the Motherhouse.

I know: it's all the same reddish colour, the walls, the hills, the houses.

This is a bowava tree. Now these have got to be seen to be believed. This picture gives no idea of the scale… Wait a minute, yes, this is better. That tiny speck down there, believe it or not, is me. These trees are *immense* and they pollinate in an extraordinary way. You see these orange things along the branches? Can you see they are *above* the branches and not below them? Well, they're balloons. Natural balloons. They rise up into the stratosphere and then burst, dispersing pollen over… well, I don't know… most of the planet I should think.

This is a *mootha. Moothai* in the plural. Quite a beast, eh? But not indigenous, actually. It's a modified version of a terrestrial animal from prehistoric times: a brontotherium. The colonisation of Apirania coincided with what you might call the *rococo* period of genetic engineering back here. Reconstructed brontotheria were introduced as the main beast of burden. Enormous, lumbering beasts. Those tusks look nasty, but moothai are as docile as can be.

No, Apirania has no large indigenous animals.

And these are some Apiranian children. Sweet aren't they? They all just *loved* having their picture taken. The boy here is Karl, the only boy in the family, and this is his sister Kara. This is Suka, this is Bavvy, this is Yar. Yes I know: they could be your next door neighbours, couldn't they? Apiranians look pretty much like us. The chromosomal differences between us and them are quite profound but their effects aren't really visible in the children at all.

But here are a couple of adults, look. Bunnoo and Thrompin. Men or women, do you think? Hard to tell, isn't it? Well actually they're both women, but they are sexually undeveloped and always will be. They are what the Apiranians call *huthi*, which really means Ordinary People. Huthi are about ninety percent of the population. They run the economy, they raise the children, they defend the towns. Males (*merthi* – Wanderers – as they call them) are about five percent. So are the fertile women who they call *manahi* – or Mothers.

Bunnoo and Thrompin had a room they rented out. That's how we came to meet them. They were foster-parents to the children you've just seen. A sweet pair. They became real friends of ours.

Here's the two of them close up. Salt of the earth really – or salt of Apirania anyway. You'd really have a job to say if they were men or women if you met them here, wouldn't you? They are not just foster-parents to these kids, by the way, they are blood relatives too, aunts or cousins at least. Everyone in a town is related to everyone else because they are all descended from the same Mothers.

Ah, here are the twins again, Karl and Kara. Lydia took this one. Beautiful aren't they? And so alike. Ever so close to each other too. When the family were all together those two would just sort of quietly gravitate towards one another, not necessarily talking to each other or ignoring anyone else, but just preferring to be alongside each other.

Yes, twins are very common in Apirania. Much more common than singletons in fact. Even triplets and quadruplets are more common than singletons. But it is unusual apparently to have a pair of twins like Karl and Kara, where one is a boy and one is a girl. Yes, she is a *real* girl. She only discovered that while we were there in fact. Her periods started. It was all rather unexpected and painful. At least the boys know what is in store all along.

Oh these are just some of the balloons from the bowava trees I told you about. After the rainy season is over you see them all the time: hundreds of them in the sky at once, sometimes, going up and up until they're just tiny dots. They often call them merthi, funnily enough: *Wanderers*, that is, the same word that they use for men.

Lydia, would you like to open another bottle of wine? I expect our guests are thirsty.

*

Now *this* is Apiranian technology at its most advanced! It's a wind-powered generator and every one of those wheels is cast out of iron. The Apiranians seem to have settled down comfortably at the early electric stage and never felt the need to move on.

This was rather a wonderful machine actually. I mean, look at those huge gears!

(What's that? Yes, *thank* you Lydia. I hadn't forgotten.)

As Lydia says, this turned out to be rather a distressing visit. We went up there with Bunnoo and Thrompin and their children. One of the kids had a pet with him, a little mouse, or the Apiranian equivalent of a mouse anyway. The little thing jumped off his shoulder onto one of these big gear wheels. Thrompin only just managed to get hold of the kid in time before she went after it. And there was the little mouse sitting on a cog on that big wheel, not seeing its fate coming towards it until... Well, it was horrible. But it was lucky it wasn't one of the kids. Now look at this. This is Karl and Kara with their mother, Diyoo. Yes their real mother. She comes down from the Motherhouse to visit them. Isn't she *beautiful*? That wonderful bone structure. And look at that incredible dress.

Yes, she does look sad, doesn't she? All the Mothers looked a bit sad like that, I thought. A rather restricted life, I suppose. Very little opportunity to make your own choices. In fact soon after this picture was taken the sentries spotted a band of Wanderers out on the plain and she had to go hurrying back at once to get ready at the Motherhouse.

Here she is saying goodbye, look. She's left Karl and Kara a little gift of cakes. They adored her. Of course she has other children with other foster-parents, but in Bunnoo and Thrompin's house only these two were hers.

*

Right, well now we are up on the wall. There are sentries up here all the time – there's one of them here you see – always up on the wall, always looking out over the plain. They are not concerned at all about attacks from other towns but there's a constant nagging fear that the Wanderers might get out of hand and take over if they were given a chance.

I suppose if they came to a society like ours that would be how they saw it: a world where the Wanderers have taken over!

Yes, I know, an interesting thought!

Anyway, as soon as Wanderers are spotted, they blow horns and pretty soon there are horns blowing all across the town. Ah look, here's Thrompin blowing one. You can see it's all a big laugh as far as she's concerned.

There *is* a real fear of the Wanderers but there's a sort of holiday feeling too when they appear. Once the gate is securely shut and everyone is safe inside, the entire city goes up onto the walls to watch the fun. And it turns into a big party.

Here they all are look: Bunnoo and Thrompin and all the kids. You can see that Bunnoo has even thrown together a quick picnic for them to eat while they watch. And there are other families behind them look. Look, that kid there has got hold of a horn and is blowing away.

*

Aha. Now *here* is the band of Wanderers arriving below the wall. Quite a small band, only about twenty of them, and all of them very young, hardly more than boys. As you see they have got a couple of moothai loaded up with all their possessions. Look at that one riding on the mootha's back. Only about thirteen wouldn't you say? It's a hard life for them out there, walking from town to town, living on whatever they can find or beg.

And look at the reception they're getting! Here's Bunnoo and Thrompin and the kids. And they are all merrily booing and shouting out abuse, along with all the other huthi and children all along the wall.

"What sort of town put you little weaklings out to spread its seed?" they shout out.

"Call yourself men? You're just huthi kids who haven't had enough to eat!"

"No way are you going to get near *our* Mothers!"

Some folk even throw things down: bits of crust, little stones... Even young Karl is doing it, look. It doesn't seem to occur to him that quite soon he'll be out there himself.

And look how the young Wanderers stand there taking all of this! Poor mites. Twenty of them, facing the population of an entire town. Hungry too. When people threw down food scraps, some of the young Wanderers went to pick them up and eat them, at least until the older ones reprimanded them.

Ah, now this chap here was a sort of spokesman of theirs. You see he's asking for silence so he can speak. It must have taken him all of ten minutes to get any quiet at all.

And here he is making his speech.

"Esteemed townsfolk of Formara. Open your gate to us please and let us visit your Motherhouse."

Something like that, and as soon as he's spoken everyone is catcalling and whooping and shouting out 'In your dreams!' and so on.

But eventually the leaders of the town go out of the gate. Here they are look: big fat huthi grandees in robes with their escort of huthi soldiers. They spend half an hour or so with the Wanderers, then confer among themselves. Finally the leader of the grandees turns and addresses us all on the walls. Look at her fine purple robes.

"Fellow citizens of Formara. We have met these boys and decided that we will open the gate for them tomorrow."

Howls of incredulity and disgust all round.

"What?! *These* pathetic specimens! I've seen more life in a limp lettuce leaf!"

That sort of thing. Look at the faces though. It's all part of the game. The Wanderers are *never* good enough. The grandees are *always* nuts to let them in.

Anyway, the grandee in purple holds up her hands again for silence.

"We will open the gate, but it will be for a gauntlet run only! We are giving these boys an opportunity, but they must prove themselves worthy of our Mothers."

A gauntlet run! Wow! The crowd *erupts*! You've never seen anything like it. They were absolutely cock-a-hoop. And pretty soon the wall starts to empty as all the excited huthi and their foster-children run back down into the town to start getting ready.

Ah, here are some more of those bowava balloons. I don't quite know how they got in here.

The toilet? Yes of course. It's upstairs and straight across the landing.

*

And now this is the build-up for the run.

You see all the huthi are jostling for space on the street outside their houses, trying to get a good position for themselves and their foster-children. These are Bunnoo and Thrompin's neighbours and their kids. We loved that little girl, didn't we Lydia? Five years old. Look at that *grin*! That's a basket of tomatoes she's got there. Her big sister has got a bucket of mud.

Here is Bunnoo, look, with her big stick, limbering up gleefully for the sport.

"Boy are there going to be some sore arses when I'm done!" she chortles.

(Yet you couldn't imagine a milder, gentler person than Bunnoo.)

Ah, and here are Karl and Kara, look, together as usual, with a big sack of vegetable scraps. Thrompin there has some rotten eggs. Everyone seems to save up rubbish especially for these occasions.

Here's a view of the whole street. It's all a big party for them, a gauntlet run, it's like a carnival.

Here is Karl again. Oh no sorry, it's Kara. The two of them are so alike!

Down below meanwhile, the soldiers have done a bit of scouting around to make sure there aren't more Wanderers hiding out there somewhere, ready to make a surprise attack when the gate is opened. (That's always the worry. The Wanderers will take over a town, murder the huthi and set up with the Mothers. After all, no other human society has such a thing as huthi! Remote as Apirania is, they are dimly aware of that.)

Once the soldiers were satisfied there wasn't going to be an attack, the town grandees gave the order, and they let those twenty Wanderers in. We were halfway up the hill, but we knew at once when it had happened because of the shouting that went up.

Pretty soon afterwards the first of them appeared. Here he is look. Poor kid, he was already covered in eggs and tomatoes and so on, not to mention bleeding from his head. And here is kind gentle Bunnoo if you please, running out to hit him with a stick and grinning all over her jolly face. Then more eggs and tomatoes and a whole bucketful of mud. And everyone shouting out that he's not a proper man at all and you'd need a magnifying glass to see his... Well, you get the picture.

(He gave up pretty soon after, actually. He stopped and walked back down to the gate. No-one harasses them when they've given up. Someone by the gate sorts them out with food and a jug of beer and a pat on the head before shoving them back outside.)

But here's the next one. A bit more determined looking, isn't he? And the one right behind him was pretty determined too. He was the oldest of them and their spokesman the previous night.

Ah, this is another one who gave up.

"Well done, lad," goes Thrompin, who five minutes earlier was telling him he was the most pathetic excuse for a man she had ever seen.

"Better luck next time," says Bunnoo.

Poor kid, he was crying.

Only about ten of them got as far as where we were. The rest had already given up. As soon as the Wanderers had passed them all the kids would run up the narrow little steps between the houses that are a shortcut between the loops of the road so as to get ahead of them again. They wanted to chuck a few more eggs at any Wanderers who got to the top, and to see them go in at the door of the Motherhouse, if any of them got that far.

Only two actually did. The spokesman and one other. Here you are, look. (I ran up after the kids, you see, and managed to catch the moment when the door opened for the second one. Lydia wasn't quick enough, to her *great* chagrin. Not quite as young as we were, eh, Lyds?)

It's an imposing building the Motherhouse isn't it? Like the keep of some medieval castle. They hung out those green and red flags in honour of the occasion. Green for fertility, red for blood I believe. Right up at the top there you can see some of the older Mothers looking down over the battlements. The younger ones are confined inside.

Here's a closer shot. You can see that the gauntlet continued right up to the door. Got worse in fact. Those are huthi soldiers there, poking this boy with the butts of their spears.

I know. He's really bleeding quite badly.

But as soon as the door opened the jeers turned to cheers. A couple of young Mothers were in there to greet him and lead him off to wash him and tend to his wounds. You can just see him there. It's a bit dark I know, but there he is, looking forward to a week of banquets and pampering and sex with every Mother he wants, before he has to go back out again onto the plain.

No, it's not a very good shot I'm afraid. Everyone was pushing to get a view and I was being jostled. You can't really get much sense of what it might be like inside.

*

Ah yes. Now these are the Wanderers who didn't make it, back at their camp outside. At least they've all got something to eat now, and some new clothes and blankets. And the kids are up on the walls until all hours calling down questions to them.

"What town did you come from then?"

"How come you gave up so quickly?"

"How did you get that bandaged arm?"

Look at their moothai tucking into that pile of cabbages!

And here is Karl on the wall, look. He's asking them questions about what it's like on the plain. Now that the excitement of the run is over it's all become a bit more real for him. He really wants some answers.

The Wanderers are telling him it's absolutely brilliant, and how they have been into dozens of Motherhouses and been with scores of Mothers – and how they just didn't really feel like it this time or they would have completed the run with ease. Formara's nothing, apparently, compared to some of the towns they've been to. Formara is an absolute breeze.

But look at Karl's face. What's going on behind those narrowed eyes?

Does anyone need another drink? Lydia, could you do the honours?

*

Yes, now this is a few months later. A couple more groups of Wanderers have been and gone including one group that was judged too large to safely let inside the walls. And now it's the ceremony which they call the *Tukanza*. The Division.

You can see this is the Motherhouse again, but the flags are black and white this time. And here are the pubescent boys and girls going in wearing their black and white Tukanza robes. We weren't allowed inside, sadly, and people were rather vague about what went on. Actually I think the huthi honestly don't know much about it. They don't even seem to care. As far as they are concerned, the Tukanza is just a little quirk of the merthi and the manahi. Ordinary People have better things to do with their time!

Here are Karl and Kara going in. Don't they look tense? And small too, under that great towering wall of the Motherhouse.

Kara told me later that at least she would be able to be with her mother now.

Here are some more kids going in. You can see their foster-parents anxiously wishing them luck. Then the door closes.

I waited outside. It's a nice spot. This is the view over the plain. Even from the foot of the Motherhouse there's a good view in several directions. It must be wonderful from the top. And look at the balloons from the bowava trees. The wet season has been and gone and the sky is starting to fill up with them. Wanderers, the Apiranians often call them, *merthi*, just like the men. Have I mentioned that already?

Yes, it is bleak out there on the plain. Bleak and windy and dry.

Now, here they are coming out again. Haven't they *changed*? Kara has been told that in another month she'll be moving in there. And when that happens, Karl and the other boys of his age will be turned out onto the plain with a mootha or two and some provisions, and an exhortation to respect all Mothers and never besmirch the reputation of Formara, though they are never ever to return there.

Look at the strain in their faces. The others are crowding around them trying to make a fuss of them but Karl and Kara are far, far away. Another month and they'll have to say goodbye to each other and never meet again.

What's this? Oh it's that mouse on the gear wheel just before... (Why did you *take* that picture Lydia, for goodness sake?)

Now look at these balloons. It's an Apiranian custom after the Tukanza. Bunnoo and Thrompin gathered them from a bowava tree (not an easy thing to do!) and they gave them to Karl and Kara to release them from the square in front of the Motherhouse.

Here they are look, Karl and Kara releasing them one by one, while all the others watch and cheer. Look at their balloons going up into the sky, to join all the others that are blowing past.

Look: a couple quite low and then three more – can you see them? – high, high up among the clouds.

*

More drinks anyone? Are you hungry? Would you like anything else to eat?

We've got some pictures from our trip to Pazzazza up in the Pleiades that we haven't shown you.

Now that was something *really* special.

Piccadilly Circus

Clarissa Fall is heading for central London to see the lights, bumping along the potholed roads at five miles an hour in her electric invalid car, oblivious to the honking horns, the cars queuing behind her, the angry shouts. How many times has she been warned? How many times has she been humiliated? But she must see the lights.

"When I was a little girl there were still physical lights in Piccadilly Circus," she's telling everyone she can. "I remember my father taking me. They were the most wonderful thing I'd ever seen."

*

She'd always been odd. There was that business when she cut holes in the wildlife fence to let the animals into the city. There were those young consensual tearaways she used to insist on bringing home. But things really started getting bad when her husband Terence died, leaving her alone in that big old house by the perimeter, that big fake chateau with its empty fountains and those icy lights that lit it up at night like Dracula's castle. I suppose it was loneliness, though when Terence was alive he and Clarissa never seemed to do anything but fight.

"I am two hundred years old, you know," she kept saying now. "I am the very last physical human being in London."

Neither of these was true, of course, but she was certainly very old and it was certainly the case that she could go for days and even weeks without seeing another physical person. There really weren't many of us left by now and most of us had congregated for mutual support in a couple of clusters in the South London suburbs. No one lived within five miles of Clarissa's phoney chateau on the northern perimeter and no one was much inclined to go and see her. She'd always been histrionic, now she was downright crazy. What's more – and most of us found this *particularly* unforgivable – she drew unwelcome attention onto us physicals, not only from the consensuals, who already dislike us and call us 'Outsiders' and 'spooks', but also from the hidden authorities in the Hub.

Her trouble was that she didn't really feel at home in either world, physical or consensual. The stiff arthritic dignity of the physicals repelled her. She thought us stuffy and smug and she despised our assumption that our own experience was uniquely authentic and true.

"Would you rather the world itself ended than admit the possibility that there may be other kinds of life apart from ours?" she once demanded.

But really, although she always insisted to us that it wasn't so, she was equally disgusted by the superficiality of the consensuals, their uncritical willingness to accept as real whatever the Hub chose to serve up, their lack of curiosity, their wilful ignorance of where they came from or what they really were. While she might criticise us physicals, she never seriously considered the possibility of giving up her own physical being and joining the consensuals with their constructed virtual bodies. And this meant that she would still always be an Outsider to them.

She may have felt at home with no one but she became a nuisance to *everyone* – physical and consensual – as a result of her forays into the city. At first she went on foot. Then, when she became too frail, she got hold of that little invalid car, a vehicle which the consensuals of North London would soon come to know and hate. Bumping slowly along the crumbling physical roads she would switch off her Field implant so as not to be deceived by the smooth virtual surface, but this meant that she couldn't see or hear the consensual traffic going by either. She could see only the empty buildings and the cracked and pockmarked empty road. Consensual drivers just had to cope as best they could with her wanderings back and forth.

When she parked her car, though, she always turned her implant on again. This of course instantly transformed empty ruined physical London into the lively metropolis that was the Urban Consensual Field, a virtual city in imitation of London as it once was, superimposed by the Hub over what London had become. Clarissa could still just remember those old days: the crowds, the fumes, the lights, the noise, the hectic life of a city in which, bizarrely, it still seemed feasible for millions of physical human beings to casually consume what they wanted of the physical world's resources, and casually discard what they didn't. And she craved that bustle and that life, she craved it desperately.

We all had Field implants of course. They were a necessity for dealing with a civilisation that had become, whether we liked it or not, primarily digital. Spliced into our nervous system, they allowed consensual constructs to be superimposed over our perceptions of the physical world, so that we could see the same world that the consensuals saw, hear what they heard and, to a limited degree, touch what they touched. The rest of us invariably took the position that we didn't like having to deal with the consensual world, but it was sometimes a necessary evil. But for Clarissa it was different. When she switched on her implant it just wasn't a matter of practical necessity for her, it was more like injecting heroin into an artery. All at once there were people all around her, there was life, there were shop windows and market stalls piled high with colourful merchandise, and the dizzying suddenness of it was like the hit of a powerful drug.

But her addiction wasn't so much to the Field itself as to the moment of crossing over. After that first moment the experience never quite lived up to its initial promise, for however hard Clarissa tried, the consensual world shut her out. And she did try. She spent hours in the consensual city outside shops and in parks and on street corners making rather pathetic efforts to engage people in conversation, but most people avoided her and some made no secret of their contempt. It was true that a few kind souls suppressed their revulsion at her age and her physicality and briefly allowed her the illusion that she had made a friend, but it *was* only out of kindness. Even apart from being an Outsider she really wasn't very good company anyway. She talked too much; she didn't listen; and, what was worse, however much she might criticise her fellow Outsiders for our existential snobbery, she herself was as much of a snob as any of us and a lot less inhibited about it. She could never resist pointing out to consensuals the shallow and illusory nature of their existence:

"You're so *very* nice dear. It's such a pity that you're not really here."

Usually she found herself alone in a kind of lacuna, with people moving aside to pass her by at a safe distance. And in these situations she would often become distressed and start to rant and shout:

"You're not real you know! You're just bits of nervous tissue plugged into a computer! You're far away from here, suspended in jars of nutrients, and the computer is sending you pictures of the real London with all this consensual nonsense superimposed on top of it!"
Terence used to talk like that a lot when he was alive, as haughty old physicals tended to do, but in those days Clarissa always used to criticise him for it:

"Who's to say our world is more real than theirs?" I remember her demanding of him at one of the physical community's periodic gatherings, the two of them on opposite sides of a large dining table laden with silver and fine china and cut glass.

Terence declined to answer. Everyone in the room was willing Clarissa to shut up and let us return to our customary state of numbness.

"Come on Terence, who's to say?" she insisted. "At least consensuals engage with life and with one another."

She glared up and down the table.

"And what do you think would be left of *us* if we stripped away everything that had come from outside ourselves, everything that other people had made? We'd be naked. We'd be gibbering imbeciles. Think about it. Even when we talk to ourselves inside our own heads, we use words that other people gave us."

But that was then. Now it seemed that Terence had been speaking all along on behalf of another side of Clarissa's own self.

"Don't look at me like that!" she'd scold the consensuals when they pointed and laughed at her, "You sold your true bodies for the illusion of youth and plenty, but I am real!"

Sometimes, in the middle of one of these rants, she would defiantly turn off her Field implant, making the people and the traffic disappear from her view, houses become empty shells again and all the shop windows with their cheerful displays turn back into hollow caves:

"I can't even see you, you know!" she shouted, knowing that the consensuals could nevertheless still see her, for sensors across the city pick up the sights and sounds and textures of everything physical and this becomes the matrix within which the consensual city is built. They had no choice but to see her. "I'm in the real world and I can't see you at all. *That's* how unreal you are. I can turn you off with a flick of a switch."

But though she might like telling the consensuals they didn't really exist, their opinion mattered to her desperately and she couldn't resist turning the implant on again to see what impact she was having. (I've never known anyone who turned an implant on and off as often as Clarissa did.) Almost invariably they would all be carefully ignoring her.

It was in these moments, when she had thrown a tantrum and discovered that no one was impressed, that things could get out of control. Once, a month or so before her trip to Piccadilly Circus, she found she could get no one to pay attention to her in the streets outside Walthamstow underground station. Rather than admit defeat, she insisted instead on going right down the stairs, arthritic and unsteady as she was, and waiting on the Southbound platform for a train. The platform emptied around her as the consensuals crowded up to the other end.

And then when the train came in, she promptly tried to step onto it. Of course she fell straight through onto the track, it being a virtual train, part of the Field, which couldn't bear physical weight, only the notional weight of consensual projections. She broke a small bone in her ankle. It hurt a great deal and she began to hobble up and down calling out for someone to help her up. The rules under which the Field operated meant that the train could not move off with her there. Yet she herself was breaking those rules. To the consternation of the passengers she appeared to them to be wading waist deep through the solid floor of the train, looking up at their averted faces accusingly and haranguing them for their lack of compassion:

"Isn't there a single soul left in London prepared to help an old woman? Have you all lost your hearts as well as your bodies?"

Broken bones – and physical injuries in general – were completely outside their experience, so they would have had some excuse for not empathising with her plight, but actually they would have *liked* to help her, if not out of pure altruism, then out of self-interest. For she was holding up the train – not to mention the other trains behind it – and she was distressing everyone. Consensuals, unless they are destitute, are uniformly beautiful and, although they die at last, they don't age in the way we do. Spit never flies from their mouth. Snot never runs from their noses. Their make-up doesn't smudge. It must have been truly horrific to see this dreadful wrinkled smeary creature wading up and down among them with its head at knee-height, like some kind of goblin out of a fairy tale. But what could they do? They couldn't lift Clarissa back onto the platform with their consensual hands and arms, any more than the train could hold her up with its consensual floor.

So someone called the Hub, and the Hub put the word out to us in the physical community that one of our people was in difficulties and did we want to deal with it or should Agents be sent in?

Phone calls went to and fro. The physicals of London are like the members of some old dysfunctional family who have seen right through each other's limited charms, know every one of each other's dreary frailties, but who are somehow chained together in misery.

"Bloody Clarissa. Have you heard?"

"Clarissa's up to her tricks again."

"Obviously we can't let Agents in. The real people have to deal with their own."

"Bloody Clarissa. How dare she put us in this position?"

In the end I was delegated to go up there with Richard Howard to sort it out. We travelled right across London and, since of course we couldn't use the virtual escalators, climbed slowly and stiffly as Clarissa had done, down the deep concrete staircase into the station. Clarissa was still stuck on the track. She had turned off her implant again, partly out of defiance, partly to avoid being overwhelmed by the agitated consensuals around her. But as a result she had lost the lights that the Field superimposed on the deserted and unlit physical station. For the last hour she had been stumbling around crying and wailing in pitch darkness with nothing for company except rats, and no sound at all except the drip, drip of water from somewhere down the southbound tunnel.

Richard and I had our implants switched on so as to be able to see what we were doing, and so had to endure the cold gaze of the consensuals. They sat in the train watching as we clumsily extracted

Clarissa from the floor; they stood on the platform watching as we dusted her down; they craned round on the virtual escalators to watch us half-carry her up the concrete steps.

"Look at those spooks!" someone in the street said, quite loudly, as Richard and I helped Clarissa into Richard's truck. "Look at the ugly faces on them! Haven't they got *any* self-respect?"

And there was a general hum of agreement. As a rule consensuals are scared of us Outsiders and our uncanny powers over the physical world. (Richard in particular is an object of awe, with his immense height, his great mane of white hair, and his tendency to walk contemptuously through virtual walls.) But we couldn't have looked very scary just then: two breathless old men, flushed and sweaty, helping a batty old woman with an injured foot into an ancient truck.

"Don't forget my car!" wailed Clarissa.

Somehow we manhandled her invalid car into the back of the truck. God knows why we agreed to take it. We would have been within our rights to say it was too heavy and left it behind. But Clarissa was powerful in some ways. She always had been. However much you might resent it, however much you told yourself that there was no reason at all to comply, it was hard not to do what she asked.

"Don't expect us to bale you out like this again," Richard told her as he bandaged her foot up back at her house. "Next time it'll be Agents."

None of us is sure what Agents really are, except that they are the servants of the Hub in the physical world. They have no visible faces. Their smooth heads and bodies are covered all over with a costume or skin in a special shade of blue which isn't picked up by the Field sensors, and is therefore invisible to consensuals. Some of us think they are simply robots of some kind, but others maintain that they are a new kind of physical human being, bred and raised apart from us for the Hub's own purposes. But, whatever they are, we fear them almost as much as do the consensuals, who only know of them by rumour and can only infer their presence from secondary clues.

"I couldn't have borne that," Clarissa murmured, "not Agents coming for me down there in the dark."

"Well it's your choice," Richard told her. "You get yourself in a fix like that again, and that's all the help you'll get."

He had been married to her once, before the days of Terence. Absurd as it now seemed, they had once, briefly, been lovers, enchanted by the sheer fact of one another's presence in the world. And even now, absurdly, Clarissa attempted to defuse his anger by flirting with him.

"I know I've been a silly girl, Richard dearest, but I promise I won't do it again."

*

I'm thinking about what I wrote earlier:

"The rest of us took the position," I said, "that we didn't like having to deal with the consensual world, but it was sometimes a necessary evil..."

I'm imagining Clarissa reading that and snorting with derision.

"Would you prefer it then if there was just us and no consensual world at all?"

Actually that very thing is looking increasingly on the cards.

When the consensual cities were first established as a way of withdrawing human beings from an environment which they were about to destroy, it was decided that these virtual cities would be congruent with the old physical ones. There were three reasons for this. Firstly many people could only be persuaded to accept consensual status on the basis that they would still have access to what they still thought of then as the 'real world'. Secondly, it was thought important to allow consensuals to continue to be able to interact with those of us who bought an exemption from the dephysicalisation process, by paying the enormous levy and by allowing ourselves to be sterilised. (In those days, after all, physicals and consensuals might be brother and sister, father and son, schoolmates, life-long friends...) And thirdly it was because the processing capacity of the Hub, though huge, was finite and a consensual world based on the physical one was less heavy on the Hub's resources than a purely invented one.

All three of those considerations have largely ceased to apply. The Hub has grown bigger, the physicals and the consensuals have grown apart and the consensuals have long since lost any sense of the physical world as being the 'real' one. So it would now be politically and technically possible for the Hub to decouple the physical city from the consensual one. In some ways this would be much easier than maintaining the status quo with its costly network of sensors.

But I suppose, if I am honest, that when I contemplate the possibility of waking up to a London where the implants no longer work, the consensuals can no longer be encountered and we are left on our own among the ruins, then I don't welcome it. In fact what I experience is a sense of dread, abandonment, isolation. I suppose I simply rationalise this feeling by saying that we need the consensuals for practical reasons, that their presence is a necessary evil.

*

I think Clarissa's promise held for all of two days before she was off in her car again. Within a week she was back in Walthamstow, though she avoided the station and didn't make any scenes. Before the end of the month, she was charging up the battery for a major trip, right into the centre of London. And then she was off again in earnest, bumping and bouncing grimly along the road and stubbornly refusing to think about how far her battery would take her.

As ever she drove with her implant switched off. She saw empty houses, abandoned petrol stations, an empty road, badly damaged by years of frost. But once in a while she stopped for that hit she so constantly craved, that momentary burst of comfort and reassurance that came from switching on her implant and seeing a living city emerging from the silent ruins.

"I'm going down to Piccadilly Circus," she told the people outside a row of shops in Stoke Newington. "They used to take me there when I was a little girl, to look at the coloured lights."

The shoppers all turned away.

"I used to love those lights," she told a man outside a betting shop in Islington, "the way they rippled and flowed. All that electricity! All that lovely colour!"

"Why don't you go home, spook?" the betting man muttered as he hurried off.

"I expect they still have lights like that now, don't they?" she asked a young woman in King's Cross, "Not *real* ones obviously, but ones for you people to see?"

"Oh yes," said the young woman, whose name was Lily, "they're lovely lights in Piccadilly Circus, but they're *quite* real you know. They're not physical or nothing like that."

Lily was not very bright and was happy to be friendly with anyone. She had a simple round very low-res face that was quite flat and looked like something from a cartoon strip. Consensuals could choose their own appearance and be as pretty and as interesting and as high-resolution as their bank balances would allow, but some consensuals couldn't afford much in the way of looks – and Lily was very obviously poor. Her eyes were dots, her skin a completely uniform pink, her clothes mere slabs of colour and her smile a simple upward curve of the single line that was her mouth.

"I'm pretty sure they're not physical anyway," she said, in her tinny little low-res voice.

And then she realised she had been rude and the smile abruptly inverted itself into a downward curve of regret.

"Oh dear. I didn't mean to say there was something wrong with being – you know – physical. That came out all wrong."

"Oh don't worry. I get that all the time. And you're the first friendly person I've met since I left home."

Clarissa had opened a flask of coffee and, still sitting in her little car, she poured herself a small cup. It was mid-October, a fresh autumn day getting on towards evening, and she was beginning to feel the cold.

"My father took me to see the lights in Piccadilly Circus when I was a little girl. Apparently when we got there I asked him where the clowns and tigers were. 'And where are the pretty ladies in tights?' I wanted to know. He said it wasn't that kind of circus: 'Circus just means a circle for the cars to go round.' I don't remember that conversation myself, but I do remember standing there with the beautiful electric lights all round me and realising that I didn't care about the tigers and the pretty ladies. Colours are so magical when you are a child. I looked one way and then the other, but I wanted to see it all at once, so in the end I decided to spin round and round on the spot."

She lifted the coffee cup to her lips and took a sip.

"I'm Lily," Lily said helpfully, staring wonderingly at the intricate wrinkles all over Clarissa's hands, and at the brown liver-spots on them, and the way they trembled all the time so that coffee keep sloshing out down the sides of the cup. If Lily's low-res looks were short on detail, Clarissa seemed to possess detail in reckless abundance. And yet – and this was the part that puzzled Lily – it was to no apparent decorative purpose. That look must have cost a fortune, Lily thought, but why would anyone choose to look like *that*?

"I'm Clarissa, my dear. I'm Clarissa Fall," said the old lady grandly, finishing her coffee and shaking the drips out of the cup before screwing it back onto the top of the flask.

"Do you know the way?" Lily ventured. "Do you know the way to Piccadilly Circus?"

"*I* should think so," Clarissa snorted. "I'm over two hundred years old and I've lived in London since I was born. I'm the last physical person left in London, you know."

She looked at her watch. She craved company and attention and yet when she actually had it, she was always curiously impatient and off-hand.

"Oh. Two hundred," repeated Lily humbly. "That's quite old. Only otherwise I was going to suggest I could come and show you the way..."

"Yes, do come by all means," said Clarissa magnanimously.

The laws of the physical universe prevented physical people from riding on virtual vehicles, but there was nothing in the rules of the Field to prevent virtual people from riding a physical car. The only difficulty was that the invalid car was only designed for one, so Lily had to ride at the back on the little rack intended to carry bags of shopping.

"I don't mind," said Lily, who couldn't afford dignity. "It's not that far."

"I'll have to turn my implant off, I'm afraid," Clarissa told her, "so I can see the bumps on the road. You won't be able to talk to me until we're there."

"I don't mind," said Lily gamely. She had no idea what Clarissa meant, but she had long since accepted that life was largely incomprehensible.

Clarissa turned the key to start the car. As she did so she noticed the meter that showed the remaining charge in the battery. When she set out, the needle had pointed to 'Fully Charged', but now it was on the edge of the red area marked 'Warning! Very Low!' She allowed herself for a single moment to see the trouble she was in – and to feel fear – and then she pushed it firmly from her conscious mind.

*

Clarissa drove slowly down Tottenham Court Road. The shop buildings were dark and empty, their windows blank, or sometimes broken and full of dead leaves. The roads were bare and strewn with rubble. Apart from the whine of her electric car and the click of stones thrown up by its rubber wheels, there was utter silence.

But Lily saw windows full of goods for sale, cars and buses all around them, and people everywhere.

"Nearly there!" she called out cheerfully, still not fully grasping that Clarissa with her implant inactivated couldn't hear her or sense her presence in any way. Then she gave a little shriek as Clarissa nonchalantly swerved across the road directly into the path of oncoming traffic and carried on down the wrong side of the road, magnificently indifferent to honking horns and shouts of indignation.

"She's physical," Lily called out by way of explanation from her perch on the back of Clarissa's little car. "She's just physical."

Half-way along Shaftesbury Avenue, the battery gave out and the car died.

And now Clarissa was scared. It was getting towards evening; it was turning very cold; and she was an elderly woman with an injured foot in the middle of a ruined city. She had nowhere to stay, nothing to eat or drink, and no means of getting home.

But Clarissa was good at pushing things out of her mind.

"It's not far," she muttered, referring not to the fake chateau, her distant home, but to Piccadilly Circus which still lay ahead. Piccadilly Circus offered no warmth, no nourishment, no resolution at all of her difficulties, but all of that was beside the point. "I'll just have to walk," she said. "It's absurd to come this far and not get to see it."

She dismounted from her car and began, painfully, to limp the last couple of hundred metres, but then she remembered Lily and stopped.

"*I'M GOING TO WALK THE LAST BIT!*" she bellowed back, assuming correctly that Lily was trailing behind her, but erroneously that Lily's invisibility made her deaf. "*I CAN'T SEE YOU* because *MY*

IMPLANT'S TURNED OFF and I don't want to turn it on again until I get there, or it will *SPOIL THE EFFECT.*"

She had it all planned out. She would not turn on her implant until she was right in the middle of the Circus.

"*YOU'RE VERY WELCOME TO COME ALONG THOUGH!*" she shouted, as if she personally controlled access to the public streets.

She hobbled forward a few steps along the silent ruined avenue (while in the other London, cars swerved around her, pedestrians turned and stared and Lily patiently plodded behind her as if the two of them were Good King Wenceslas and his faithful page).

"I'll tell you what though," Clarissa said, pausing again. Her face was screwed up with the pain of her injured foot, but her tone was nonchalant. "If you felt like calling the council and asking them to get hold of someone physical to come and help me out, I would be grateful… Only my dratted car has *QUITE RUN OUT OF POWER* you see, so it's not going to be able to get me back."

"I don't have any money," said Lily. "Is it an emergency do you think? Shall I call the emergency number?"

But of course Clarissa couldn't hear her.

*

It was getting dark as she limped into Piccadilly Circus. The buildings were inert slabs of masonry, all those thousands of coloured light bulbs on the old advertising signs were cold and still, and the statue of Eros was more like the angel of death on a mausoleum than the god of physical love.

Some gusts of rain came blowing down Regent Street. Clarissa's lips and fingers were blue with cold and her whole body was trembling. (Lily was amazed: she had never seen such a thing, for consensuals are never cold.) Clarissa was in great pain too – the broken bone in her ankle had slipped out of place and felt like a blade being twisted in her flesh – and she was tired and hungry and thirsty. Too late she realised she had left her flask of coffee behind in her abandoned car.

"You're a fool, Clarissa Fall," she told herself. "You don't look after yourself. One of these days you'll just keel over and the rats will come and eat you up. And it will be your own stupid fault."

Then she remembered her low-res companion.

"*ARE YOU STILL THERE LILY?*" she bellowed. "Did you make that *CALL FOR ME*? I'm just going to get across to the statue there and then I'll turn my implant on and *WE CAN TALK.*"

She hobbled to the base of Eros and then reached up to the implant switch behind her ear. The colour, the electricity, the teeming life of a great city at night came flooding instantly into the desolate scene. There were people everywhere, and cars with shining headlamps and glowing tail-lights, and black taxis and red double-decker buses full of passengers, lit upstairs and down with a cheery yellow glow. But above all there were *the* lights, the wonderful electric streams of colour that made shining moving pictures and glittering logos and words that flowed across fields of pure colour in purple and red and green and yellow and blue and white.

"Ah!" cried Clarissa in rapture, "almost like when I was a little girl and the lights were real!"

"I told you they was lovely," Lily said, like a pet dog that will wait an hour, two hours, three hours for its mistress to glance in its direction, and still be no less grateful when the longed-for attention finally comes.

Clarissa turned, smiling, but the sight of Lily's cartoonish moon-face had an unexpected effect on her. She felt a stab of pity for Lily and at the same time revulsion. Her smile ceased to be real. Her pleasure vanished. She felt the bitter cold of the physical world pushing through, the needle-sharp physical pain nagging at her from her foot, the physical ache in her head that came from tiredness and dehydration.

Lily sensed her change of mood and the simple line that represented her mouth was just starting to curve downwards when Clarissa switched off her implant again. Lily vanished, along with lights, taxis, buses and crowds. It was very dark and quite silent and the buildings were dim shadows.

"The thing is, Lily," Clarissa announced to the empty darkness, "that you consensuals are all just like these lights. Just moving pictures made out of little dots. Just pictures of buses, pictures of cars, pictures of people, pictures of shop windows."

Deliberately turning away from where Lily had been, Clarissa turned the implant on again and watched the lights come back. But there was no thrill this time, no exhilarating shock, nothing to offset the cold and the pain. It was no different really from changing channels on a TV set, she thought bitterly, and straight away reached up to flick the implant off again. But now the switch, which was designed to be turned on and off a couple of times a day, finally broke under the strain of her constant fiddling with it and refused to stay in one position or the other. Clarissa's perceptual field now flickered randomly every few seconds from the consensual to the physical world and back again – and she couldn't make it stop. She stood helplessly and ineffectually fingering the switch for a short time, then gave up and sank down to the ground at the foot of the statue. What else was there to do?

"Did you call up the council, Li..." she began, and then the consensual world disappeared. "Oh dear. *LILY, ARE YOU STILL THERE?*... Oh you are, good. Did you call the council only I think I ought to go home now... Lily? *LILY! ARE THE COUNCIL GETTING HELP?*... Tell them I don't want Agents mind. Tell them to get some physicals out. They'll be cross with me, but they'll come anyway. I don't care what Richard said."

*

Actually, whether she liked it or not, Agents were coming, four of them, from different directions, from different errands in different parts of London. They were still some way off but they were on their way. The Hub had sent them, having contacted Richard Howard and been told by him that we physicals wouldn't come out again.

Later Richard began to worry about what he'd done and called me.

"I know it seems harsh," he said, rather defensively, "but I do feel we've got to keep out of this, don't you agree? Clarissa's got to learn that when we say something we mean it, or she'll keep doing this stuff over and over again. I mean she's in *Piccadilly Circus* for god's sake! Even Clarissa must be perfectly well aware that she couldn't go into central London and get back again in that silly little car of hers. She obviously just assumed that we would come and fetch her. She just banked on it."

I was as furious with Clarissa as he was. I had spent the afternoon raking leaves and tidying up in my secluded little garden. I had just eaten a small meal and taken a glass of port and was looking forward to a quiet evening alone in the warm behind drawn curtains, making some preparatory notes for Chapter 62 of my book 'The Decline and Fall of Reality'. (I had dealt in Chapters 60 and 61 with the advent of the Internet and the mobile telephone and was just getting to what was to be the great central set-piece of my whole account: the moment where the human race is presented for the first time with incontrovertible evidence that its own activity will destroy the planet, not in centuries or even decades but in years, unless it can reduce its physical presence to a fraction of its current levels.)

"Bloody Clarissa! *Bloody bloody* Clarissa!"

Why *should* I give up the treat of a quiet evening and a new chapter, when she herself had deliberately engineered her own difficulties? I absolutely dreaded going into the centre of London at any time, as Clarissa surely knew, and yet here she was calmly assuming that I could and should be dragged there whenever it suited her convenience. And yet I knew I had to go to her.

"I can't leave her to the Agents, though, Richard. I know she's a pain, I know we're being used, but I can't just leave her."

"Oh for goodness' sake, Tom, it'll teach her a lesson," Richard said, hardening in his resolve now he had my own flabbiness of will to kick against. "How will she *ever* learn if we don't stay firm now? It's for her own good really. And anyway, the Agents can't be called off now. You know what they're like."

"Well if they're going to be there anyway, I'd better be there too," I said. "They scare her silly. I'll drive up there now, so at least there's someone on hand that she knows."

I went out into the cold and started up my car. I resented Clarissa bitterly. I dreaded the dark feelings that trips into London invariably churned up in me, the shame, the embarrassment, the sense of loss, the envy, the deep, deep grief that is like the grief of facing a former lover who belongs now to another and will never never be yours again... I was exhausted by the very thought of the effort of it all, not to mention the discomfort and the cold.

When I got to Piccadilly Circus, Agents were just arriving, one emerging from Shaftesbury Avenue, one from Piccadilly and one each from the northern and southern branches of Regent Street. But, huddled up under the statue of Eros, Clarissa couldn't see them, for when she was in purely physical mode it was too dark and when she was in consensual mode they were invisible. Beside her squatted Lily with her consensual arm round Clarissa's physical shoulder. Sometimes Clarissa could see Lily and sometimes she couldn't, but either way she could get no warmth from the embrace, however much Lily might want to give it.

As my physical headlights swept across the physical space, the first thing Clarissa saw was two of the Agents looming out of the darkness and advancing towards her. It felt like some nightmare from her childhood, and she screamed. Then her implant switched on by itself and the lights and the buses and the crowds returned to screen them out. But that was even worse because she knew that behind this glossy facade the Agents were still really there, slowly advancing, though now unseen.

She screamed again.

"Keep away from me, you hear me! Just keep away."

"Don't be scared, Clarissa," said Lily. "I'm here for you."

But Lily didn't have a clue. She had never experienced cold. She had never known physical pain. She wasn't aware of the presence of the Agents. She had no inkling of the other world of silence and shadow that lay behind the bright lights of Piccadilly Circus.

I got out of my car. I had my own implant switched on and I picked my way gingerly over the ground between me and Clarissa, knowing only too well how easily nasty physical potholes can be concealed by the virtual road surface. I was doing my best to ignore the many consensual eyes watching me with disapproval and dislike and I was seething all the while with rage at self-obsessed Clarissa for putting me through all this yet again. How dare she drag me out here into the cold night? How dare she expose me to the illusion of the consensual city and to the disapproving gaze of the consensual people, when all I ever wanted was to be at home behind my high hedges that I had cut into the shape of castle walls, behind my locked doors, behind my tightly drawn curtains, writing about reality.

"You know her do you?" a man asked me. "Well, you want to do something about her, mate. She's nuts. She's mental. She needs help."

I didn't respond. I had never known how to speak to these people, so manifestly unreal and yet so obviously alive. I both despised and envied them. How tawdry their constructed world was and how craven their meek acceptance of it. Yet how narrow and dull my own world was by comparison, my bleak garden, my clipped hedges, my book, my nightly glass of port, my weekly sally down the road to the Horse and Hounds, the Last Real Pub, to drink Real Beer with the diminishing band of decrepit and barren old men and woman who call themselves the Last Real People.

"She needs locking up more like," said a woman. "That's the same one that blocked the Northern Line last month with her carrying on. I saw her face in the paper."

I picked my way through the traffic.

"Alight Clarissa," I called coldly as I came up to her, "I'm here again for you. Muggins is here again as you no doubt expected he would be. I've come to fetch you home."

"Muggins? Who's that?" she quavered. She was afraid it was one of the Agents.

"It's just me, Clarissa. It's just Tom."

"It's who?" muttered Clarissa, straining to see me.

"He said Tom, dear," Lily told her.

Clarissa glanced sideways at the cartoon face with its little black dot eyes and its downward curved mouth. Then Lily vanished again, along with the whole Field, and Clarissa was back in the dark physical world. But the lights of my car were there now and, without the distraction of the Field, Clarissa could clearly see me approaching as well as the Agents around me, waiting to step in if I couldn't resolve things.

Awkwardly, wincing with pain, she rose to her feet.

"I just wanted to see the lights again, like they were when I was a child," she said stubbornly.

And then she began to spin round on the spot like children sometimes do in play, but very very slowly, shuffling round and round with her feet and grimacing all the while with pain. And as she revolved, the faulty switch on her implant continued to flicker on and off so that, for a few seconds the bright lights and the buses and the cars span around her, and then it was the turn of the darkness that was the source of her coldness and her pain, and it was the dim cold walls of the empty buildings that moved round her, lit only by the headlights of my car.

Lily appeared and disappeared. When she was there the Agents vanished. When she vanished, they appeared. The one constant was me, who like Clarissa could both feel the physical cold, and see the consensual lights.

"Come on Clarrie," I said to her gently. "Come on Clarrie."

The old lady ignored me for a while, carrying on with her strange slow-motion spinning and singing a tuneless little song under her breath. People were craning round in cars and buses to look at us. Pedestrians were standing across the road and watching us as frankly as if this really *was* a Circus and we were there expressly to put on a show.

Then abruptly Clarissa stopped spinning. She tottered with dizziness, but her eyes were blazing like the eyes of a cornered animal.

"Who are you?" she demanded. "Who exactly are you?"

It was odd because in that moment everything around me seemed to intensify: the sharpness of the cold night air in the physical world, the brilliance of the coloured lights in the consensual one, the strange collision of the two worlds that my Clarrie had single-handedly brought about... And I found that I didn't feel angry any more, didn't even mind that she'd brought me all this way.

I switched off the implant behind my ear, so that I could check up on what the Agents were doing. But they were still standing back and waiting for me to deal with things.

"It's me, Clarrie dear," I said to her. "It's Tom. Your brother."

The Agent nearest me stiffened slightly and inclined its head towards me, as if I had half-reminded it of something.

"I reckon you've had enough adventure for one day, my dear," I told my sister, flicking my implant on again to shut the Agents out of my sight. "Enough for one day, don't you agree? Don't mind the Agents. I've brought the car for you. I've come to take you home."

She let me lead her to the car and help her inside. She was in a very bad state, trembling, bloodless, befuddled, her injured foot swollen to nearly twice its normal size. I was glad I had thought to bring a rug for her, and a flask of hot cocoa, and a bottle of brandy.

That strange moon-faced creature, Lily, a human soul inside a cartoon, followed us over and stood anxiously watching.

"Is she alright?" she asked. "She's gone so strange. What is it that's the matter with her?"

"Yes, she'll be alright. She's just old and tired," I told her, shutting the passenger door and walking round the car to get in myself.

I flipped off my implant, cutting off Lily and the sights and sounds of Piccadilly Circus. In the dark dead space, the four Agents were silhouetted in the beam of my headlights. They had moved together and were standing in a row. I had the odd idea that they wished they could come with us, that they wished that someone would come to meet *them* with rugs and brandy and hot cocoa.

I got my sister comfortable and started up the car. I was going to drive like she always did, with my implant deactivated, unable to see the consensual traffic. I didn't like doing it. I knew how arrogant it must seem to the consensuals and how much they must resent it – it was things like that, I knew, that gave us Outsiders a bad name – but I just couldn't risk a broken axle on the way home on top of everything else.

"Really, we're no different when you come to think of it," said Clarrie after a while. Her implant was off at that moment and she looked out at abandoned streets as lonely as canyons on some lifeless planet in space. "*That's* the physical world out there, that's physical matter. But we're not like that, are we? People are patterns. We're just patterns rippling across the surface."

"Have a bit more brandy, Clarrie," I told her, "and then put the seat back and try to get some sleep. It's going to be some time before we get back."

She nodded and tugged the rug up around herself. Her implant switched itself on again and she saw a taxi swerve to avoid us and heard the angry blast of its horn. Briefly the busy night life of the Consensual Field was all around her. And then it was gone again.

"Just the same," she said sleepily. "Just like the lights in Piccadilly Circus."

Jazamine in the Green Wood

Memorial Day.

I got out of bed and opened the window. Birdsong rippled through the mild creamy air and a fat old woman pushed her bike up from the allotments with its basket laden with a spring harvest of leeks and sprouting broccoli.

"Morning has broken, like the first morning..."

She was singing that old hymn.

Well, yes, I thought. I suppose it is on days like this that we should thank God for all Her munificence: for light, for air, for sunlight, for the great dance of the planets and stars... But let us not forget to mention tuberculosis too, and beriberi and cholera and TTX.

(TTX. Ah yes, now, there is proof, if any more were needed, that God is truly a *She*!)

I pulled on my jumper and jeans and struggled into my specially adapted boots.

And do I thank God for my feet? I demanded. Do I thank Her for the curse of being born a boy? Do I thank Her for my good kind reasonable parents, who have cut me off from the whole world with their good intentions, their damned principles?

I closed the door of my flat and hobbled off down the road towards Peace Square, where the Memorial Statues wait under the cherry blossom for the annual speeches and tears.

On the way I met Harry Higgins, a big burly man with a red beard, always wearing the same brown jacket with the little MRP badge on the lapel.

"Going to the ceremony, eh, Jack?"

I nodded guiltily. "Well, yes. My mum and dad, you know…"

He winked.

"Yeah, of course. Don't worry mate, I understand. But pop over to the Men's Pub later, eh Jack? At the end of the day we blokes have got to stick together."

"Yes, sure, I'll be there."

"Good man, good man," Harry said, patting my arm. "Well, enjoy the ceremony. Your mum is sure to make a good speech. She's a strong woman, your mum. I admire her. Even if we are on opposite sides."

I noticed he didn't mention my dad.

*

Outside the Mother-Church I saw Beatrice walking with a girl-friend: Beatrice with her curly blonde hair and her milk-white teeth, Beatrice with her beads and her many rings and her lacy dresses, so nonchalantly flung together but always so stylish and funny and graceful.

God, she is so beautiful that she makes my blood run cold.

"Morning, Beatrice," I croaked.

She smiled and waved, "Hello Jack!"

I wanted to say something else. I actually stopped to do it. But before I could think of anything, she'd turned away, slipping her arm through her friend's and giving her a kiss. They were probably lovers.

Alone in a cruel cage of sunlight and blossom and birdsong, I watched them go.

*

Under the cherry trees, Mother was giving her customary speech as Town Convenor.

"We're here to remember the victims of the plague: our husbands, brothers, fathers, sons…"

She touched the statue of the sad woman who looks down at her dead male shadow. Plenty of women there cried. Apart from my father and me, no other men were there. My father was getting ready to speak. I looked away down the square. It was quite empty except for the group under the trees.

"But secondly we're here to remember the women victims of men in the long centuries before…"

She moved to the second statue: that terrified girl who is groped and clawed eternally by coarse male hands.

"Males are the weaker sex," my mother said. "More die in the womb, more die as babies and they live shorter lives, perhaps because of the conflict that is hard-wired into their brains. They are not less able, they are not more evil, but they are weaker and for that reason we must never let them take control from us again…"

"Thanks, Mum," I muttered, and looked away again down the empty square.

But now it was *not* empty! As if he had fallen from a sky, a young man stood tottering only a few metres from me. He was thin, unshaven, dressed in oddly-cut jeans and a torn blue T-shirt.

There was a faint ozone smell.

"That man is magic, mum," said a little girl calmly, "He can appear out of the air." But her mother didn't hear her.

The stranger looked scared when he saw that the little girl and I had noticed him, so I quickly turned away. I felt as if he was some sort of forest animal who would easily startle.

"It's not as if we should hate men," Mum was saying, "I myself love one young man more than I love anyone in the world…"

Here she looked across at me smiling. I blushed and everyone looked at me, knowingly, benevolently. I felt naked, consumed, infantilised.

"But their numbers must be maintained at the present level," my mother said, "for the good of all of us, men as well as women, boys as well as girls."

Everyone clapped. Women nearby looked at me as if they expected me to be proud. Some of them glanced at the stranger behind me, but at that moment my father Timothy, with his kindly beard and his twinkly eyes, was climbing up onto the box and they all turned back to see what he would say.

"Thanks my dear," he said, giving Mum a little kiss as she made way for him.

He is the chair of the Men's Committee. He and Mum didn't live together but they were good friends. Now, on behalf of the men of the town, he acknowledged Mum's speech.

"We men behaved badly in the past," he said, "but we are learning. Generation after generation, we are learning. And I want to ask all of you to keep your minds open to the possibility that a time will come when men can be trusted again, and our numbers allowed to rise naturally to the proportion that nature intended..."

A middle-aged woman turned to her friend.

"Oh but he is gentle," she said, "he is a *good* man. It would be different if they were all like him!"

*

"What is this place?" the stranger asked, quietly coming up beside me.

His eyes were very large and blue and he spoke with an odd accent which was not foreign but which I had never heard before.

"It's Peace Square," I said. "It's Memorial Day."

He stared at me.

"I'm hungry."

"Do you want me to get you something to eat?"

He still just stared, as if his brain was incapable of processing the sounds that reached his ears.

A cold breeze rustled the cherry blossom. My father's gentle voice went on about Aggression Control programmes and the need to construct Positive Masculinities.

"Where do you come from?" I asked the stranger. "How did you get here?"

He stared across my shoulder, looking at my father without really seeing him. Then he rubbed his face with his hands.

"I'm so hungry."

"Like I said, I'll get you something to eat. But I think we should get away from here."

He nodded and followed me through the sunlit streets, gazing around at trees, at houses, at people, at notices and signs. We passed an election poster for the RadFems and he stopped to look at it. It showed a frightened woman cowering in a huge male shadow. "NEVER AGAIN!" the poster declaimed, "REDUCE THE QUOTA NOW!"

"Reduce – the – quota – " the stranger read very slowly aloud, as if he was a child.

"They don't want us any more, mate," I said. "That's what it boils down to. They don't want us and they don't need us much either."

He looked at me, frowning, then turned away from the poster and carried on walking. I had to hobble my quickest just to keep up.

"No cars," he said after a while.

"No. Well we hardly have any. Not since…"

But he wasn't listening. We had come to the Mother-Church and he was absorbed in studying the sign outside with its rose-pink mandala. Petals within petals, softly unfolding, and blossoming, and thriving, free from danger at last…

He looked at me.

"Where do I come from?" he said, repeating the question to himself that I'd asked him some time previously. "I don't remember. So many… So many places."

Frowning, he started to feel about in his pockets as if they might hold some clues.

"The trees *danced*," he said. "The ground *boiled*…"

He found a penny coin in his pocket and handed it to me, then he pulled out some dried up bits of leaves and flowers. Little blue flowers, they were: forget-me-nots.

Tears brimmed from his eyes.

"What's the matter?"

He held out the bits of flower, as if he thought these shrivelled scraps could somehow speak to me and provide some kind of explanation. Tears ran down his cheeks as his whole face screwed up with the effort of remembering and then, quite suddenly, he seemed to relax.

"Jazamine!" he cried. "Jazamine! I was with her by that pool!"

"Who is Jazamine?" I asked him.

"She said she'd wait for me there. In the green wood. But… but I keep *falling*."

"*Falling*? How do you mean?"

He flinched. He'd become agitated again. More agitated than before. His breathing had become quicker, his eyes constantly on the move.

"I don't know who you are! I've never met you before! Why do you keep asking me all these questions?"

He started to run. With my stupid feet and my stick, it was useless for me to try and follow.

"Stop! Come back! I won't hurt you!" I cried out after him, but he didn't even look back.

*

The penny piece had the head of a king on it, like an old coin from before the plague, but it was new coin, an English coin, minted only a year ago. The trouble was we'd had no king in England for over forty years.

I had a strange moment of terror, as if the world had suddenly turned out to be nothing but a painted backdrop and I had glimpsed for one moment what lay behind.

Two women passed by me hand in hand, both laughing.

"...anyway Mandy went round to Gill and Sarah's," one of them said, "and there was the most God-awful row. Typical Mandy, Gill said, but she's hardly the one to talk. Anyway, what *Liz* said about it was..."

Jazamine in the green wood, who the stranger loved. Who was she? What kind of world did she inhabit?

I stooped to pick up one of the crumpled forget-me-nots that had fallen at my feet.

*

Later I went over to the Men's Pub. It was very quiet. At the back some boys were playing *Ninja Assassin*, the pub's one surviving video game. At the bar Harry Higgins was conferring with his diminutive sidekick Peter Hemlock and with Rod Stone, the landlord.

They looked up with irritation as I came in. They were MRP activists, all three, and had no doubt been discussing politics. Like most people, they didn't feel able to talk freely about such things in front of me because of who my parents were.

I belong to neither camp. Neither the men nor the women accept me as their own.

But Harry was an instinctive, compulsive networker. He made it his business to be friendly to *everyone*, to cultivate every possible connection.

"Jack! Nice to see you mate!" he exclaimed. "Let me buy you a pint. I expect you need it!"

I accepted the drink, but I could see his welcome was ambiguous. His face smiled but not really his eyes and he was anxious to resume his talk with Peter and Rod out of my hearing. So after Rod had pulled my pint for me, I carefully chose a seat some distance away from them and put some music on the antique jukebox so they could plot and scheme in peace.

"I want you / I want you so bad / I want you-ou-ou / I want you so bad it's driving me mad, it's driving me mad...."

The jukebox and the music on it, like *Ninja Assassin*, was old stuff, from the golden age, the days before the Plague.

"...I want you..."

I thought about a girl like Beatrice in a green wood, bathing in a woodland pool, with the green leaf-light on her skin.

Presently Lily Tulip came in, balancing precariously on her high heels. She wore a tight silver dress slashed to the very top of her silk-envaginated thigh. Her eyelashes were heavy with mascara, her ear-lobes hung with fake jewels.

The three men greeted her from the bar. Harry whistled.

"Hi guys," Lily simpered at them, then glanced across at me, knowingly, like an old fisherman casting out his line. I looked quickly away.

But I watched her all the same, in little furtive glances, as she settled down at her accustomed table, crossing her long legs sheathed in blue silk, and sipping her blue curacao.

"...I want you so bad..."

God help me, Lily wasn't what I wanted at all, yet I could see myself going to her before the night was out.

Then the door flew open and in burst the stranger.

*

143

"The wood," he blurted out to the room in general, "I'm trying to find my way into that wood…"

"The *wood*?" asked Rod Stone.

"Over behind here," he gabbled in that impossible-to-place accent of his. "You can see the green branches over the rooftops. I keep following roads that seem to lead there but they always turn out to be dead-ends."

He turned to me.

"There was a public baths at the end of the first road," he told me, without giving any sign that he remembered our earlier meeting. "I went in and it was full of naked old women. It was strange. They didn't even try and cover themselves. They just laughed. And then at the end of the next road I tried there was a couple arm in arm on a bench in a garden, watching their children play, but *both* of them were women."

"That seemed unusual to you, did it?" Harry asked, with a quizzical glance towards Peter and Rod.

The stranger stared at him blankly.

"There's a little scrap of a wood just behind here," said Rod with a shrug, "if that's the one you mean. You can get to it through the back door there. There's a gate at the bottom of the beer garden. Just follow the hedge."

"And in the middle of the wood there's a pool?"

Again I thought of a girl like Beatrice wading in a warm pool, with rushes and willowherb and forget-me-nots.

Harry frowned: "I don't remember a pool down there."

"There isn't one," said Rod.

But the stranger was already heading off.

"Wait a minute!" Harry called. "Can't I get you a drink? You're new in town aren't you?"

He never missed a chance to make a contact.

"How about something to eat?" I asked, getting up to join them. I remembered how hungry he'd been several hours ago and I doubted he'd eaten since. "You must be famished."

He looked at me. I don't know if he remembered me or not, but he nodded anyway and I bought him a couple of pies while Harry got him a pint and introduced us all.

"Harry Higgins, mate. Convenor of the local Men's Rights crowd for my sins. Anything you need, let me know. We blokes have got to stick together these days, eh?"

The stranger stared blankly.

"This is Peter, my treasurer," Harry went on, "and Rod here is my deputy when he's not too busy pulling the only decent pint in town."

He glanced at me.

"Oh, and this is Jack," he said, his voice perceptibly cooler. "He's one of us too at heart, aren't you Jack my old mate? It's just that his mum's on the other side and his dad...well, Timothy's a lovely bloke of course but he's sort of *gone native*, as they used to say in the old days. Fair comment, Jack?'

I grinned painfully.

"Oh, but he's such a *good* man," squeaked Rod in a cruel falsetto.

*

"So what do you call yourself, my friend?" asked Harry. "Whereabouts do you hail from?"

The visitor's mouth was full of pie and he had his eye on the door at the back of the pub. He mumbled a name that no one heard and said he came from Birmingham.

"Birmingham, eh? Well I couldn't quite place that accent of yours, but I'd never have had you down as a Brummie!"

"And how do the slits treat you up there these days?" asked Rod Stone.

"Slits?"

"Slits," Rod repeated impatiently. "*You* know! Bumpies, pussycats..."

"...doublebums..." offered Peter Hemlock.

"...women!" exclaimed Rod.

Understanding dawned. "Oh... women... well..."

He glanced uncomfortably between their faces, wondering what sort of reply they wanted. "Well, you know..."

"We know, mate, we know," said Harry sympathetically. "Still you've got a strong champion there in John Thompson."

The stranger looked blank.

"You don't know who John Thompson is?" asked Harry, very surprised. "You come from Brum and you don't know about the chair of the Birmingham Men's Committee? Good God man, they say he's the most powerful man left in England!

"Oh yes... *that* John Thompson... he's..."

"In a different mould entirely from our own dear Timothy Brown," Harry said, winking at me to show no hard feelings.

"Oh but Timothy's such a *good* man," said Rod Stone again in a soft falsetto. And *he* didn't bother to wink.

"He's a pussy-licker," said Peter Hemlock, avoiding my eye. He tipped back a glass of vodka. His eyes glazed over as the ethanol hit his bloodstream.

Rod Stone refilled his glass.

"Drink up," Harry said to the stranger, "You look like you could use another. What on Earth were you hoping to find in that wood there anyway?"

"Jazamine. She said she'd..."

All three of them snorted with disapproval.

"A girl? What do you want a girl for?" Harry asked. "Listen mate, if it's a little nooky you're after, you be much better off with the likes of Lily here."

Lily had come up behind us in an overpowering blast of sickly sweet scent.

"Hi there," she purred.

"She's got everything a woman has got," said Harry with a wink at me. "I think we can all vouch for that, eh lads? But she's got the brain of a man, and that means she knows what a man really wants."

Lily fluttered her eyelashes at the stranger. Comprehension slowly dawned in his dazed blue eyes. Her female face was nothing more than a mask of paint and mascara. Through it looked out the solid heavy face of a man, burning with a bottomless rage.

So the stranger had come looking for Jazamine in the green wood – and he was offered *this*.

He reddened violently and turned away. The others laughed at him. He tried to shift the conversation onto other ground.

"What... what is TTX?" he blurted out. "I saw it written on a sign."

The laughter died instantaneously. The four of them stared at him in shocked silence.

"You mean you don't *know*?" asked Harry quietly, all friendliness gone.

The stranger could see he had made some kind of blunder and tried to recover.

"No – I mean yes... I mean I just forgot for a moment..."

"Well, if you really know what it is sweetie," said Lily in a hard male voice, "why don't you tell us?"

The stranger looked at me desperately. I tried to mouth the word 'plague'.

"It's an... illness," he said.

"Yes," said Harry grimly, "an illness. So now tell us what it does to a man."

"It's... like flu to start with and then..."

"It makes your balls go purple and swell up like footballs," snapped Rod Stone from behind the bar, "and then they burst and you die."

"Everyone knows that, my friend," said Harry reprovingly, "everyone knows *that*."

There was a moment of silence.

*

"You know what he is, don't you?" said Rod. "He's one of those shifters you hear about. He doesn't belong here. He's slipped in from another world."

Harry whistled softly.

The stranger stood there like a prisoner in the dock.

Harry spoke very quietly "So you come from a place where TTX never happened, do you? The women never took over?"

"Maybe he's got some of that stuff on him," Rod said. "You know, that shifter drug they use, maybe he's got some."

"Well let's see if he has," said Peter Hemlock.

"You know what they say, don't you?" said Lily. "If a shifter's swallowed all his stuff, you can still get it out of him by drinking his blood!"

Her painted lips parted, revealing yellow fangs. The stranger gave a sort of low groan and started to back away.

"Not so fast," Harry said, "we haven't finished with you."

He and Peter took hold of the stranger's arms.

"Hey!" I yelled. "He hasn't done you any harm. Leave him alone!"

"Or you'll tell your mummy, eh?" snarled Peter.

But they loosed their grip all the same, for my mother had power. The stranger broke free and ran, out of the door at the back, off in the direction of the wood.

Harry and Peter settled back onto their bar-stools, both a little flushed and breathless. Lily gave a cold snort of contempt. None of them looked at me.

"Do you think he was really a shifter, or was he just off his head?" asked Rod, after a moment.

"Just some nutter more likely," said Harry with a shrug. "I mean I've heard these rumours about shifters the same as you have, but I've never been able to see how a drug could make people cross to another world. Even if there *are* such things. I mean I know the slits have abolished science and we don't know squat about *anything* anymore, but it just doesn't sound plausible does it?"

"I suppose not," said Peter, "but I wish we'd searched him all the same."

"I wished we'd sucked him dry," hissed Lily.

She glanced venomously in my direction. So did Peter.

"Pussy-licker!" he whispered.

I picked up my stick and hobbled away from them with as much dignity as I could manage, through the back door, following after the stranger.

*

There *was* no pool in the wood. He was standing by a small concrete reservoir with a locked metal lid. He jerked round in alarm as he heard me coming, preparing to run again.

"Don't worry," I said, "I'm not about to drink your blood."

He nodded and turned away from me. "This *is* the place. The pool was here. Jazamine was here. But it was another world I suppose."

Tears came to his eyes but I laughed harshly.

"Well, even if you *could* find her, so what? You don't believe men and women can really get on together do you? You don't really believe that? Harry and his crew – okay I don't like them and they don't like me – but they're right really. So are the RadFems. We're rivals. It all boils down to one thing: them or us."

I lashed out at a nettle with my stick.

"The fools are the ones like my dad, the good men, the gentle men, the ones who try to smooth things over by denying their own nature…"

I grinned at him.

"What…" he began. "What are you…"

He voice tailed off. He stared at me with those dazed eyes of his and I felt ashamed of what I was doing but carried on anyway, determined to crush his dream, and even more determined to stamp out in myself the cruel impossible hope that opposites could be reconciled.

"Oh I know, I know. You and that girlfriend of yours made sweet music together. It happens even here sometimes. But all that's based on a delusion, isn't it? What you wanted and what she wanted weren't really the same thing. Just for a moment they seemed to coincide, that's all."

Still he stared, wide-eyed. He was confused, a little frightened, but even more than that (I now realise in shame) he was just plain *puzzled* by my hostility.

Well, I was puzzled by it too, but my bile boiled up inside me anyway. I grinned mirthlessly in his face, I waved my stick at him. There in that little scrap of a wood with evening falling, I – who knew better than most what it was to be alone and to be picked on – ruthlessly attacked a young man who was completely alone in the world, and had done nothing to harm me at all:

"We think that if we long for something there must be a someone out there in the world that's there to quench our longing. But why should that be?"

I laughed. "Do you know what a lamprey is? Do you know what it longs to do? A lamprey longs to fasten itself onto the skin of a fish and suck out its insides. That's its heart's desire! But do you think that the fishes it preys on are longing to be eaten alive? No, of course not. If the fishes had their way, the lamprey would go hungry. He could pine himself away with longing, for all they care. He could fucking starve."

I gave a bark of loud triumphant laughter. The stranger shivered. It was getting cold and he had only his jeans and his torn shirt, while I had my jumper and my sensible green anorak. I suppose my thought was that when I'd finished tearing his dreams to shreds, I would offer him a bed for the night.

"That's biology for you, mate." I chuckled grimly. "That's life. Not harmony and resolution, not peace – just conflict and desperation and struggle …"

Suddenly he winced. Ah good, I thought, I've made him cry.

But no, that wasn't it. It was nothing to do with me. He winced again, gave a groan – then grabbed out wildly at the air.

Slow-witted as I am, it was only at that moment that I realised what was happening.

"No!" I found myself crying out. "Don't leave me! Please! I didn't mean…"

But it was too late. He was gone. There was a popping sound as the air rushed into the empty space. And then: nothing, no trace of him, only a faint electric smell.

*

I was alone. It was growing dark. A cold wind had begun to blow through the branches above my head.

"Come back!" I cried into the empty little wood.

It was pointless of course. He was somewhere else entirely.

He was searching for Jazamine in the green wood.

He was falling. He was falling through the worlds.

Dark Eden

Tommy:

Space is a very dangerous place but for me personally it always felt like a safe haven. And especially this time. In the final days before our mission, it seemed to me, just about every newspaper and TV station on the planet had been carrying revelations from Yvette. I couldn't pull back a curtain without a storm of flashbulbs and a chorus of voices. I couldn't pass a newsstand without seeing my own name:

TOMMY SCHNEIDER'S EX TELLS ALL

SEX-MAD SCHNEIDER BROKE MY HEART

The void between the stars, sub-Euclidean nothingness, life in a metal box with nothing but vacuum beyond its thin skin – all that was fine with me. It always had been fine. Living in space was simple and straightforward compared to trying to live on earth. But now it was beginning to look as if this sanctuary of mine would soon be closed off.

"I think this could be one of the last trips before they shut down the program, yes?" said my crewmate Mehmet Haribey on the shuttle out.

He was a Turkish Air Force officer. We usually had one non-American seeing as the program was nominally international. I'd worked with Mehmet several times before and liked him. He was an open sort of guy, and he had warmth.

"I guess, but I *so* hope not," I said. "Who in God's name would I be if I had to spend my life on Earth?

Mehmet grunted sympathetically.

"Or it *would* be one of the last trips," said our captain, Dixon Thorley, "if it wasn't for the fact that this time we are going to find life."

Mehmet and I exchanged glances. Dixon Thorley was okay when he was just being himself, but he found it very hard to forget that God Almighty had called him personally to carry the good news of Jesus Christ to alien civilizations. It was a tale he had told to many a rapt congregation and many a respectful interviewer on the religious networks: God had put him on Earth to perform this one task. And for him it was just inconceivable that the program could end without contact with any other life form.

Poor guy, I suddenly thought. He's in for quite a fall.

The fact was that over two hundred fantastically expensive missions had traversed the galaxy and found no trace of any living thing. Human beings had trodden lifeless planets right across the Milky Way and now it looked as if their footprints would just fill up with stardust again. Silence would return like nightfall to all those empty solar systems whose planets held nothing but rock and gas and ice and sterile water.

I say 'like nightfall', but really it's not the right word to use because of course in any solar system it's really always *daytime*, always sunny everywhere, except in the tiny slivers of space that lie on the lee side of planets, and in the even more miniscule areas on planetary surfaces that are cut off from the light by clouds. As we approached it in the shuttle, the galactic ship *Defiant* basked ahead of us in a perpetual noontime, an enormous cylinder half a kilometre long, covered in gigantic pylons that made it look like some kind of weird spiny sea-slug. It was huge, but 99% of it was engine. The habitable portion was a cramped little cabin in the middle. We crawled through into it from the shuttle, closed the airlock doors behind us, and gratefully breathed in the familiar space smell of dirty socks, stale urine and potato mash. How I loved that smell! It was the smell of freedom. It was like coming home.

"God I'll miss this," I said as I began switching on monitors.

(I've been thinking about this recently – I've had a *lot* of time to think – and what I've come to realize is that I have always been most at home in transient, and dangerous places. Even when I was a kid, danger was always somehow reassuring to me. Safety and security always made me feel uneasy and afraid.)

Dixon flicked the radio on to a county music station and we settled into our positions and started running through the pre-activation procedures. Soon we'd start the ship's gravitonic engine and then we'd head out into deeper space while the engine built up power for the leap. Finally – *blam!* – we'd let it loose. In a single gigantic surge of energy it would drive us out in a direction that was perpendicular to all three dimensions of Euclidian space. A few seconds later, we'd bob up again like a cork. We'd be back in Euclidean space but we'd be a thousand light-years away from home.

"*The spaceman who wrecked my life,*" said the radio, "*New revelations from Yvette Schneider! Exclusively in tomorrow's Daily Lance.*"

"Poor Tommy," Mehmet said. "You can't get away from it, can you?"

Dixon gave a snort, but refrained from saying anything. He'd already told me that as far as he was concerned I'd only got what I deserved. And of course he was right. I didn't expect sympathy. But I couldn't help responding to the self-righteous baying of the radio ad.

"There's always another side to the story," I muttered. "I behaved badly, yes. But there were things she did too."

This was too much for Dixon.

"Tommy, you just can't…"

But he was interrupted by a voice from Mission Control.

"Tommy, Dixon, Mehmet, this is going to come as a shock…"

It was Kate Grantham, the director of the Galaxy Project, in person.

"The mission is cancelled boys. The whole project has been terminated. Sorry, but the President has decided to pull the plug, and as the US funds 95% of the project, that means the end of the project itself. We all knew this was likely to happen soon but I'm afraid it's happening now. The shuttle is coming back for you. Please shut all systems down again with immediate effect. The *Defiant* will be mothballed pending further decisions."

"But excuse me the project has barely started!" Mehmet protested. "*Of course* we haven't found life yet. Doesn't the President know how *big* space is? The galaxy would have to have been bursting at the seams with life for us to have found it already."

"The President has been thoroughly briefed," the director said shortly. "He has a number of competing priorities to consider." And she couldn't help adding: "The bad publicity around Tommy hasn't helped."

"Oh that *is* logical!" I burst out. "One of the explorers gets caught cheating on his wife, so cancel the exploration of the entire galaxy."

Dixon switched off the radio.

"I must say," he said, "I've never been able to understand how people can do things they *know* are wrong and then still get indignant when it causes problems for them and other people. But that's for another time. Right now, crewmates, I've got a simple proposition to make. We have power and provisions enough for one trip. Why not do it anyway?"

"Dixon!" Mehmet gave an incredulous laugh. "This isn't like you!"

"I'm quite serious," he said. "How can they stop us?"

"How about by sending an interceptor after us?" I said.

There were interceptors in Earth orbit, a dozen of them at least at any one time, looking out for illegally launched communications satellites and for the killer satellites which big business and organized crime sent up to disrupt the communications of rivals.

"It'll take them an hour to figure out what we're doing," said Dixon, "and an hour after that to decide what to do about it. By then we'll only be about six hours from the leap point. And it could take six hours at least for one of them to catch up with us. It's not as if they are going to try and laser us."

"Yes but..." Mehmet stopped himself and laughed. "Well, okay. This is a very stupid idea. But, yes, I'm up for it if Tommy is."

I thought about the alternative. Going back to live among daily revelations of my own duplicity. Walking down a street in which every passerby knew what, *precisely*, I liked to do in bed. And maybe never again coming up to this place – or maybe *non-place* would be a better word – which was where, more than anywhere else, I actually felt at home.

"Yeah," I said. "I'm in. Even though it'll mean a court martial when we get back. Who cares?"

"Oh *we'll* be okay," Mehmet said. "The public will *love* us won't they? The public will think we're heroes."

"It's the goddam taxpaying public who've pulled the plug on us," I pointed out.

"Yes, I know," said Mehmet. "But that makes no difference. When they see us defying the bureaucrats they'll yell at the bureaucrats to leave us alone and get off our backs. They won't remember that the bureaucrats were acting at their own request. They never do!"

So we were agreed. Contrary to our orders we started charging up the engine.

Angela:

People laughed at me when I put myself forward for secondment to the UN's 'space-cop' service. The British police forces had only been given a quota of four secondees altogether and I was only twenty-five, black and a woman. Plus I was only an ordinary uniformed cop and had no training as a pilot beyond what I'd done with the air cadets at school. But then my mum and dad had always taught me to believe in myself.

Yeah and look at me now, I thought, as our hundred million dollar interceptor passed five thousand miles above India. Who says a black girl from Peckham can't get on in the world?

This was my third patrol. My captain Mike Tennison and I were looking for Mafia satellites, which we would either tow to destruction points or, if they were very small, simply nudge down into the atmosphere to burn up like meteorites.

Mike was an air force secondee, a former RAF fighter pilot. He was decent, sporty, stiff upper lipped. He was a brave man too. He'd served and won medals in several recent wars. But something was happening to him that neither he nor anyone else could have predicted. He was becoming a cosmophobe. Space was starting to scare him.

"It's a silly thing," he'd confided on our previous mission, "I've flown in all kinds of dangerous situations and never thought twice about it. I didn't think twice about this at first either. But now I can't seem to forget that out here I'm not really flying at all, I'm just constantly *falling*. Please don't tell anyone, Angela. I'll get over it I'm sure."

But it was getting pretty obvious to me that he wasn't going to get over it. His face streamed with sweat. He kept wiping his hands so as to be able to grip properly on the controls. And his eyes, his weary frightened eyes, were just unbearable to look at. I was going to have to confront him about it at the end of this mission, I knew. I couldn't sweep this under the carpet any more. He was putting us both in danger.

But that was for later. Right now we were heading towards a rogue satellite which had been launched a few days ago from Kazakhstan. We were just about to get close enough to actually see the thing when we received an unexpected order from ground base. The intergalactic ship *Defiant* had been hi-jacked by its own crew and they were taking it out of orbit. We were the nearest interceptor and we were to go after it, grapple it if necessary and prevent it from making a leap.

"Jesus!" I breathed.

Mike gave a kind of groan. I realized that up to that point he'd coping by counting off the minutes until we could drop out of orbit and return to base.

But he was a professional. He put his fear to one side, located the *Defiant* and calculated a trajectory which would intercept theirs in about three and a half hours. Then off we went, me leaning out of the window to stick a flashing blue light on the roof.

Well, okay, I made that last bit up.

Tommy:

They used to say there were only five people on Earth who really understood how a gravitonic engine worked, and I certainly wasn't one of them. What I do know is that, for a few seconds at the point of leap, what an engine does is generate an artificial gravitational field that converts the space around it into the equivalent of a black hole. And because an engine works by gravity, it can't be used too close to any large object with a gravitational field of its own. This would distort the field and would result, at minimum, in the ship emerging in a completely different place from the target area. At maximum it could result in the field failing to properly enclose the ship, so that the ship itself would be damaged or destroyed.

This was why, at the rate of acceleration that the *Defiant* could achieve with its conventional Euclidean drive, it would be eight hours before we could reach the nearest safe point to make our leap through sub-Euclidean space: the so-called leap point. It would take half that time in any case for the engine to build up a sufficient charge.

It was after we'd been going for about an hour that we became aware that we were being followed.

"It's gaining on us too," Mehmet said.

"Shall we talk to them?" Dixon asked.

I thought better not. But the others decided we should call and tell them if they didn't back off, they might get sucked down into sub-E with us when the time came to make a leap.

We were surprised to hear the voice of a self-assured young Englishwoman in reply.

"We'll reach you long before you get to your leap point," she said in response to our threat, "and we are certainly *not* going to back off."

Dixon winked at us.

"Listen," he radioed back, "When you get close to us, we leap, even if we're four hours short of the leap point. It's up to you."

Mehmet looked at me with an expression that said, "He's bluffing, yeah?"

But he hadn't seen the gleam in Dixon's eye, the mad religious gleam as he turned back to watch the power monitor.

The interceptor drew closer. There was no sign of them backing off.

"I meant what I said," Dixon told the orbit-cops.

"So did I," said the young woman who we now knew to be Sergeant Angela Young.

Dixon shrugged.

"Okay, then," he said, "here goes or it'll be too late! God save us all."

"*What!*" Mehmet and I simultaneously yelled. We were still three and a half hours short of a safe leap point!

But Dixon laughed as he switched on the field.

"Thy will be done!" he hollered as we plunged into the pit.

Angela:

Purple lightening prickled up and down the *Defiant's* pylons, and the stars all around it shuddered like a mirage. Our vehicle shook violently, its metal groaning with the strain as it was sucked towards the artificial gravity the galactic ship was generating. And then suddenly the stars and moon and sun and earth all vanished and all around us, in every direction, was something like a huge distorting mirror. It was like when you're under water and look up and you can't see the sky or the world outside, only the silvery undersides of waves. Our own faces were there in front of us, little distorted reflections of our frightened faces maybe fifty yards away, peering back at us from a distorted reflection of our cabin window. There was a jolt like an explosion and I vaguely remember hearing a hissing noise coming from somewhere and Mike giving out a despairing groan. Then I blacked out

When I came round again I was in the *Defiant*, and those three famous galactonauts were looking guiltily down at me like naughty little boys who've done a stupid dare and it's gone wrong.

"Hi, you okay? Listen, I'm…"

"Where's Mike?"

"Your partner? He's okay. He's not come round yet, but he's okay. Listen, I'm Mehmet Harribey and…"

"…and I'm Dixon Thorley."

"…and I'm…"

"I know. You're Tommy Schneider. The famous love rat."

My head was killing me, and I was very scared and feeling sick, but I was damned if I was going to show any sign of weakness.

"I meant to leap before you got too close to us," said Dixon, "but I must have left it too late because we pulled your interceptor vehicle through sub-E with us. It was very badly damaged but the three of us came over and managed to get you and your crewmate out before the pressure dropped too low."

"So we did complete the leap then?"

"Yeah, I'm afraid we're kind of…"

"So where the *hell* are we?"

"Well, we're…"

"The truth is," Mehmet said, "that we don't exactly know. We're in intergalactic space, I'm afraid, which… um… is kind of a first. But we believe that the nearest galaxy is our own. So it should still be possible to…um…"

"…to get back to Earth and not suffocate or freeze to death in space – although that *is* the most likely outcome. Is that how it is?"

"Well, yes, I'm afraid so," Mehmet laughed ruefully. (I grew to like him best of the three. He was nice-looking, had natural friendly manners, and didn't come with a reputation either as a religious nut or a serial adulterer. I remembered seeing a photo of him in some magazine with a pretty wife by the Aegean somewhere and three or four pretty little Turkish kids.)

I looked around. The cramped little cabin was about as big as the back of a small delivery truck and it smelled like the boys' changing room at school, but as far as we knew it was the only habitable place for thousands and thousands of light years: the only place in which a human being could remain intact and alive even for a single second.

"You arseholes," I told the three of them, and I felt like I was a copper back on the streets of London, pulling up three silly naughty little boys. "You selfish, childish, thoughtless little arseholes."

They never had a chance to respond because suddenly Mike screamed. He'd opened his eyes and the first thing he saw was the wheel of the galaxy outside the porthole.

Tommy:

It was pure hell there for a while. The British guy hollered and roared and grabbed us and snatched at the controls and swore and wept. I got a black eye, Mehmet got his shirt torn, Angela was yelling at us to back off and not make things even worse (but where the hell were we supposed to back off *to*?) and all of us were getting dangerously close to seeing ourselves just like the Englishman saw us: doomed, doomed to die slowly and horribly in a stuffy tin can with nothing but nothingness outside.

Eventually Dixon managed to get to the medical box and whack a sedative into the guy's ass.

"He's afraid of space," Angela explained as he slumped down.

"A space-cop who's afraid of *space*?"

Even Angela reluctantly laughed.

I'd never gone for black girls particularly before, but I found myself noticing that this was one attractive young woman. She was tough, and funny, and sharp – and she looked *great*. Maybe *this* was what I'd been looking for all this time, I couldn't help thinking (as, God help me, I'd thought so many times before). Maybe I'd just been looking in the wrong place?

Yeah, I know, I know. We were in a damaged ship in intergalactic space and so far from home that, if we could pick out our own sun in that billion-star wheel, we'd be seeing it as it was back in the Pleistocene era. And yet even *then* I was thinking about *sex*. I guess that *is* what you call an obsession.

I mean we had a month's supplies at most. Maybe six week's oxygen.

But I caught her eye anyway and smiled at her, just to let her know she was appreciated.

Angela:

It turned out that their stupid leap had not only sucked through our interceptor and turned it into scrap, it had also damaged the *Defiant* itself. Because they'd made the leap too early the artificial gravity of the field had been pulled back toward the Earth by real gravity – that was why Mike and I had been caught inside it. Some of the pylons at the front end of the ship had actually remained outside of the field, and so literally ceased to exist, while others further back had been bent and twisted. This was very bad news. To get home from this distance would take a minimum of three or four leaps, which was pushing things at the best of times, even *without* a defective engine.

So Dixon, Mehmet and Tommy suited up and went outside to see what repairs they could make, Tommy cheesily asking me if I was *sure* I'd be okay minding the fort and keeping an eye on Mike. Can you believe that he'd already given me the eye several times? Was this bloke *entirely* ruled by his dick?

"I'll be okay," I said, "and I promise not to answer the phone or to let in any strangers."

Answer the phone! Even if my mum and dad could have called me up from Earth – even if there was a signal strong enough to reach this far, I mean – I'd have been dead a million years by the time their message got to me.

Pretty soon all three gallant galactonauts were back. They'd been able to straighten out a few bent pylons. But now something else was on their minds and they rushed to the sensor panel and started playing around with frequencies and filters like kids with a new video game.

"There was this dark disc in front of the galaxy," Tommy explained to me eventually, "Mehmet spotted it first…"

"Never seen anything like it!" Mehmet interrupted. "It was…"

"Here it is!" called Dixon, pointing to a screen.

He'd used radar on whatever it was and it turned out to be a solid object the size of earth, a planet in other words.

"There's a thing called the Ballantyne effect," Mehmet explained to me. "A ship's trajectory through sub-E space is always twisted in the direction of any large mass that's in the vicinity of its notional exit point. It means that you always end up nearer to stars that you would predict on chance alone. But who'd have thought there would be any sort of object out *here* to pull us towards it, eh?"

"So it's a planet with no sun," I said.

"Yes," Dixon told me excitedly. "A planet all on its own. It's been assumed for a long time that they existed, but we've never found one before."

"Well so what?" I said. "What use is it to us? Even Pluto would be hospitable by comparison with a planet that has no sun at all and Pluto is so cold it's covered with solid methane. We're trying to *survive*, remember? What use is a dismal place like that?"

"But the thing is, Angela," Mehmet said excitedly, "the thing is that this planet *isn't* cold!"

"And it's not completely dark either!" said Tommy.

They were all over one another in their haste to show me the evidence. Somehow, even without a sun, this strange object had a surface as warm as Earth's. Seen in infrared it glowed. In fact, even in the *visible* spectrum it glowed, though very softly, so softly that against the blazing mass of stars it still seemed dark.

And when Dixon did the spectrometry on the starlight passing round the planet's edge, he made the most sensational discovery yet. This was a planet with breathable air.

Tommy:

Mehmet, Dixon and I had made a whole career of looking for habitable planets. And now, with very little chance of ever being able to bring the news back to Earth, it looked like we'd finally succeeded, by accident and in the least likely place imaginable.

Of course we had to go and look at it. The thing was only few days away across Euclidean space and a short delay wouldn't make our next leap any more or less likely to succeed. The only difficulty was Angela and Mike, but she shrugged and said okay, if she was going to die, she might as well see this first – and he was strapped to a bunk and peacefully off with the fairies.

Angela:

When we'd got the *Defiant* in orbit, we climbed into the ship's landing capsule and sank down towards a surface that we could now clearly see to be gently glowing over much of its area, as if the planet was covered by a huge candle-lit city. But it wasn't a city. It was a forest. It was a shining forest of glowing trees and luminous streams and pools, that filled up all but the highest ground.

The trees were like gnarled oaks, leafless but with shining flowers along their branches. Their trunks were warm to the touch and they constantly pulsed. You could feel it if you touched them. You could even hear it. *Hmmmmph – hmmmmph – hmmmmph*, they went, and the sound of all of them together combined into a constant hum that pervaded the whole forest. The ground under the trees grew strange leafless flowers that shone like stars. Under the surface of pools and streams waving waterweed carried more shining flowers that made the water luminous, like a swimming pool lit up by underwater lights. And the whole forest was mild and scented like a summer evening on Earth.

"Look at that!" cried Mehmet as something bird-like with neon blue wings swept by overhead.

"Hey, come and see this!" called Dixon, squatting down to look at a clump of small shining flowers like miniature sodium streetlights.

Tommy wandered off in one direction, Mehmet in another. Neither of them said where they were going, and no one asked. Dixon settled down under a tree with his back to its warm trunk. I settled down on the mossy banks of a nearby stream. Strange melodious cries came to us from other parts of the forest. All around us the trees throbbed and hummed and shone under the great wheel of the Milky Way galaxy that filled up most of the sky. Fluttering creatures resembling fluorescent butterflies fed on the shining flowers and in the warm air vents that many of the trees had on their trunks. Bird- and batlike creatures swooped and dived among them.

I was lying by the stream watching little shining fish-things darting around in the water when I remembered that Mike was still inside the capsule.

"Dixon," I said, "would you mind giving me a hand?"

My voice sounded very strange and looming, like when someone suddenly speaks after a long silence during a night journey in a car. It was as if this planet wasn't used to human voices.

Tommy:

Angela and Dixon fetched Mike down from the capsule and settled him on the ground, still fast asleep. He came round a few hours later. There was no screaming and yelling this time. He just wandered through the trees like the rest of us and found a place to sit down and stare and try and take it all in. It turned out that he was some kind of amateur naturalist back home – he went on bird-watching holidays and stuff like that with his wife and kids – and now he had a whole new set of plants and animals to explore. It was him that came up with the theory that the trees worked like radiators, pumping water through hot rocks underground, circulating it through their branches, and warming the surrounding air. They got their energy from the planet's core, he reckoned, instead of from a sun.

Eventually everyone got hungry and we reconvened round the capsule for a share of the rations we'd brought down with us. We supplemented this cautiously with fruit we'd found on the trees. Most of it turned out to be good to eat.

"Isn't this great?" exclaimed Dixon, munching contentedly, his back against a warm tree-trunk. "This is what it must have been like in Eden before the Fall."

And Eden is what we decided to call the place.

Angela:

Mehmet was the one I got on best with. He was friendly and interested and fun to be with. Dixon was okay I suppose but I was really angry with him for selfishly doing the leap when Mike and I were so close. I'm not a person that likes to hold grudges but I really did need to get some of that anger off my chest before I could get along with him – and he *simply wouldn't let me*. Whenever I tried to challenge him, he just said that God had told him to make the leap: the fact that we'd found Eden was proof of it.

"I'm sorry I dragged you away from your family and your friends Angela," would have been nice, or even: "I quite understand why you're so angry."

But I wasn't going to get any of that. Instead it was: "Angela, you need to try and accept the will of God."

The will of God! The arrogant prig! It seems wrong to talk about him like that now, after what's happened since to the poor bloke, but that's how I felt at the time.

Mike, on the hand, was really sweet in this context. Free of the role of RAF officer and free of the fear of space, he became a sort of gentle, dreamy, solitary child. He'd spend his time making lists of all the animals and plants he could find, and giving them names.

But Tommy, he *really* got on my nerves. He tried to be charming and helpful but he was this world-famous lady-killer and he couldn't forget it. In one way I felt that he just took it for granted that I'd want to fall at his feet, yet in another way he was quite afraid of me and needed to keep testing me out all the time to see if he could get a reaction and work out where he stood with me. So he was complacent and insecure, both at the same time, a weird and seriously irritating combination.

Annoyingly, though, he was just as handsome as he'd always looked on TV, so you couldn't help looking at him, whether you wanted to or not.

Tommy:

Angela was graceful, funny, natural. I thought she was wonderful. Stranded a million light-years away from home and very probably in the final days of her life, she was dignified and undefeated and unbowed.

I've been with all kinds of women in my life – models, film stars, university professors, athletes and, yes, I admit it, even whores – and I guess what everyone says about me is true in a way. Women are not just people to me: they are also a kind of addictive drug. But, and I guess this is the part that many people don't understand, I really do like women. I mean I just like being with them, I like them as human beings – and I always have. I remember when I was five years old my teacher asked the whole class one day to pair up for a walk in the local park – and all the boys looked for other boys and all the girls looked for other girls, but I risked the ridicule of everyone to ask a girl called Susan if I could hold her hand. I remember another time I was chasing round the school yard with a bunch of boys, yelling and hollering and waving sticks around, when I noticed a bunch of girls quietly playing in a tree. And suddenly I wanted to be in their game with them, their quiet game, and not with the boys at all. That's how I felt about Angela. I just wanted her to let me join in her game.

The sad thing was, she didn't like me at all. Every time I tried to talk to her, she ended the conversation as quickly as she could. Whatever tack I tried with her, I could see she saw it all as some kind of trick. Yet she would sit for hours with that goddamned Turk, talking and laughing away like they'd known each other forever.

Angela:

When we'd been there the equivalent of two or three Earth days we started to ask each other the question 'What happens next?'

I wanted to know what the chances were of getting successfully back to Earth. Dixon immediately said that he had no doubt at all that God would see us safely home to bear witness to the new Eden. But Mehmet and Tommy thought that it would take at least three leaps to get back to Earth and that each leap would have no more than a 25% chance of success. A quarter of a quarter of a quarter: that was a one in sixty-four chance of getting back alive. A fourth leap, which we'd quite likely need, would knock those odds down to one in two hundred and fifty-six. A fifth leap was apparently out of the question. We just didn't have the power.

"There is an alternative, though," I said. "We could stay here."

"That's true," said Tommy. "Or some of us could stay here while the others tried to get back. If they succeeded, they could send out another crew in the *Reckless* or the *Maverick*, to fetch back the ones who'd stayed."

"But if they failed, the ones who'd stayed would have to grow old and die alone," said Mehmet with a shudder. "Okay I know it's pretty here, but to live a whole lifetime here and die here and ..."

He broke off, and no one spoke for a little bit.

"Not necessarily grow old and die alone," I eventually said. "Not if I was one of the ones who stayed and one of you stayed with me. We could have babies, and then we wouldn't be alone. We could start a whole new race."

Men are funny prudish creatures in some ways. They all visibly squirmed – and then they all laughed loudly to cover up their unease.

I told them I wasn't kidding. I'd stay here with any one of them, or more than one if they liked, and if the *Defiant* didn't make it back and the *Reckless* and the *Maverick* never came, I would make babies with whoever was with me.

Tommy:

I wanted to shout, 'Me! I'll stay!', but I honestly wasn't sure whether I was included in the invitation. Dixon put on his religious voice and said he was married. Mike and Mehmet both said they had to at least try to get back to their kids.

"How about you, then Tommy?" Angela asked.

I was amazed.

Angela:

Tommy and I gave them two months, two Earth months. If no one had come back for us by then, it would mean the *Defiant* had definitely failed to get through.

Two Earth months was April 8th. The date didn't mean anything, of course, in constant Eden, which has no days or nights or sun or moon and (as it turns out) doesn't even change its own position relative to the distant galaxy, or not so you'd notice. But we still followed Earth time on our watches, and hung onto some kind of notion of months and days. And both of us started keeping a diary record on pocket recorders.

On April the 1st there was a small earth tremor and mountains appeared in the distance that we'd never seen before, illuminated by the lava streaming down the side of a volcano in their midst: big mountains covered in snow, that up to now had been in permanent darkness. For a while a hot sulphurous wind blew and the galaxy was hidden behind black dust. Tommy and I spent a few hours laying out a circle on the ground, using big round stones from the bottom of one of the streams, to mark the site of our original landing. It was my idea. It struck me that whether we stayed or whether we returned to Earth, this was a fairly important historic site for the human race. It was a good spot to be in. There were large pools around it, and streams, with fish in them that were good to eat if you could catch them.

April 3rd it rained. We sheltered in a small cave in one of the rocky outcrops around the pools. The cave was even more full of life than the forest outside. When we finally lay down and tried to sleep – Tommy at one end, me at the other, listening to the rain outside – Tommy said that life on Eden must have begun deep down in underground caves when the surface was still covered in deep ice. You get little pockets of geothermal life even on Earth, he pointed out, in deep caves and on the bottom of the sea beyond the reach of the sun. There was even life in Lake Vostok two miles down under the Antarctic ice. Life here could have begun like that and then spread upwards when it discovered how to heat its own environment. Any life form that could reach the surface and melt the ice would get an advantage because it would be able to spread more quickly than was possible in underground caves.

Tommy was trying really hard to be nice to me and not to slip into his smooth lady-killer routine which he knew I hated. In fact we were weirdly formal with each other. It was such a strange position to be in. I was quite clear in my mind that if we got back to Earth I most probably wouldn't want to have anything more to do with him. His celebrity as such didn't impress me and as a person he really wasn't the type I chose to spend my time with.

But if no one came for us? Well then he would be my life's companion and this really would be a marriage which nothing could end but death, a marriage more total than almost any other that has ever existed.

Tommy:

April 4th we saw a new animal a bit like a cat, only it had luminous spots and its eyes were round and flat, not spherical. The weird thing was that when it moved its spots could ripple backwards along its sides at exactly the same speed as its forward motion, so as to create the illusion that its skin was standing still. It also had six limbs, like other Eden creatures. The bird-like and bat-like animals, for example, had hands as well as feet and wings. The little bats stood upright on their hind feet on branches and looked down at us curiously, stroking their wrinkled little noseless but oddly human faces with their oddly human hands while they fanned their membranous wings.

April 5th, I shot a pig-like six-legged animal and we skinned it and cooked it over a fire. It was the first thing we had killed, but we knew we couldn't live on fruit and space-food for much longer. It tasted a bit like mutton, but kind of sweet and fatty.

We didn't talk much, but I guess we both did a lot of thinking. I've never noticed *myself* as much as I did then. I'd often been told I was selfish, self-centered and self-absorbed – by Yvette among others, though I'm not sure she was really in a position to talk – and I guess I was, yet I'd never reflected much before on *me*, on this strange being that happens to be myself. I'd always just *been* this person, blundering and trampling around like some kind of wounded beast, without ever thinking about who he was or why.

Angela:

April 6th I woke up loathing the perpetual night of Eden. It's not cold, it's not pitch dark, it looks pretty enough with its lantern-flowers – quite lovely in fact, like a garden forever decked out with Chinese lanterns for a midsummer night's party. But to think that there would never be a sunrise here, never a blue sky, never a clear sunny day when you could see for miles. Never. Never. Never. For a while I felt so claustrophobic it was all I could do not to scream.

Tommy and I hardly said a word. We'd said we'd wait to April 8th so we did, but really we knew already that no one was going to come back to us, and that Mehmet and Mike and Dixon had not got through. We just weren't going to allow ourselves to say it yet.

Tommy:

April 7th I tried to fill up the time by following starbirds through the forest. Starbirds was the name Mike gave to those peacock-like creatures with luminous stars on their tails. I liked the creatures, even though they were basically carrion eaters. I liked the way they crashed noisily through the trees. I liked the way that pairs of them would move through the forest some way apart, but in parallel, calling out to each other in loud voices that carried over the humming of the trees, and over the cries of all the other creatures.

"*Hoom – hoom – hoom*," goes one.

Then the other, maybe a mile away, goes "*Aaaah! – Aaaah! – Aaaah!*"

I liked the way that that was all they'd got to say but they were happy anyway to say it for hours and hours, back and forth across the forest.

Starbirds don't know they're in Eden, I said to myself several times, as if it was something I couldn't quite get through my head. They don't know Eden is in intergalactic space. They don't know that this ground isn't the base of the universe itself. To them this is just how the world is.

Angela:

And then it was April 8th. We were both awake watching the GMT click over from 23:59:59 to 00:00:00.

"They didn't make it," we admitted to one another at 00:05:00. "They didn't get through."

I wondered how it had ended for Dixon and Mehmet and Mike. It was possible that in mid-leap they had been swallowed up inside one of those weird mirror-lined bubbles of sub-E, which are really tiny little temporary universes which shrink back to nothing when the engine stops pulling them into being. But I think it was more likely that the engine died on them after a leap or two and left them stranded: stranded in that smelly little box in the middle of the void, while the food and water ran out, the ship gradually grew cold and Mike's last sedative shot was finally used up. Poor gentle Mike with nothing between him and his worst fear. Poor friendly, positive Mehmet. Poor Dixon, having to come to terms in the end with the fact that God had let him down. He had found proof that there was life beyond Earth, proof that would undoubtedly have ensured that the Galactic Project would continue and that the gospel could be carried out across the stars, but God had not let him take that news home.

But there was no point in going on and on thinking these thoughts, was there? There was simply no point.

I took Tommy by the hand and we went to a pool we knew and which, without actually speaking of it, we'd somehow both set aside for this moment. It was surrounded by pulsing trees. A soft cool moss grew on its banks, small bats swooped over the water and there always seemed to be starbirds in the vicinity, calling to each other across the forest. It sounds romantic but really for me it was a case of Plan A has failed so let's move quickly on to Plan B – to Plan Baby. This just seemed the best place to put it into effect.

But then again I really did feel a sort of closeness to Tommy because of the weird experience that just the two of us had shared, and because there were so many strong emotions going around in my head, and because there was never going to be anyone else to turn to *but* Tommy – and whoever else he and I managed to summon up between us inside my body.

After we'd done, we looked around and I noticed that there was a tree by the pool with ripe fruits high up in its branches. I've always been good at climbing trees and so I separated myself from Tommy and scrambled up to get something to eat for us. Tommy stood up and waited for me below. I could just make him out in the soft glow of the tree's white lanterns, smiling up at me. Like a little boy, I thought, and then I suddenly felt incredibly angry with him. He was nothing but a silly over-indulged little boy, I thought, who does silly selfish thoughtless things and expects to be instantly forgiven.

I got the fruit and clambered back down, pausing before the last bit to toss it to Tommy so I could use both hands. As I dropped to the ground beside him, Tommy, without any warning, kissed me profusely and then burst out that he loved me and that he'd loved me from the day he saw me. In fact he'd never loved *anyone* as he loved me, he told me. He hadn't known until now what love was really like.

Jesus!

Well, of course I told him not to talk crap. I mean I didn't ask to come here, did I? I didn't ask to be stuck with bloody love-rat Schneider. I would have much preferred Mehmet. Yes and I didn't ask never to see my mum and my dad and my sister Kayley again. I didn't ask to be cut off forever from my friends, and the sun, and green leaves, and the friendly streets of London. And if it wasn't for Tommy Schneider here and his selfish friends I would still have had all of those things. Most likely I would have had them for years and years to come.

So I was angry. I ignored what he had said completely. I started instead to tell him all the grimmest things I could think of about what lay ahead of us.

If we got sick here there would be no one to cure us, I told him. I told him we'd go blind one day in this dim light. I told him I could easily die in childbirth, die in agony and leave him alone here with nothing for company but mine and the baby's corpses. Yes, and I told him – I pointed out to him – that if we *did* have children that lived, they would have to turn to each other for sex partners – unless of course they turned to us – because there would be no one else there for them.

And I told him that after a couple of generations of inbreeding our descendants would have to cope with all the hereditary diseases and deformities that were now hidden away harmlessly in his and my genes. There's sickle cell in my family, I told him, and diabetes too, and my grandmother on my mum's side and two of my aunties were born with a cleft palate. (Did Tommy Schneider know what a cleft palate looked like, or how to surgically correct it, of course without the use of anaesthetics?) Many of these things would become rife in a few generations, when inbreeding brought recessive genes together again and again, along with whatever little genetic contributions Tommy's family might have to make. That was assuming of course that there actually were future generations at all and that the line didn't simply die out, as was quite likely, leaving some poor devil at the end of it all to face the experience of being completely alone in this ghostly forest where day would never come, and no other human being would ever come again.

"This isn't some kind of happy ever after story, Tommy," I told him. "This is *very very* far from happy ever after. The best you can say for it is that it's the only way we've got of going on living and finding out what happens next."

(And, though I didn't speak about it to him, I thought, as I sometimes do, about my ancestors, my great-great-great-great-grandparents, taken from Africa in chains to the Caribbean to cut cane under a slave driver's lash. Horrific as it must have been they went on living, they kept going. If they hadn't, I would never have been born.)

Tommy nodded. He seemed quite calm about everything I'd said, which was disappointing because I wanted to upset him. I wanted to trample over his lovey-dovey daydream so as to pay him back for what he and his friends had done to me. Those three men had stolen my life from me, stolen my home, stolen everyone I really loved.

"So it was all a cold calculation?" he asked, quite calmly. "You staying with me. You making out with me here beside the pool. There wasn't any feeling involved, just a clinical assessment of the situation. Is that right? Is that what you are trying to tell me?"

I'd thought a lot about this. I'd been thinking hard about it for days.

Of course I didn't love the man. He didn't love me either, whatever he'd decided to tell himself. (What did he know of me, after all, except that I'm pretty and that I have a brave face I've learnt to put on when I'm scared?) But there was a bond between us now, I'd decided, which in a way was much stronger than love. And love could grow from that bond, is what I'd thought, maybe not constantly like the lantern flowers of Eden, but perhaps, if we were very lucky, on a recurring basis like the flowers back on Earth.

That is what I'd decided in those strange quiet days of waiting. If we stayed on Eden there would be a bond between us of necessity, stronger in a way than ever existed in almost any marriage on Earth. Necessity was as deep as love and maybe deeper; that was what I had told myself, and perhaps love could grow from it. That was what I'd made up my mind to believe.

But right now I still wanted to hurt him.

"A calculation?" I sneered. "Yes, that's about right, mate, a calculation. If Mehmet had stayed, it would have been him who had laid down here with me just now. If…"

But he didn't let me finish.

Tommy:

It was bad enough to look at her up in the tree, just like I watched those girls in the tree all those years ago when I was a kid at school, asking for them to accept me into their game. It was worse when I tried to tell her how I felt and she trampled on that (just like those little girls did when they all laughed at me and told me to leave them alone). But it was when she mentioned Mehmet that I got *really* mad.

"You goddam women are all the same!" I found myself yelling at her. "You fool us, you lie to us, you twist us round your fingers. You offer us something sweet, something so sweet that we'd give up everything we have just to possess it – *everything*! – and then you take it away again and trample on it, and tell us it doesn't mean anything to you at all!"

I've been told I'm ugly when I get like that. My eyes bulge and spit comes flying out of my mouth. She looked at me with disgust.

"I suppose this is what happened with all your other women," she said, speaking very quietly and coldly. "As soon as they try to inject a tiny note of reality, as soon as they admit that Tommy Schneider isn't the one thing they've been pining for since the day they were born, then Tommy Schneider flies into a rage and runs off to find some other woman who doesn't know him yet, so that she can dry his tears and take him to bed and tell him he's perfect and wonderful. That's it, isn't it? That's what always happens, yes? Well, you've got no one else to run to now!"

"You don't get it!" I told her. It was such an old, old script she'd recited there and I felt so weary of it: "*None* of you get it. I don't *want* you to think I'm perfect. I know I'm not. I'm nothing special at all. I'm good at flying space ships, that's all. I've *never* asked anyone to think I'm perfect. I've just wanted someone to make me feel that I'm wanted anyway for what I am. Why is that so hard to understand?"

And then I grabbed her. I honestly don't know what I intended to do next. To shake her? To beat her against the ground? To rape her?

I never found out because next thing I was in the pool with those little shining fishes darting away all around me.

"I don't think I told you I was in the British national judo team," said Angela from the bank.

"No. Now that you mention it, I don't believe you did."

Angela:

There was a moment there, looking down at him in the water, when I really panicked. I'd made the wrong decision! I was trapped with a violent brutal man without any possibility of escape!

Then I got a hold on myself. Don't be so silly, I told myself. You made a choice between this and death, that's all, and death will *always* be an option. (Maybe that's how my ancestors thought too, out in the cane fields? It's this or death – and death will always be there for us, death will never let us down)

Tommy:

I climbed out of the stream. My anger had vanished, the way anger does, so you wonder where it comes from and where it goes to and whether it's got anything to do with you at all.

"Since we're the entire population of this planet," I said, "I guess we've just had World War One."

That made her laugh. She took my hand again and then we lay down together again in the moss, as if nothing else had happened in between.

Angela:

"*Hoom – hoom – hoom*" went a starbird far off the forest as we pulled back from each other.

I thought to myself, well there is something about him that is okay. And I cast back in my mind and realised that I'd read many, many bad things about Tommy – that he was a serial adulterer and a liar and all of that – but I'd never actually heard it said, or even hinted at, that he ever hit a woman or beat her up.

And I thought too that, after all, I had been a fool to go straight for the place that would hurt him and frighten him the most, even though, God knows, I had a right to be angry. No one reacts well when you deliberately prod their deepest wounds. And there was some wound in Tommy, some old wound to do with love.

Of course I knew that the time would soon enough come again when I would hate him again and want to do everything in my power to hurt him. There would be a World War Two and a World War Three and a World War Four. But this peaceful place we were in now would still be there, I thought. With any luck it would still be somewhere to come back to.

"*Aaaah! – Aaaah! – Aaaah!*" called back a second starbird, far off in the opposite direction to the first one.

"*Hoom – hoom – hoom,*" returned the first. It had got nearer since it last called. It was just across the pool.

"They don't give a damn, those starbirds, do they?" Tommy said. "They don't even notice that great wheel burning up there in the sky."

Tommy:

Angela didn't answer. I didn't expect her to. I was just speaking my thoughts aloud.

But then, five or ten minutes later, after we'd been lying there in silence all that time looking up at the stars, she spoke:

"No they don't," she said. "You're right. This dark Eden, it's just life to them, isn't it? It's just the way things have to be."

We Could Be Sisters

Nature is profligate. All possible worlds exist. In one of them there was once an art gallery in Red Lion Street, London WC1, and its manager was a woman called Jessica Ferne. On one particular grey November day, when Jessica was thirty three, she spent the morning in her office as usual. She made phone calls about her next exhibition and then experimented on her PC with images of the art objects that she planned to exhibit, trying out different arrangements and juxtapositions. Then at lunchtime she put on her jacket, gave some instructions to her secretary, and walked through her gallery and out onto the street. As ever each exhibit stood alone – a pair of mummified hands, a flashing light, an assemblage of human bones – each one contained and separated from the rest of the world by its frame, its label, its pedestal.

Outside an electric cleaning vehicle went by and then some lawyers in robes. Red Lion Street was part of a subscriber area, but at the end of it were the open streets of London, where anyone could go. The boundary between the two areas was marked by a gate with a uniformed security guard in attendance. As Jessica approached it an elderly woman tried to walk in through the gate and it started bleeping. The guard stepped forward and politely refused her entry.

"But I am a subscriber," she complained. "There's some mistake."

A jet fighter passed high overhead   it was part of the city's ever-present shield against aerial attack. The guard suggested to the elderly lady that perhaps her clearance was out of date and that she needed to

175

check with the network. Meanwhile Jessica passed through the gate in the other direction, unimpeded, and there she was, in High Holborn, in the open area. She was not frightened exactly but she quickened her pace and, without even thinking about it, she began to monitor the people around her, checking for sudden movements or suspicious glances.

*

When Jessica was a child, growing up with her adoptive parents in Highgate, you could travel from one side of London to another, on a bus, on foot, in a car. But Jessica was thirty-three now and the map of London had become a patchwork of subscriber areas, reserved for those who could pay, and open areas in between for the rest.

Jessica lived in a subscriber area in Docklands: the Docklands Secure Community. It was managed by a syndicate of subscription companies called LSN, which now controlled almost all the subscriber areas in London apart from a few exceptionally expensive ones for the seriously rich. And Jessica had just walked out of another LSN area, the West Central Safe Street Zone, where her art gallery was located. Within the Zones, burglaries and street crime were almost at zero. Beggars, illegal immigrants, known criminals and suspected trouble-makers were all excluded. Everyone you met had been checked out. And there were TV cameras on every street and LSN detectives constantly on patrol.

'It's *not* like the good old days,' said the LSN ad in the Tube. 'It's *much, much* better.'

The syndicate even ran special trains between the Zones, which didn't stop at the stations in between. There was even talk of special freeways.

*

Outside, in the open areas, things were different. Violent crime was commonplace and in some neighbourhoods there was more-or-less constant low level warfare between rival gangs and religious groupings. Holborn, where Jessica was now, was not an especially rough area –

LSN was actually in the process of negotiating its absorption into the West Central Zone and, in preparation, had already begun augmenting policing there with its own security force – but still, as soon as you passed the gate you could feel the difference. There were beggars for one thing and there were street performers who did not confine themselves, as in the Zones, to designated Street Entertainment Areas.

Today there was a pair of jugglers. They were very adept, making their spinning clubs pass between them so smoothly that it gave the impression of a constant stream, as if the clubs were flowing of their own accord round some kind of force field. If either juggler had faltered for an instant the pattern and the illusion would collapse, but neither of them ever did. The appearance of smooth flow was created by precise rhythm, thought Jessica, and the illusion of weightlessness depended on the law of gravity to bring the clubs back to the jugglers' hands. These little paradoxes pleased her. She smiled and tossed a coin into their hat. A sharp-eyed beggar noticed this largesse and at once shot out his hand.

"Any spare change, love? I haven't eaten yet today."

Jessica looked away, quickening her pace.

"Go on, surprise yourself!" said the next beggar along, this time a woman.

"Sorry, no change," said Jessica.

She noticed the woman beggar had extremely fine blonde hair, very like her own.

High up in the cold blue sky, a pilotless surveillance plane passed above them.

*

Jessica was having lunch in a Laotian restaurant with an artist called Julian Smart. He had told her that, on principle, he only ever ate outside the safe zones. Inside, apparently, the food had no flavour. He was about her own age, currently enjoying a rapidly growing reputation in the art world, and he was very good looking. Last night Jessica had been so excited about this meeting that she'd not been able to sleep. It was true that this morning in the gallery that feeling had vanished and she'd felt strangely indifferent, unable to connect at all with her previous night's excitement, but now once again she felt as excited as an infatuated teenager.

"Jessica! Hi!"

He kissed her. She trembled. He seemed ten times more beautiful than she had remembered him, passionate and fiery. She could not believe that he was interested in her. She could not believe that she had ever doubted her interest in him.

But Jessica was exceptionally ambivalent in matters of the heart. She had never had a sustained relationship with a man of her own age, though she had several affairs with older men, and had recently ended a two-year arrangement with a motorcycle courier ten years her junior, who she had taken in to live with her. Equality was the hardest thing, and yet what she longed for the most.

They ordered fish soup and braised quail. He showed her some pictures of his latest work. It consisted of a sequence of images, the first of which was a banal photograph of a couple feeding pigeons in a park. In succeeding stages, Julian had first drained the scene of colour and then gradually disassembled it into small numbered components like the parts in a child's construction kit. The final image showed the pieces lined up for assembly: rows and rows of grey pigeons numbered 1 to 45 on a grey plastic stem, grey plastic flowers (50 to 62), grey plastic trees (80 to 82), grey plastic hands and heads and feet…

"You'll have to come and see it though," he said as she leafed though the pictures. "Come over and see it. Come up and look at my etchings. We can go for a drink or something."

Wanting to share something of herself in return, she told him about the jugglers she had watched on the way.

"I found it a bit disturbing," she said, "I found that I'd rather watch the two of them than look at any of the stuff we've got in the gallery at the moment. They had something that most artists now have lost: style, virtuosity, defiance… Do you know what I mean?"

The soup arrived. No, he didn't know what she meant at all. He suggested using the jugglers as a basis for a video piece, or making them into one of his plastic kits – a row of grey clubs numbered 1-10, and a chart to show what colours to paint them – or getting the jugglers themselves to stand in the gallery and perform as a sort of living *objet trouvé*. And then this reminded him of a plan of his to stage an exhibition in which the museum attendants themselves were the sole exhibits, with nothing to guard but themselves.

He laughed loudly and, with that laugh, he finally lost her: it had such a callous sound. He no longer looked beautiful to her. She saw in his eyes a kind of greedy gleam and it occurred to her that Julian Smart couldn't really see *her* at all except only as a pleasing receptacle for his own words. She wondered how she could have ever failed to notice that greedy gleam and how once again she had managed to deceive herself into thinking she had found a fellow spirit.

As she headed back to Red Lion Street she asked herself why this happened so often. She thought perhaps it came from being adopted, raised by beings whose blood was strange to her, and hers to them, so that she had learnt from the beginning to work at imagining a connection that wasn't really there. But then again it might just be the world she lived in. All the art in her gallery seemed to mock the possibility of meaning, of connection. It was all very subversive but without a cause. It exposed artifice but put nothing in its place.

Even the jugglers, when she saw them again, seemed weary, as if they longed to let the clubs fall to the ground and leave them to lie there in peace.

*

"Surprise yourself!" said the woman beggar, right in front of her.

Jessica gave a little cry of shock, not just because she was startled, though she was, but also because for a moment she felt as if she was looking into a mirror and seeing her own reflection. But once having collected herself she realised this face was altogether leaner, and had different and deeper lines in it. She is not like me at all, thought Jessica taking out her purse, except superficially in the hair colour and the eyes. And the hair was thinner, the eyes more bloodshot.

But the beggar said, "We could be sisters couldn't we?"

Two jet fighters hurtled by above them.

Jessica pressed bank notes into the beggar's hands.

*

Well I *could* have a sister, Jessica thought as she hurried back to the gallery. It's not impossible.

She had met her natural mother once, a haggard icy-hearted creature called Liz.

"Brothers or sisters?" her mother had said. "You must be *joking*. I had my tubes done after you. No way was I going through *that* again."

But Liz could quite well have been lying. She'd struck Jessica as a woman who spoke and believed whatever seemed at that particular moment to further her own ends. In that one meeting Liz had given Jessica three different accounts of why she had given Jessica up, discarding each one when Jessica had presented her with contradictory facts she'd read in her file.

Then again, the files had not mentioned a sister either.

*

At six o'clock Jessica went back down Red Lion Street to look for the beggar, but she wasn't there. She drove home through North London and lay awake planning to search the homeless hostels and the soup kitchens, all over London if necessary, all over England. The beggar had a West Country accent she thought. Like Liz, who came from Bristol.

In the morning, after she'd parked the car, Jessica went down to the end of Red Lion Street again, and again at lunchtime. She spent half the afternoon in her office in the gallery phoning hostels and charities and welfare agencies, asking how she would go about finding someone she had met in the street. They all said they couldn't tell her anything. Jessica could have been anyone after all: a dealer, a blackmailer, a slave trader looking for a runaway. And anyway Jessica couldn't even give a name for the woman she was looking for.

She nearly wept with frustration, furious with herself for not finding out more when she met the woman yesterday. And now it seemed to her that if she could find the blonde beggar again it would be the turning point of her whole life. That's no exaggeration, she thought. If necessary, I really will give the rest of my life to this search. This is my purpose, this is the quest which I've so long wanted to begin.

When she went down Red Lion Street for the third time, though, the beggar was there again – and this turned out to be a bit of a disappointment. It had really been *far* too short a time for this to have been a satisfactory life's quest. And anyway, when it came down to it, who was the beggar but just some stranger? Once again, Jessica thought, I've blown up a great big bubble of anticipation, and she would have walked away from the whole thing at once had she not known herself well enough to realise that, as soon as she turned her back, she would immediately want to begin again.

So she made herself go forward, even though she was full of hostility and resentment.

"We could be sisters?" she demanded.

The beggar woman looked up, recognising Jessica at once.

"Yes!" she exclaimed, and she appealed to her male companion. "Look Jim. This is the woman I was telling you about. We *could* be sisters don't you reckon?"

The man looked up.

"Yeah," he said indifferently, "the spitting image..."

Then he really looked.

"Fucking *hell*, Tamsin! You're right. You could be fucking *twins.*"

Jessica felt dizzy, as if she had taken a blow to the head.

"Tamsin?" she asked. "Tamsin? Is that your name?"

"Yeah, Tamsin."

"Tamsin's my name too. My middle name. The name my mother gave me before she had me adopted."

Tamsin the beggar gave a small whistle.

"We need to talk, don't we?" said Jessica. "There's a coffee shop over there. Let me buy you some coffee and something to eat."

"Coffee and something to eat?" said the male beggar. "Yummy. Can anyone come?"

"Fuck off Jim," said Tamsin.

A powerful helicopter crossed very low over the street. It was painted dark green and armed like a tank.

*

In the coffee shop Jessica said, "Could we really be sisters?"

"No chance," said Tamsin, "my mum had herself sterilised right after I was born."

"But how old are you?" asked Jessica.

"Thirty three."

"When is your birthday?"

"April the second," said the beggar. "*What*? What's the matter?"

Jessica had gone white.

"It's mine too," she said. "April the second. And I'm thirty-three. We must be twins."

Tamsin laughed.

"We're not you know."

"Same name, same birthday, same looks, I'm adopted. What other explanation can there be?"

"I've never heard of twins with the same name," said Tamsin.

"Well no but…" Jessica was genuinely at a loss.

"Haven't you ever heard of shifters you posh git?"

"Shifters?"

Jessica had heard of them of course. She'd never knowingly met one. The word had eerie, uncomfortable connotations. People said shifters moved sideways across time by taking some kind of drug. She'd heard it came in pills they called 'slip' or 'seeds'. A few years ago there had been something of a moral panic about shifters and there had been talk about how they were a mortal threat to law and to civilisation and to humanity's whole understanding of its place in space and time. But oddly people seemed to have rather forgotten about them since then. It was like flying to the moon, or having conversations with people on the far side of the world: impossible things happened and people soon got used to them (though in the case of shifters there were still those who maintained the whole phenomenon was some sort of elaborate hoax).

"*I'm* a shifter," said Tamsin. "I don't come from this world. I must have been in a hundred worlds at least."

"But if you don't come from this world how can…?"

Tamsin made an exasperated gesture. "Don't you get it? I'm not your twin. I *am* you. You and me were once the same person."

For some reason Jessica leapt to her feet with a small cry. Everyone in the coffee shop looked round. She sat down again. She stood up.

"Give me your phone a minute," said Tamsin.

Like most pocket phones at that time, Jessica's had a security lock which could only be deactivated by her own thumbprint. Tamsin pressed her thumb on the pad and they watched the little screen light up.

Jessica couldn't bear to stay still.

"Let's go out," she said. "Let's walk in the street."

*

The world splits like cells on agar jelly. Just in the short space of time you've been reading this, countless new worlds have come into being. In some of those worlds you've tossed this story aside already. In others you have been interrupted by the phone, or the doorbell, or a jet plane crashing through the ceiling. But it seems that you – this particular version of you – were one of the ones who carried on reading.

When Tamsin was born, her mother Liz had her placed for adoption. Tamsin was not a wanted child. She was the child of a rape for one thing and this did not help, but as a matter of fact she wouldn't have been wanted anyway, for Liz didn't have an ounce of maternal feeling in her. But Liz's mother and her sister and her brother and the people in the pub where she drank every night, they all told her she was a selfish cow and how could she give up her own flesh and blood? They all told her they didn't want anything to do with a selfish cow who would give away a little baby that never asked to be brought into the world. And all this was not easy for someone like Liz to withstand.

Time split and in some of its branches, Liz gave way to the pressure and asked for Tamsin to be returned to her, as was her legal right, before the adoption went through. In other branches Tamsin was adopted by the couple who'd been caring for her since birth, two earnest young doctors who couldn't have children of their own. They renamed her Jessica. Jessica Tamsin Ferne. This is what Tamsin and Jessica worked out between them as they walked in the open streets.

Tamsin had not had an easy time of it. After getting her back, her mother had grossly neglected her. One of her mother's boyfriends had abused her. In the end the authorities had taken her back into care. But they left it too late and were unable to settle her anywhere. She moved between many different foster-homes and residential units, in and around the big social housing project outside Bristol where she had originally lived with Liz.

Jessica on the other hand had been raised in Highgate by the two earnest doctors, who sent her to private schools and took her in the car to ballet classes every Saturday morning and violin lessons on Wednesdays and extra French every second Thursday.

But once, thirty-three years ago a single baby girl had lain in a crib with these two different futures simultaneously ahead of her. Not to mention other futures that neither of them knew about.

"You must come home with me," said Jessica. "I'll phone my work and say I've had to go home."

Tamsin smiled as she listened to Jessica lying to her secretary. When Jessica had finished they looked at each other and burst out laughing, like co-conspirators, both of them noticing how alike they were, how at some deep level they understood one another, whatever their different histories. And each of them was thinking simultaneously that at last she'd no longer be alone.

Both of them, however, had thought this many times before, if only ever very briefly. In Jessica's case she'd thought it for a short while just a few hours previously in the Laotian restaurant with Julian. And yet Julian hadn't entered her thoughts, even for a moment, since Tamsin said, 'We could be sisters'.

Jessica led the way to her car, but as they turned up Red Lion Street the gate began to bleep, for only Jessica had an LSN card in her pocket.

"Excuse me!" called out the guard. "Can you…"

When they turned towards him, each with the same irritated expression, he was speechless. He knew both of them by sight, for Jessica often walked through his gate and Tamsin often begged outside it, but it had never until now occurred to him to compare them.

*

As the guard wouldn't let Tamsin into the West Central Safe Streets Zone, Jessica had to fetch the car and pick Tamsin up outside it. There were problems at the other end too. As a resident subscriber of the Docklands Zone, Jessica was allowed to bring in visitors, but they were still required to show their national ID card at the gate. Tamsin had no ID of any sort. She may have been born in Bristol but this didn't alter the fact that she was an illegal immigrant from another universe.

So she hid in the luggage compartment of the car, and in that way Jessica smuggled her deviant alter ego through the security barrier within which she herself had, at considerable expense, chosen to live. She was taking quite a risk in doing so, for the penalty for deliberately violating the LSN security rules was to be automatically barred not only from the Docklands Safe Streets Zone but from all the other LSN Zones in London as well. So she would lose both her home and her job if she was caught.

An elderly neighbour from two floors up stared at them in the lift: Jessica in her chic outfit and Tamsin in a jumper and jeans which gave off the sickly odour of clothes that have been slept in. They were both giggly and excited, each in her own way feeling released from a long oppression.

"People usually call me Jess," said Jessica.

"People usually call me Tammy."

"Do you want some wine?"

"You are so fucking *posh* aren't you?"

"Well you're so fucking common. Do you want wine or not?"

"Yeah great. Haven't you got a bloke or kids or nothing?"

"Nope. I did have a bloke but I chucked him out. I never wanted kids."

"Me neither. Like mum."

Tamsin sipped the wine and looked around.

"You must be *rich*! I bet you're one of those that go on foreign holidays every year. Thailand, India… all that…"

"Well I've never been to another *world*, though. I can't even imagine what that's like."

"They're just the same as this one, except for stupid little things, like the phone boxes are a different colour, or the money looks different, or the estates have different names. Just stupid little things. When you start shifting you think you are going to find a place where it will be better, a magical place. But you soon give that idea up when you've done a few shifts. It's always the same old shit. It's always the bloody same."

"So why did you keep doing it?"

Tamsin walked to the doorway of the room and looked out, clutching her wineglass against her body with both hands.

"Once you start its hard to stop," she said. "You're not looking to get anywhere any more, not really. It's the shift itself that's the thing. All these worlds going by and you're not in any of them, you're just falling and falling through them. In the middle of a shift the worlds go by so fast that it's just a blur."

She looked into the kitchen, into the bathroom, into the main bedroom. Jessica followed her patiently.

"I'll tell you a weird thing about shifting, though," Tamsin said at length. "You know those little flick-books you can get? The ones where you flick the pages and it looks like one picture that's moving? Well, it's a bit like that. All those blurry worlds sort of merge together and you see something else which isn't in any of them. And it's like a huge tree, a massive great tree, but with no roots or leaves or nothing, no ground or sky, just branches growing all the time in the dark, growing and growing, and splitting off from each other all the time as quick as anything…"

She looked into Jessica's spare bedroom, which had once been the den of Jessica's motorcycle courier boyfriend, Jeff.

"And you think if only you could see that tree properly," she said. "If only you could see it you'd, like, *understand*. But it only ever lasts a second or two and the next thing you're in some other shitty world and you're thinking, *oh crap*, now I'm all on my own again, and I've got to get some money and somewhere to sleep, and why the fuck did I give myself all this grief all over again? Yeah, but even *then* you're already thinking about your next shift. Where am I going to get some more seeds? That's what you're thinking. Who can I nick them from? Who've I got to have sex with to get him to give them me?"

Tamsin looked into Jessica's study. As she entered it the large wall-mounted computer screen came to life and there was Jessica's virtual p.a., 'Elsie', life-sized, smiling out at her in the form of a friendly, slightly overweight Scottish woman in her middle thirties. Everyone had one these days – or at least everyone who had an exceptionally expensive, state-of-the-art computer like Jessica. The things copied and spread themselves through the internet and you could customise them at will.

"Hi Jessica," Elsie said to Tamsin. "Have you had a good day?"

Tamsin dropped her glass.

"What the *fuck*?"

The electronic face furrowed with concern.

"Are you *okay*, Jessica. You look very pale. Is everything alright?"

Tamsin looked to the real Jessica outside the doorway for support. Jessica laughed.

"Don't worry Tammy, it's only a computer graphic."

She came into the room, identified herself as the real Jessica, and told Elsie to shut herself down.

"Creepy," muttered Tamsin as the screen blanked.

"You're right," said Jessica. "I think it's about time I uninstalled her."

She went for a cloth to mop up the spilled wine.

"That computer can't have come cheap," Tamsin said looking round, while Jessica cleared up the mess, at the elegantly minimal furnishings, the shelves of art books, the signed painting on the wall. "What the fuck do you do to get all this money?"

"I manage an art gallery."

"What, paintings and that?"

"Not many paintings actually. Body pieces mainly these days."

"What?"

"Pieces made from human bodies."

"Ugh."

"Listen Tammy. Don't do any more shifts. Stay with me. Please. Promise me you will. I'll look after you. I'll make everything alright for you."

"Have you got a bath? I'd really like a bath."

"Of course. And take some of my clothes. They can be our clothes. I'll change too. We could have a bath together and dress the same. Let's see how alike we are when we dress the same. Let's take pictures of ourselves together."

*

They slept together that night in Jessica's double bed. Tamsin went to sleep very quickly. It was a long time since she had lain down in a real warm bed after a bath with a belly-full of food. Like some small forest animal, she had learnt to exploit such moments when they came.

Perhaps she's not like me at all, thought Jessica suddenly in the dark, listening to Tamsin's wheezy breathing. A person's body and brain were just empty vessels waiting to be filled, or so the earnest doctors had told her. Personality was in the programming, not in the machine. What did a shoot 'em up game and a word processor have in common just because they could be run with the same hardware? This was a complete stranger lying beside her: a dangerous, unpredictable interloper who, in a moment of madness, she had brought into the safe zone and into her flat and her bedroom and her bed – yes, and then made extravagant promises to as well: 'Stay with me. I'll look after you. I'll make everything all right.' What had she been thinking? Had she gone completely mad?

But then she thought: yes, but the same things made us laugh. She and I both noticed it. We noticed each other noticing it. So there *is* something in common. Whatever the different paths we have travelled, deep down Tammy and I are still the same.

But *then* she thought: why I am so obsessed anyway with finding someone who is the *same*? Why this constant obsessive longing for a soul-mate? Suppose I did find someone who was identical to me in every way. Wouldn't that just be another way of being alone?

Tamsin whimpered in her sleep.

"Tex! Don't do that!" she pleaded with someone in her dream. "Please! Please! *Please*!…You're scaring me Tex. Oh shit, *no*! *Please*!"

"It's okay sweetheart," whispered Jessica. "It's okay Tammy. You're only dreaming. You're safe here with me."

She took Tammy in her arms. Tenderness such as she had never felt came welling up in the darkness. She remembered Tammy's body in the bath, thin and pale, worn and scratched and bruised, with dozens of deep scars where Tammy had cut herself with razor blades and knives and broken glass. What sort of pain would you need to have suffered to make you do that to your own flesh?

What did it matter how alike or unalike Tammy was to her? The point was that they were connected. They were inextricably connected.

*

Next morning, as it happened, Britain embarked on a war. Few people even remarked on it. It took place in a small country far beyond the imaginative universe of most British people. Even the brave warriors themselves fought from ten thousand metres up and never once saw the faces of those they attacked.

A war had begun. What last night had been solid buildings in that small faraway country – houses, offices, factories – this morning were scattered stones and bricks and bits of wood. On TV, if Jessica had chosen to watch it, the safely returned warriors were being asked how they felt ('How was it for you?' 'Was it your first time?' 'Was it like what you expected?') But Jessica didn't watch TV and, though she woke abruptly with a sense of loss and dread, it came from quite another source. She was alone. While she slept, Tamsin had gone.

"Tammy!" cried Jessica, leaping out of bed, but she already knew what she would find: her purse emptied on the floor, her money gone, the front door left open, no note, no explanation...

Jessica threw on some clothes. She wasn't angry. She knew that Tamsin had gone to buy 'seeds' and she understood this perfectly, for she knew that, if she had been the one that had woken first and had found Tamsin still there, then she would have resented the intruder, and it would have been *her* who would have been desperate to put distance between them.

She ran out into the street.

"Tammy! Tammy!"

It was 7am. Only a few people were about, most of them workers – LSN-vetted workers – who travelled into the Zone from far away to make the cappuccinos and empty the dishwashers and clean the streets. They observed Jessica with surprise. A Turkish newsvendor setting up his stand paused and asked her if she was alright. Jessica ran past him to the gate.

"Are you running round in circles?" asked the LSN guard. "It was only twenty minutes ago you last ran through."

He frowned.

"And weren't you wearing *red* last time?"

*

Jessica arrived an hour late at the gallery. She hurried through that pure white space in which each exhibit was isolated and quarantined by a frame, by glass, by a neatly printed label: a preserved human face, a self-portrait made in blood, a scribbled page from a diary reproduced in relief on a slab of marble, a row of grainy snapshots of an ordinary London street, elaborately framed and labelled with Roman numerals like the stations of the cross...

Barely even speaking to her secretary, she shut herself away in her office and went at once to her PC to download the photographs she had taken the previous night. There they were on the screen, a dozen pictures of Tammy, in Jessica's bath robe, in Jessica's pyjamas, laughing and pulling faces and striking poses.

She clicked the print icon. She gathered up the printed images one by one as they emerged and then laid them out on her desk. Last night, when she and Tamsin had been together what these twelve pictures showed had been reality. But now each of them had already become an object in its own right, separate from the past, separate from each other, separate from Jessica, separate above all from Tamsin.

Jessica felt nothing. She moved the photos this way and that on the desk, over and over again, trying different arrangements, as if she thought she might find a pattern, a resolution, if only she tried long enough.

La Macchina

On the first day I thought I'd go and see the *David* at the Accademia, but what really caught my imagination there wasn't the *David* at all but the *Captives*. You've probably seen pictures of them. They were intended for a Pope's tomb, but Michelangelo never finished them. The half-made figures seem to be struggling to free themselves from the lifeless stone. I liked them so much that I went back again in the afternoon. And while I was standing there for the second time, someone spoke quietly beside me:

"This is my favourite too."

I turned smiling. Beside me was a robot.

I had noticed it in the morning. It was a security guard, humanoid in shape and size, with silver eyes and a transparent skin beneath which you could see tubes, wires, sheets of synthetic muscle...

"Move out of my way!" I said. (You know how it is? Like when you say Hello to an ansaphone? You feel like an idiot. You need to establish the correct relationship again between human and inanimate object.) "Move out of the way," I snapped. "I want to stand there."

The automaton obediently stepped back and I moved in front of it, thinking that this would be the end of the encounter. But the thing spoke again, very softly.

"I am sorry. I thought you might understand."

"*What?*"

I wheeled round angrily.

But the robot was walking away from me.

*

You know how Italians drive? Round the corner from the Accademia some idiot in a Fiat took it into his head to try and overtake a delivery van, just as a young woman was stepping out into the road. He smashed her into the path of the van, whose left wheel crushed her head.

A wail of horror went up from the onlookers. One second there had been a living woman, the next only an ugly physical object, a broken doll: limbs twisted, brains splattered across the tarmac...

I waited there for a short while, dazed and sick but thinking vaguely that they might want me for a witness. Among the bystanders an appalled and vociferous debate was building up. The Fiat driver had hit and run, but strangely the recriminations seemed to centre not on him but on the robot driver of the delivery van, which remained motionless in the cab, obviously programmed in the event of an accident to sit tight and wait for human instructions.

"*La macchina,*" I kept hearing people say, "*La macchina diabolica.*"

One forgets that in all its gleaming Euro-modernity, Italy is still a Catholic country.

*

I went back to the hotel.

It was one of those cheap mass-market places. Through the little window of the lift, you could see that every floor was identical: the same claustrophobically narrow and low-ceilinged corridor, the same rows of plywood doors painted in alternating red, white and green. The delayed shock of the road accident suddenly hit me and I felt almost tearfully lonely.

"Ninth floor, Signor," creaked the tinny voice of the lift.

I went down the windowless corridor from number 901 to number 963 and opened the door, dreading the empty anonymous room. But Freddie was already there.

"Fred! Am I glad to see you!"

Freddie laughed. "Yeah? Beer's over there Tom. Help yourself."

He was lying on the bed playing with his Gameboy and had already surrounded himself with a sordid detritus of empty beer-cans, ashtrays, pizza cartons and dirty socks. He had the TV on without the sound.

My little brother doesn't speak Italian and has no interest whatsoever in art. He had spent his day in the streets around the hotel, trying out bars and ice cream parlours and throwing away Euros in the local VR arcades. I told him about seeing the girl killed outside the Accademia.

"Jesus Tom, that's a bit heavy. First day of the holiday too!" He thumbed back the ring-pull of another can. "Still, nothing you could have done."

I had a shower and we went out for something to eat. We were just finishing off our first bottle of wine when I remembered the robot.

"I meant to tell you. A weird thing happened to me in a museum. This robot security guard tried to talk to me about one of the sculptures."

Freddie laughed. "Probably just some dumb random choice program," he said with a mouth full of spaghetti. "Easy to set up. Every hundred visitors or whatever it spins random numbers and makes one of a hundred possible remarks..."

"But this was the *Accademia*, Fred, not Disneyland!"

Fred shoved a big chunk of hard Italian bread into his mouth and washed it down with a swig of wine. "What did it say exactly?"

My brother acts like a complete dickhead most of the time – he is a complete dickhead most of the time – but cybernetics is his special interest. He reads all the mags and catalogues. He visits the chatrooms. His accumulated knowledge is immense. And by the time I had told him the whole story, he had stopped eating and was looking uncharacteristically serious.

"It sounds very much like you met a Rogue there, Tom. You'd better call the police."

I laughed. "Come on Fred, you're putting me on!"

"No really. Those things can be dangerous. They're out of control. People can get killed."

I got up ("I'm warning you. This'd better not be a joke!") and asked to use the phone. The police said that regretfully *cibernetica* were not under their jurisdiction and I should contact the *carabinieri*. (What other country would have two separate police forces operating in parallel!) I phoned the carabinieri and got through to a Sergeant Savonari in their *Dipartimento di Cibernetica*. He took the whole thing alarmingly seriously. There had been several reports already, he said, about the same *macchina*. He asked me to stay at the trattoria and he would come out immediately to see me.

*

Somewhat shaken I went back to our table.

"Christ Freddie, I had no idea. I obviously should have contacted them this morning. Is it *really* likely to kill someone?"

Fred laughed. "No, not at all likely. But a Rogue is out of control. So you just don't know what it'll do."

"So what *is* a Rogue exactly? Like a Robot that's picked up a virus?"

"Not really. A virus is something deliberately introduced. Robots go Rogue by accident. It's like a monkey playing with a typewriter. A sophisticated robot is bombarded with sensory information all the time – they've got much better senses than ours mostly – and every now and then a combination of stimuli happens by chance which screws up the robot's internal logic, unlocks the feedback loops…"

"And the robot comes alive?"

"No it *doesn't*," Freddie was irritated by my naivety, "no more than your electric razor comes alive if the switch gets broken and you can't turn it off. It's still just a machine but it's running out of control." He wiped tomato sauce from his plate with his last piece of bread. "Well if we're going to have to wait here for this guy, you'd better buy us another bottle of wine…"

Savonari arrived soon afterwards, a small dark man with deep-set eyes and a great beak of a Roman nose. He shook us both by the hand, then reversed a chair and straddled it, leaning towards me intently across the remains of our meal. It was only after he had been with us for some minutes that I registered that he himself had a robot with him, standing motionless by the doorway, hammerheaded, inhuman, ready to leap into action in an instant if anyone should try and attack the sergeant, its master. (It was what the American police call a 'dumb buddy' – three hundred and sixty degree vision, ultrafast reactions, a lethal weapon built into each hand...)

Several people, it seemed, had witnessed and reported the robot's attempt to converse with me in the Accademia – and seen it slipping away from the gallery soon afterwards – but no one else had been able to report the exact words spoken. Apparently my account confirmed beyond doubt that there had been a fundamental breakdown in the thing's functioning, rather than, say, a simple hardware fault. The sergeant noted, for instance, that it had continued to try to talk to me when I had clearly ordered it out of the way.

"These security machines are unfortunately very prone to this problem," said Savonari with a resigned gesture, addressing himself to Freddie. "Their senses and analytical apparatus are so very acute."

Freddie, unable to understand a word, smiled vaguely and offered the sergeant a cigarette, which was declined.

"Our own machines are totally reprogrammed every week to avoid this," the Sergeant said, nodding towards his sleek minder by the door, "but not everyone is so aware of the dangers."

He made a little movement of exasperation and told me of a case he had dealt with recently where a robot farm hand had suddenly tossed its owner's ten-year-old son into a threshing machine.

I shuddered. "What did you do?"

"Like all Rogues," (the Italian word, it seems, is *Incontrollabile*), "the machine had to be destroyed. But that was no help to the little boy."

Again the angry gesture.

"I am a Catholic, Signor Philips. Like the Holy Father, I believe that to make machines in the likeness of people is a sin against the Holy Spirit. I would like to see them *all* destroyed."

He snorted: "My little son had a machine once that taught him how to spell. I put it out for the dustman when I discovered he had given it a human name."

Then he shrugged and got up: "But I can only enforce the law as it stands, Signor Philips. Thank you for getting in touch. I am sure we will find the *macchina* very soon."

He shook our hands again and left. We heard him outside the door barking angrily at his 'buddy': "*Pronto, bruto, pronto!*"

*

Later as we leaned comfortably on a wall watching the bats looping and diving over the river Arno, Freddie enthused about that police machine. Apparently the things are actually made in Florence in the Olivetti labs out at the *Citta Scientifica*.

"Beautiful design," Freddie said. "Nothing wasted. A really Italian machine."

I liked that concept and proceeded to spout a lot of drunken nonsense about how the taut police minder was in a direct line of descent from Michelangelo's David – how the wires and tubes under the transparent skin of the robot in the Accademia echoed the nerves and muscles in da Vinci's sketches of dissected limbs...

Freddie just laughed.

*

Our days settled into a routine. We were woken in the morning by the humming of a little box-shaped domestic robot, which let itself in through a hatch in the door (and drove Freddie crazy by trying to vacuum up coins, paperbacks, socks and anything else which he'd left on the floor). Then we wandered round the corner to a café and had breakfast together before splitting up for the day: me heading for the museums and churches, Freddie for the Virtual Reality arcades.

In the evening I'd meet him in one or other of the arcades (looking like a gentle Nordic giant among the wiry Italian kids as he piloted a landing on Mars, or led a column of armoured sno-cats through an Alpine pass). He'd take off the headset and we'd go to a trattoria for a meal. Then we'd find a bar on some busy street or square, so we could sit outside and watch the city go by.

After a while you start to see not just a single city but several quite separate ones. There is the city of the Florentines themselves... There are the high-tech pan-Europeans from the *Citta Scientifica*, wearing Japanese fashions and speaking Brussels English, larded with German catchphrases... There is the city of the tourists: Americans, Japanese, foul-mouthed British kids on school trips, earnest Swedes clutching guide-books (all different, but all of them alike in the way that they move through the famous sights as if they were a VR simulation)... And then there is the city of the dispossessed: the Arabs, the Ethiopians, the Black Africans from Chad and Burkina Faso and Niger – hawkers, beggars, hustlers, climatic refugees from the burnt-out continent, climbing up into the belly of Europa along the long gangway of the Italian peninsula...

About the fifth or sixth day into the holiday, Freddie picked up a book somewhere called *Illicit Italy* (with a cover photo of a transvestite hooker, leaning on a Roman bar). While we sat drinking in our roadside café in the evening he kept chuckling and reading passages out loud.

"Listen to this, Tom! 'The *Bordello Sano*, or Safe Brothel, recently legalised by the Italian government in an attempt to curb the AIDS epidemic, can now be found on the outskirts of all the major Italian cities, staffed entirely by what the Italians call *sinteticas*, robots with living human skin...'"

I shifted uncomfortably in my seat. Freddie read on cheerfully:

"'The obvious advantages of sinteticas are (a) that they are very beautiful and (b) that they are completely safe. But some say that the biggest advantage is the fact that they have no soul...'"

He read on a bit to himself, then looked up. "Hey, we should go and have a go Tom. It'd be a laugh!"

*

I have to admit that I knew about the Bordello Sano in Florence and had already considered a discreet visit, just to have a *look*. But discretion is not my little brother's style. The whole way over there in a crowded bus, he chatted cheerfully about the sinteticas in an embarrassingly loud voice.

"Apparently they build them to look like famous models and film-stars. There's some old woman who used to star in porn-movies when she was young and then got elected an MP. She sold her genes to a sintetica manufacturer. She said she was bequeathing her body to the men of Italy!"

I grunted.

"Another thing," Freddie said, "there's actually been cases of women *pretending* to be sinteticas because sinteticas are more popular and make more money. Weird isn't it? A real woman pretending to be a fake?"

But when we actually got there, Freddie went very quiet. It was ruthlessly hygienic and efficient, quite terrifying in its cool matter-of-factness. You walked through the door and a receptionist gave you a sort of menu, illustrated and in the language of your choice. Then you went through into the lounge where the sinteticas waited under reproduction Boticellis in fake gilt frames, with canned Vivaldi twiddling away in the background.

They were extremely beautiful – and looked totally human too, except for the licence plates on their foreheads. (According to Freddie's book you can check whether you've got a real sintetica by seeing if the licence plate is bolted on or just glued.)

A tall blonde in a black leather miniskirt came over to Freddie and offered her – its – services.

In a small dry voice he muttered: "English… No capito…"

"Oh I'm sorry," it said in faultless Euro-English, "I said would you like to come upstairs with me?"

Freddie looked round at me helplessly. (The kid is only eighteen years old. I could at least have *tried* to keep him out of this.) I shrugged and attempted to smile as the sintetica led him away.

Then it was my turn. The creature that approached me was curvaceous and dusky-skinned, with a face so sweet it set my teeth on edge. And she wore a dress of white lace which left her graceful shoulders bare and showed most of the rest of her through pretty little patterned peepholes.

"Hi, I'm Maria. I'd be pleased if you decided to choose me."

I felt myself smiling apologetically, shrivelling in the cool frankness of her gaze. I had to struggle to remind myself that this was not a 'her' at all. Under the veneer of real human skin and flesh was a machine: a thing of metal and plastic and wires…

Upstairs in a room full of mirrors and plastic roses and pink ribbons, the beautiful robot spread itself appealingly on the bed and asked me for my order. I remembered the menu thing clutched in my hand and started to read it. You could choose various 'activities' and various states of dress or undress. And you could choose from a selection of 'personalities' with names like 'Nympho', '*La contessa*' and 'Virgin Bride'.

You could ask this thing to be whatever kind of lover you wanted. But instead (God knows why) I blurted out: "I don't want any of those. Just be yourself."

The friendly smile vanished at once from the syntetica's face. It sagged. Its mouth half-opened. Its eyes became hollow. I have never seen such terrifying emptiness and desolation.

Freddie told me later that I read too much into that expression. It was no different from the blank TV screen you get when you push a spare button on the channel selector... Well, perhaps. But at the time I was so appalled that I actually cried out. And then I fled. I literally ran from the room, and would have run straight outside into the street if the bouncer at the door hadn't stopped me: "*Excusi, Signor. Il conto!*"

There was a bill to pay and I had to wait to pay it because the receptionist was settling up with another customer who was paying extra for damage to the equipment. ("A hundred Euros, signor, for a cut lip, and fifty each for the black eyes... Thank you, Signor – oh, thank you very much, you are most kind – we look forward to seeing you again as usual...")

As the other customer turned to go I saw the Roman nose and realised it was Sergeant Savonari of the Carabinieri, the very same who lined up with the Pope on the Robot Question.

*

I didn't wait for Freddie. Male human company seemed about the last thing in the world I needed just then – and I guessed he would feel the same. So I spent a couple of hours wandering the streets by myself, in between those different cities that occupy the same space but hardly touch each other at all: the city of the Florentines, the city of the Euro-techs, the city of the tourists, the city of the displaced...

And it suddenly struck me that there was another city too which I hadn't noticed before, though it had been there all the time:

Outside a tourist pizza place on the Piazza del Duomo, a little street cleaner trundles along on rubber tyres, peering about for litter and scooping up the discarded cardboard and polystyrene with long spindly arms...

Through the steamy window of a tiny bohemian restaurant, a waiter made of plastic and silicon quietly clears tables and serves coffee, while its bearded owner dispenses cigarettes and largesse to his customers...

Following behind a pair of carabinieri on the Ponte Vecchio, a robot minder guards the officers' backs while they keep an eye on the beggars and pickpockets...

At the door of a Renaissance Palazzo, a sintetica housemaid in a blue uniform presses the entryphone button, a prestige domestic appliance clothed in human flesh, returning from an errand for its aristocratic masters...

The City of Machines.

I thought about the robot from the Accademia. I wondered whether it had been caught. I found myself having the irrational thought that I'd like to see it again.

*

Two days from the end of the holiday, I was sitting by the fountain on the Piazza della Signoria, eating a strawberry ice cream and wondering where to have my lunch when a taxi, driving too fast in what is basically a pedestrian precinct, snagged one of the little municipal cleaning machines with the corner of its bumper. The thing keeled over and lay there unable to right itself, its wheels spinning and its arms and eye-stalks waving ineffectively in the air.

I laughed, as did several other on-lookers. No one felt obliged to do anything. But a robot security guard and a sintetica servant, coming from different directions, lifted the thing gently back onto its wheels. They dusted it down and the sintetica squatted briefly beside it as if asking it whether it was okay. Everyone laughed: tourists, Florentines, African hustlers. The cleaner trundled away and the other two *macchine* headed off on their different errands.

I was suddenly seized by a crazy conviction.

"Hey you!" I shouted, dropping my ice cream and chasing after the security guard. "I know you, don't I? I met you in the Accademia!"

People stared at me and exchanged incredulous glances, half-shocked, half-delighted at the outlandishness of the spectacle.

And there was more in store for them. It was the robot from the Accademia. It stopped. It turned to face me. It spoke.

"Yes... The Captives..."

It was so obviously a machine voice – flat and creaking – that it was hard to believe that I could ever have taken it for a human. Maybe as the programmed order of its brain gradually unravelled, its control over its voice was weakening? But strangely the very creakiness of it seemed touching, like something struggling against all odds to break through.

Hardly believing what I was doing, I touched its cold plastic hand.

"That afternoon in the Accademia – what was it you thought I understood?"

But before the automaton could answer me, it was interrupted by a shout.

"*Alt! Polizia!*"

A fat policeman was running up, followed by his hammerheaded minder. The Incontrollabile turned and ran.

"Shoot it!" the policeman ordered.

"No don't shoot!" I pleaded. "It's harmless! It's just come alive!"

But the minder did not take orders from me. It lifted its hand – which must have contained some sort of EMP weapon – and the Incontrollabile fell writhing to the ground.

The policeman ran over. His thick moustache twitched as he looked down at the broken machine. Then he lifted his booted heel and brought it down hard on the robot's plastic head.

A loud, totally inhuman roar of white noise blasted momentarily from the voice-box and the head shattered, spilling a mass of tiny components out onto the square.

The policeman looked up at me triumphantly.

"Don't talk to me about these things being alive. Look! It's a machine. It's just bits of plastic and wire."

*

I dreamed that the broken machine was taken to the monastery at Vallombrosa, where the simple monks mended it and gave it sanctuary. Somehow I found it there.

"I have come to see the macchina," I told an old friar who was working among the bee-hives.

There was a smell of honey and smoke and flowers, and the old man's hands and shining pate were crawling with fat black bees. He smiled and led me through a wrought iron gate into an inner garden.

The macchina was sitting quietly in the shade of a flowering cherry tree, almost hidden by its thick pink clouds of blossom, which were alive with the buzzing of foraging bees. Quivering lozenges of shade and pinkish light dappled its translucent skin. An old dog lay snoozing on its left side, a tortoiseshell cat on its right.

And it spoke to me about the Great Chain of Being.

"The first level is simple matter. The second is vegetative life. The third is animal life which can act and move. Then somehow the fourth level emerges, the level of self-awareness, which distinguishes human beings from animals. And then comes a fifth level."

"Which is what?"

The macchina seemed to smile.

"Ah, that is hard to say in human words…"

*

"Gotcha!"

Bees and cherry blossom vanished.

Freddie had leapt out of bed onto the little domestic robot, trapping it beneath a duvet.

"Thought you'd pinch my ciggies again did you, you little bugger?"

He beamed up at me from the floor, expecting me to laugh.

But suddenly I had seized him by the throat and was ramming him up against the wall.

"*Leave it alone, you bastard, alright?* Just leave the poor bloody thing alone!"

Karel's Prayer

The first thing Karel Slade noticed when he woke up was an odd smell in his hotel room. It was like the plasticky smell of a new car which has just had the polythene taken off its seats, but with a hint too of something antiseptic, a hint of hospital. And it was entangled in his mind with the mood of a fading dream in which he was drowning or suffocating, or being held down.

The second thing he noticed was that the radio alarm hadn't gone off. It was now 8.00 and his plane home flew at 8.45.

"Shit!"

He leapt out of bed naked – a big, broad-chested, athletic man in his late forties, with thick silvery hair – and grabbed the phone to get a taxi. But the line, unaccountably, was dead.

"I do *not* believe it!"

He pulled on his trousers and headed for the bathroom. But it was locked.

8.03, said the clock as he went to the door of the room and found that locked too. The phone rang.

"Mr Slade, please come to the door of your room."

"It's locked."

"Please come to the door and walk through."

Beyond the door, where the hotel corridor should have been, was a large almost empty room, entirely white, with three chairs in the middle of it. Two of them were occupied by men in cheap suits. The third, a tall straight-backed thing which reminded Karel both of a throne and of an electric chair, was empty.

The two men rose.

One of them, the tall, wiry black man with the gloomy, pock-marked and deeply-lined face, went to the door that Karel had just come through, closed it and locked it. The other, the rotund Anglo-Saxon with the curly yellow hair and the affable expression, came forward in greeting.

"Mr Slade, good to meet you, my name is Mr Thomas. My friend here is Mr Occam."

Karel did not take the extended hand.

"Who the fuck are you and what the fuck do you think you're playing at?"

There were those who said that Karel was surprisingly foul-mouthed for a prominent Christian leader, but as he often pointed out to his family and his friends, coarse language might be undesirable but it *wasn't* swearing and had nothing whatever to do with the third commandment. You had to have *some* way of expressing your negative feelings, he always argued.

"Sit down," said Mr Occam shortly, returning to stand beside his colleague.

Mr Thomas gestured to the throne.

"No," Karel told him. "I don't feel like sitting. I *do* feel like listening to your explanation."

"Sit!" commanded Mr Occam.

"Yes, do sit," said Mr Thomas, "and then we can talk sensibly."

He returned to his own chair. He was one of those people who manage to be both plump and nimble. His quick, graceful movements were almost camp.

Karel shrugged, went to the chair and sat down.

With a buzz and an abrupt *click*, shackles came out of the chair legs and fastened themselves around his shins.

"Lay your arms down on the rests," Mr Occam told him.

"What? And have them shackled too!"

The black man approached him.

"I will hit you Mr Slade if you don't put your arms on the rests."

Karel did as he was asked.

Buzz. Click. The shackles slid into position.

Mr Occam nodded curtly – a taciturn man acknowledging a small courtesy – and took his seat alongside Mr Thomas.

"Now Mr Slade," said the more amiable of the two men, "let's see if we can answer your questions for you. Who the fuck are we? Well, suffice to say that we work for a government agency. What the fuck are we playing at? That's easy. We're carrying out an investigation. An investigation concerning a terrorist organisation. And we believe you may be able to help us with our inquiries."

Mr Occam gave a small snort.

"He is going to help us with our inquiries."

Mr Thomas turned to his colleague gravely.

"Do you know what Mr Occam? I think you may be right."

*

God help me, Karel prayed.

He was very very afraid but trying hard not to show it.

Please God, help me!

As ever, when he needed it most, his faith seemed to have deserted him. *But we should expect that,* he reminded himself. In the darkness and confusion of a fallen world, we should expect that. After all, if the world wasn't fallen, people wouldn't *need* belief. They would just *know.*

Please God, help me! he tried again and this time help did seem to come. For a merciful moment he was able to hold the thought in his mind that all this was only happening to one man at one particular point in space and one particular moment in time. Beyond this room, outside of this moment, the world was still the world. And beyond the world, that tiny inconsequential speck, there was eternity. There was always eternity. The same as it ever was.

"I have rights," Karel said. "You can't detain me and shackle me and question me without a warrant."

"With respect," said Mr Thomas, "I think we've just demonstrated to you that we can."

"But you're breaking the law. You're violating my constitutional rights. Sooner or later you'll have to release me, and then this will get out. I'm a prominent man. I head an organisation with more than two million members. I have connections. I…"

"Why do you think we'll have to release you?" queried Mr Thomas with what seemed like genuine curiosity.

"Well of course you..." Karel broke off, realising that there were, after all, other theoretical possibilities.

"Listen," he said, "if I'm not out of here very soon, my family and colleagues will start demanding explanations. And they'll go on until they *get* explanations. And then you two men are going to be in deep trouble."

"You think so?" Mr Thomas wiggled his head from side to side doubtfully, weighing up the merits and demerits of a questionable argument. "Well who knows? Who knows? But you should let us worry about that. After all, you've got other things to consider."

"Yes," said Mr Occam. "Like for example your membership of the SHG."

"The Soldiers of the Holy Ghost," said Mr Thomas regretfully, almost as if embarrassed to bring it up, "an illegal terrorist organisation responsible for several hundred deaths over the past five years."

"I don't know what you're talking about," said Karel. "I'm Executive Director of Christians for Human Integrity. It shares some theology with the SHG, yes. But it's an entirely legitimate organisation, properly registered with all the appropriate authorities."

"It's a front for the SHG," stated Mr Occam.

"And you, Mr Slade," his colleague continued, "are a leading member of the SHG's strategic command. Why deny it? You can see for yourself that we know it, so what would be the point?"

While Mr Thomas was speaking, Mr Occam leant forward and stared intently at Karel's eyes.

Don't try too hard to look sincere, Karel told himself. It was the mistake that liars always made, like drunkards trying too hard to act sober, like unfaithful husbands trying too hard to appear uxorious, rushing home from their mistresses with chocolates and bunches of flowers for their wives.

"I do deny it," he said. "I deny it completely. Now let me call my lawyer."

"No, Mr Slade," said Mr Thomas. "That's not going to happen. And *don't* lets go on and on about it, eh? Or it will get so..."

Mr Occam broke rudely across him, leaning forward to bark a question into Karel's face.

"Do you deny you support the aims of the SHG?"

"No I don't deny that. Like the SHG, I'm opposed to any form of artificial life or artificial reproduction of life. I'm opposed to artificial intelligence, I'm opposed to cloning, I'm opposed to designer babies and I'm opposed to field-induced copying of human tissues. But it's not a crime to object to tinkering with human identity. Millions agree with me. A majority of the population quite possibly."

"And do you deny that you support the *methods* of the SHG?" asked Mr Thomas.

Tell the truth whenever possible, Karel told himself. *The less lies the better*. But he'd need to choose his words carefully.

"I believe that their use of violence is *in principle* justified by the cause. Most Christians for the last two thousand years – including all the Christian members of the present government – have believed that violence in some circumstances is justified. It's the traditional doctrine of the Just War. If Christians can legitimately invoke that doctrine to justify war in defence of purely national interests then they are certainly entitled to invoke it when it comes to defending the integrity of the human person. But that's an intellectual and theological position. It doesn't mean that…"

"You are a member of the strategic command of the SHG," Mr Occam said. "Not intellectual position. Not theological position. *Fact*. You know that. We know that. We're not even going to discuss it. You've been actively involved in funding and planning attacks on laboratories and laboratory staff for the past five years at least. What we want from you are names, code words, bank accounts, structures and systems. And you're going to tell us all of them, Mr Slade. One way or the other you're going to tell us the whole lot."

"No I'm not, because I don't know them."

"Oh for *Christ's* sake man," grumbled Mr Occam, rising wearily from his chair and hitting Karel very hard across his face.

"You can't *do* that!" Karel yelled at him.

It had hurt. It had frightened him. But more than anything he was shaken by his own baby-like helplessness. He was a man who liked to be in charge of his own life.

Mr Occam hit him again, this time so hard that the entire chair toppled sideways and crashed to the floor.

Help me God, prayed Karel, shackled to the fallen chair. He could feel blood running down his cheek. He could taste the rusty tang of it in his mouth. *Help me remember that this is just pain. It's essentially trivial. It's just something that's happening for a very short time indeed to the most temporary part of me.*

They'd had a training course in the SHG – 'Using Faith to Withstand Torture' – and a set of guidelines that they'd instilled into all their members. But they also knew very well that, faced with the agony of the Cross, even the Son of God had lost faith for a moment. So they'd set themselves a limited goal: you can't hold out forever but try at least to hold out for one day to give the rest of the organisation time to go underground.

One day, Karel thought, *just one day*. That had to be manageable.

The guidelines proposed two stages. Stage A was to stonewall as long as possible, denying all knowledge. Stage B, when the torture got too much to bear, was to give false information. There were various fake addresses and phone numbers which would keep the enemy busy for a few hours, and tip off the people outside that they were under threat...

But for now Karel needed to try and stick to Stage A. Actually, as long as they stuck to hitting him, he felt quite confident he could cope. Hitting just hurt after all. It was only if they got onto needles and blades that he would start to be vulnerable because, brave though he was about most things in life, he was absolutely terrified of being pierced or cut. He always had been. Ever since he sliced open his knee when he was a kid and had looked inside before the blood came, and seen his own white bone.

"Names, code words, bank accounts, structures and systems," repeated Mr Occam. "Starting, *now*, with the names of the other four members of the strategic command group. The real names, not the crappy fake ones that you and your pathetic friends have dreamed up. We know all about Mr French of Dawson Street. We know about Mr Gray of Oldham Road."

Parallel to the floor in his toppled throne, like the fallen king at the end of a game of chess, Karel quailed. Telling them about the fictitious Mr French and Mr Gray had been Stage B. So now there was nothing pre-prepared to fall back on.

"I told you," he said, "I don't know any names. I don't even know what the strategic command group *is*."

Wham. Intense pain and nausea. Bright lights in his eyes. Mr Occam had kicked him in the stomach.

"Don't *lie* to us you murderous piece of shit. We aren't just guessing here. We *know* you're high up in the SHG. We know that since the death of Leon Schultz, there's no one senior to you in the whole gang."

A sour strand of vomit, mixed with blood, dribbled from the corner of Karel's mouth. The mention of Leon Schultz had shocked him. A wealthy hotelier who had died suddenly and unexpectedly of a heart attack three weeks ago, Schultz had indeed been the leader of the SHG, but Karel had thought this was known only to himself and his four colleagues in the strategic command group.

"Names," said Mr Occam, "*now!*"

He kicked Karel again.

"Hey!" protested Mr Thomas, standing up. "Easy Mr Occam now. Easy! You're letting it get to you again. Maybe you should take five while I have a quiet word with Mr Slade here?"

"Quiet fucking word be damned," grumbled the black man. "Let's stop pussyfooting around."

It was hard for Karel to see what Mr Occam was doing because he had moved into a part of the room which was nearly above his head, but there was some kind of cabinet there against the wall, like one of those cabinets with many narrow drawers that you get in museums, holding fossils or sea-shells or pressed flowers. Mr Occam was opening and closing drawers, muttering. And then something silvery glittered in his hand and he turned and advanced across the room.

Oh shit God, Karel prayed. *Help me please. If you love me God, make him put that back.*

"Come on Mr Occam," said the fat man, standing in front of his colleague and reaching up to lay his hands on his shoulders. "You *know* it's not time for that yet. We need to give Mr Slade a *little* space. A man takes a few minutes to figure out how he's going to get round his entire system of belief."

Mr Occam made a disgruntled noise.

"Come on man, take five," said Mr Thomas. "You know I'm talking sense."

Mr Occam hesitated and then, to Karel's surprise and huge relief, he nodded. Returning the blade to the cabinet, he strode across the room, opened a door and went out, out into the mythical world which lay beyond these four white walls, its existence almost as hard to believe in now as that of the Kingdom of Heaven itself. The door slammed.

Ten minutes must have gone by already, Karel told himself. *Just six times that and I'll already have done one hour.*

*

"Mr Occam's got all kinds of nasty things in that cabinet there," said Mr Thomas, returning to his seat and leaning forward to peer down concernedly into his prisoner's face. "Knives, razors, pliers, even a blow torch. You know, like one of those little ones people use to make that crunchy caramel crust on a crème brulée? Nice in a kitchen but, man, it *hurts* when you use it like he does, with the vinegar splashed on afterwards and all. But I think those sort of things should be the very last resort. I'm not a sadist. Maybe I'm in the wrong job but I honestly don't like causing pain."

Karel, the fallen chessman in his sideways throne, said nothing. Of course he had heard of the good-cop bad-cop routine and he understood that a game was being played. But he desperately *desperately* wanted to keep the good will of the reasonable Mr Thomas and to keep the ruthless Mr Occam at bay.

"Actually," said Mr Thomas, "Mr Occam isn't a sadist either. You should see him with his grandchildren. He's gentleness itself. But he's an angry man, that's the thing. His little brother was maimed by your people, you see. Bomb went off at the lab where he worked. Concrete beam fell on top of him. Legs mashed to a pulp. Had to have them both off at the hip. Girl beside him – nice girl, Gloria: as a matter of fact they were talking about getting married – she was decapitated by the blast. He was trapped in there for an hour and a half next to her headless corpse. Well, need I go on? Just imagine it was your little brother Mr Slade."

Karel said nothing.

"He can't stop thinking about it actually," Mr Thomas said. "You wouldn't believe how it eats him up."

He got up with a sigh.

"Come on now, let's get you upright. I really shouldn't do this with my bad back, but I just can't talk to a man in that position."

With a grunt of effort he levered Karel and his throne back up, then returned to his own seat, puffed and red-faced.

"I know you people sincerely believe what you are doing is right," he said. "I know you sincerely believe that what Mr Occam's brother was doing was wrong. But, man, he was working on ways of duplicating human organs for transplants. He was only trying to help. You can see why Mr Occam is angry, can't you? You can see why he feels entitled to hurt you. Your people didn't seem to care much about his brother's feelings after all."

Karel still said nothing. Intellectually his position was that the SHG should feel no more and no less responsible for the individual tragedies that resulted from their operations than the bomber pilots who helped rid the world of Nazi death camps should feel responsible for the individual tragedies that befell German civilians in the cities they bombed. There would have been mashed legs there as well. There would have been many decapitated girlfriends. But he couldn't say that without incriminating himself further. After all, his position was supposed to be that the SHG weren't 'his people' at all.

"Yes. I can see why he's angry," he said. "I would be too in his place. But those laboratories, those technologies, they're brewing up all kinds of horrors for the future. They're blurring the boundaries between a human being and a thing. You don't have to be a Christian to see that, surely? Without that distinction, there..."

He broke off.

"But I'm not going to change your mind here am I?"

Mr Thomas laughed pleasantly.

"I'm a public servant, Mr Slade. My opinions are neither here nor there."

"How can you be a public servant if you don't obey the law?"

"Ah, but those are the *written* laws you're talking about Mr Slade, aren't they? Laws for the daylight, laws for the public stage. You've got to bear in mind that every public stage also needs a behind-the-scenes, a backstage. There's got to be a place where it can be a bit messy and untidy, and where it's okay to leave the ropes and props and bits of scenery lying about. Do you know what I mean? The show's the thing, the show's what it's all about – that's indisputable – but it's what goes on behind the scenes that keeps it all going."

Mr Thomas stood up.

"I'll tell you what. Why don't I leave you here to think for a little while? You think about what you could do to help us, and I'll nip out and have a quick word with Mr Occam there, see if I can persuade him to cut you a little bit of slack."

*

Fifteen minutes at least, thought Karel, sitting in the middle of the empty room. *Get through three more times what I've done so far and that will be an hour ticked off already.*

And it would only be another hour before Caroline realised he wasn't on the plane. She'd know at once that something was wrong. She'd know to inform Matthew using the agreed code. Matthew would set the wheels moving to get everything in the SHG battened down in readiness for the coming storm, and Caroline meanwhile would do the worried wife routine, using all the formidable resources she possessed as a TV celebrity and famous beauty: phoning the TV stations and the international press, phoning lawyers and churches and civil rights groups, e-mailing the two million members of Christians for Human Integrity. Twenty-four hours? Who needed twenty-four hours? It would be a couple of hours at most before the light of day began to break through into Mr Thomas's 'behind-the-scenes' and Messrs Occam and Thomas began to feel the heat.

It was worrying that they knew about Leon Schultz though. How had they found out? How did they know about Mr French and Mr Gray? What else did they already know?

The door opened. Mr Thomas came back in, followed by a sombre Mr Occam. They both sat down in their chairs in front of him. It was as if Karel was being interviewed for a job.

"We've decided to give you a bit of information," said Mr Thomas. "Something we've been holding back from you. We think it may help you come to a conclusion."

Mr Occam stood up, walked slowly over to Karel's throne. Karel braced himself for another blow. But instead the sombre black man leant forward and placed his hands on the ends of the chair arms, so that his face and Karel's were no more than a foot apart.

"You're not Karel Slade," he said, and for the first time he very faintly smiled.

His breath smelled of tobacco and peppermint and garlic.

"What do you mean I'm not Karel Slade? Of course I am!"

Instinctively Karel looked past the implacable Mr Occam to the accommodating Mr Thomas. But Mr Thomas made the regretful grimace of a person who reluctantly confirms bad news

"It's very hard to take in I know," he said, "but it's true. You're actually a copy of Karel Slade; you're not Karel Slade himself. In fact the real Karel Slade knows nothing of you at all. He knows nothing of any of this."

Mr Thomas paused like an experienced psychotherapist giving a client some space to process a difficult truth. Karel needed it. He was frozen in the sense that a computer can be frozen when so overloaded with tasks that it can't proceed with any of them.

"Incidentally," Mr Thomas said, "it's actually a lot later in the day than you probably think it is. It's actually early evening. The real Karel Slade got up at 6.30 this morning, caught his plane and is now back with his wife, Caroline. They're at a restaurant with Caroline's brother John and his new fiancée Sue. I believe the meal is in celebration of John and Sue's engagement."

"Not without me, they're not. That was my idea."

"It was actually Karel Slade's idea. You *think* it was your idea because your brain is an exact copy of Slade's and contains all his memories and thoughts."

"Oh come on," said the man who still believed himself to be Karel Slade, "I can see you're trying to disorientate me, but to suggest I'm some sort of clone is really absurd."

"Not a *clone*," said Mr Occam.

"No of course not," said Mr Thomas. "That *would* be absurd. A cloned copy of you would take forty-eight years to grow – and even then it would only be a body copy of you. It wouldn't have your memories. And it's your memories that we're after."

He leaned closer.

"No, you're not a clone, Mr Slade, you're a field-induced copy. Last night when Karel Slade got into that hotel bed he didn't know it but he was actually getting into a scanner. The precise imprint of his body on the surface of space-time was recorded, right down to the subatomic level. And then this imprint – this field – was reproduced by an Inducer in the mineral bath from which you eventually emerged. It's a bit like dropping a crystal into a solution. It takes a bit of time, though, which was why we had to tinker with the clocks before we put you back in that fake-up of your hotel room and waited for you to wake up."

Karel knew about the field induction process. Like artificial intelligence and genetically engineered babies, it was one of the things that Christians for Human Integrity and the SHG were both fiercely opposed to.

"But no one's ever copied more than a few cells," he said, "and the government declared a moratorium on the whole thing a year ago, pending the report of the Inter-House Committee on Ethics."

Mr Thomas nodded.

"But we're back to what we were talking about earlier, aren't we? About the difference between the public stage and behind-the-scenes? There is a moratorium on field induction research and it's perfectly appropriate in a civilised society that there should be, but behind-the-scenes has its own needs."

"You mean you just went ahead with field-induction in secret?"

"Well we couldn't pass up on a technology like that, could we? Not in all conscience. As you pointed out yourself at the beginning of this session, suspects have all kinds of rights – and properly so. They can't be physically hurt. They've got to have a lawyer present. They can't be held for more than a short period of time. It's all very laudable. But we've got a responsibility to protect the public and if we can work with a *copy* of the suspect, none of those problems need apply. What's more, if we do it right, the suspect and his associates need never even know that we're onto them. Karel Slade for example has no *idea* you're here and that you're about to incriminate him and the entire leadership of the SHG by telling us everything he knows."

"I *am* Karel Slade, and I'm not going to tell you anything about the SHG because I don't *know* anything."

"I know it's hard to grasp. I know it's just too much. But you're not

Karel Slade. It's just that you have no other memories except for the ones that were copied from Karel Slade's brain."

"You're a copy," said Mr Occam bluntly. "Get used to it. A couple of hours ago we fished you out of the tank and dried you down with a towel. Two hours earlier you were a lump of meat. Two hours before *that* you were just soup."

"Perhaps it would help to clarify things if we gave you another name," said Mr Thomas. "Let's call you... I don't know... let's call you Heinz."

Mr Occam seemed to find this amusing.

"You always call them Heinz," he complained. "You always call them Heinz or Campbell."

"Not *always*," protested Mr Thomas. "I sometimes call them Baxter."

There was a TV set in the corner of the room. He strolled over to it and switched it on.

"Something I'd like to show you Heinz. We have one of our sleuths at the restaurant where Karel and his wife are dining at the moment. The Red Scallop. Only just opened this week, I understand..."

Karel – or Heinz – could see them on the screen: Caroline, John, Sue round the restaurant table... and Karel Slade, large and voluble, teasing his future brother-in-law about something or other while the women laughed.

"This is a fake," he said, "you've done this with computer graphics."

"What, since *yesterday*? It *was* only yesterday you phoned Caroline and suggested this restaurant, remember? Previously you had a table booked at the Beijing Emperor."

"Somehow you've done it since yesterday."

"Dear God, Heinz, we're good but we're not *that* good."

"I'm not called Heinz, I'm Karel Slade. And that isn't a live transmission. It's a fake."

"Okay, let's test it," said Mr Thomas. "What's your cell phone number?"

Karel told him. Mr Thomas punched the number into his own phone and paused with his finger on the 'call' button.

On the screen John was replying to Karel's banter. Caroline and Sue were watching Karel to see how he would react. They were smiling in anticipation. Karel could be a very funny man. They were looking forward to a laugh. Caroline's hand was resting affectionately on his arm.

"Now you tell me when to push the button," said Mr Thomas. "You choose the moment."

In the restaurant Karel was acting the outraged innocent in response to whatever John had jokingly accused him of. They were all laughing now. The waiter had just arrived with the starters.

"Now," said Karel-in-the-throne.

Mr Thomas pushed the button.

Karel-on-the-TV reacted at once. The smile faded to an irritated 'What now?' expression as he felt his jacket pockets for the ringing phone. When Mr Thomas hung up, Karel-on-the-TV examined his phone to see who the call had come from, shrugged, replaced it in his pocket and, muttering something to Caroline in passing, turned his attention first back to the others and then to the generous plate of seafood in front of him.

Karel-in-the-throne shrugged, as far as a man can shrug when his arms are shackled.

"You could do all that with computers. You could easily do all that." Mr Thomas smiled.

"Okay, demonstration number two coming up."

He took out of his pocket a device like a TV remote controller and pointed it at Karel's throne, which rose about an inch as small wheels emerged from the bottom of each leg. Mr Thomas and Mr Occam got up from their own seats. Then, with Mr Thomas leading the way, Mr Occam pushed Karel back through into the room where he had woken up, as if he was some elderly invalid in a wheelchair.

It seemed incredible to Karel now that he hadn't realised at once when he woke up that the alleged hotel room was simply a crude stage set. The walls were plywood panels, in some places not even properly screwed back onto the frame. There was a blank white screen outside the window where there was supposed to be a view of the city. But you see what you expect to see.

Only the sense of smell, it seemed, was not so easy to fool. All that had troubled him on waking had been that plasticky, slightly disinfectant smell.

However it wasn't the room that Messrs Occam and Thomas wanted to show him. Using his remote, Mr Thomas unlocked the bathroom door and they passed through. Of course there was no bathroom. In fact what lay beyond wasn't so much a room at all as a hangar or a factory floor. Its dull metallic walls rose to the height of two ordinary rooms and it was the length and width of a soccer pitch. Down the centre of it was a row of five large ovoid objects lying lengthways, each about three metres long and two metres high. They were complex structures, made predominantly of metal. A thick mass of cables – red, green, black, blue, yellow, multi-coloured – fed into plugs across their surface and trailed back across the floor to a bank of monitors against the wall. There was an ozone smell and a soft electrical humming.

"In case you're wondering, Heinz," said Mr Thomas. "These giant Easter eggs are Field Inducers."

They approached the nearest inducer and Mr Thomas pressed a button on its surface to make a segment of the egg slide upwards to create an opening. Inside, beautifully illuminated by lights both above and within it, was a bath of clear liquid. It smelt of iron, like blood. Karel could feel the warmth of it in his face.

"So you're trying to say you grew me in there?"

"You don't *grow* things in a Field Inducer," said Mr Thomas. "You *assemble* them. Field induction isn't a biological process. It's a physical one. Think of making a recording of a sound. You don't try and reproduce the same conditions that led up to the sound being produced in the first place, do you? You by-pass all that. You construct a device that can copy the sound waves themselves."

"But yeah," said Mr Occam. "That's what we fished you out of. When you'd got a face, that is, when you'd got past the stage of just being a big clot of blood. We fished you out, put you on the recovery table and got you going with a jolt of current. Then we gave you a shot to put you to sleep for a bit and took you through to the bed."

Mr Thomas nodded.

"So what we're saying, Heinz, is that this is the soup can you came out of."

Karel couldn't help remembering his dream of drowning and of hands holding him down, but he managed a derisive snort.

"It's all a film set," he said. "Like the hotel room."

All of this was actually *good*, he tried to tell himself. It was good because it was taking up time. The longer he could keep Mr Thomas and Mr Occam busy with trying to prove he was a copy, the nearer he'd get to his twenty-four hour deadline before having to face the challenge of physical pain.

"Hang on, Heinz, hang on," laughed Mr Thomas, "we haven't finished yet."

Mr Occam pushed him forward to the second Field Inducer. Once again Mr Thomas touched a button. Once again a warm metallic smell wafted out as the device opened up...

Then Karel gasped. Suspended in the fluid, neither floating nor sinking, was a flayed human corpse.

"Dear God," he whispered. "What have you done?"

"*That* thing bothers you does it?" growled Mr Occam. "You should have seen my brother's girlfriend after you lot blew her head off."

The thing suspended in the water was dark red like congealed blood, its half-formed face an eyeless, orifice-less sculpture made of blood. All over its surface were hundreds of fine, branching strands, which at first seemed to be some kind of growth like seaweed, but then turned out not to be solid outgrowths at all but patterns of inward movement, rivulets of matter being drawn from the surrounding fluid and streaming into the solid mass of the body.

"Recognise the face at all?" asked Mr Thomas.

Karel looked at the eyeless mask. Red as it was, eyeless and hairless as it was, covered as it was by the little branching rivulets, the resemblance wasn't immediately obvious, but now that he looked more closely it was unmistakeable. This thing was a likeness of himself.

"We always make several copies," said Mr Thomas. "It gives us a margin of error. If we're too rough with the first copy and it goes and dies on us, we can fall back on one of the others. Copies aren't quite as resilient as originals unfortunately. In fact, in about ten per cent of cases, you can't even get the heart to start and we just have to bin the things."

He looked down thoughtfully into the mineral bath.

"It's funny. It doesn't matter how many times I've seen this, I still always find myself wondering why they don't drown down there, and why they don't float or sink to the bottom. It's hard to get your head round the fact that it isn't a living entity at all at this stage. *Nothing* is moving in there. The field is a rigid template, the matter flows into it, and once every particle is in place, it is locked there, completely and utterly motionless. It's the ultimate in suspended animation."

They moved towards the third Inducer.

"This will only have been started a short time ago," said Mr Thomas as the panel slid open.

At first this one seemed empty – there was certainly no solid object in there – but after a moment Karel made out a faint reddish vaguely man-shaped blur. Mr Thomas took an aluminium pole which rested against the Inducer and stirred the liquid until the reddish mist had disappeared. Then he laid down the pole again and they watched as the wispy shape slowly began to reassert itself.

"Suppose what you say is true," said Karel/Heinz. "Suppose that I *am* only a copy of Karel Slade. Why tell me?"

Mr Thomas glanced at Mr Occam.

"Well in a certain sense, Heinz, it doesn't make much difference to us whether you believe yourself to be the original or the copy. Either way you have the information we want and we're going to extract it from you by any means possible. And if that involves razors, that's too bad. If it involves putting vinegar on your scalded flesh or pulling off your nails with pliers, that's too bad too. But it does seem *unfair*. So Mr Occam and I, when we talked outside earlier, we agreed that you might like to reflect on your position a bit before we go any further."

"What do you mean, my position?"

"Think about it Heinz. Think it through. If you resist and we have to hurt you, you won't be suffering on your own account but on behalf of Karel Slade. *You've* never been part of the SHG. We know that. In fact we're your alibi. We can vouch for the fact that we fished you out of the soup ourselves, only a few hours ago. So there's no doubt about it, *you've* never ordered anyone's death. *You've* never harmed anyone at all."

Mr Thomas took hold of Karel's throne by the arms and turned it to face him.

"You're an innocent man, Heinz," he said. "Why should you suffer on behalf of someone else? Why should Mr Slade be protected by the law while we torture you to try and stop *his* wrong-doing."

"Even if I am... Even if I'm not..."

Karel glanced at the misty red phantom of himself suspended in the mineral bath. Tears came welling up into his eyes.

"I mean *whatever* I am," he persisted, fighting them back, "my beliefs are still the same."

"Hey, hang on a minute there, Heinz, are you quite sure about that?" protested Mr Thomas. "Your beliefs the same? Think about that for a minute. Think, for instance, about what Karel Slade would think of you."

"What do you mean?"

"Wake up Heinz!" said Mr Occam giving the throne a rough shake. "Wakey wakey! You're a *copy*, remember? You're an *abomination against God*. That's what Karel Slade thinks, doesn't he? He thinks that even the lab technicians who *make* things like you deserve to be killed. And as for you yourself, well you're just an *object* to him, aren't you? You're just a *thing*."

"That's right isn't it Heinz?" asked Mr Thomas. "In Slade's book you're not even a person. You have no soul and no feelings. You have no rights, not even a right to pity. Think about it. That man we watched in the restaurant earlier on, if he knew what was going on here, would be pretty worried. But he wouldn't be worried about *you*. He wouldn't give a damn about you. Your feelings just wouldn't come into it."

"So if you don't tell us what we need to know," said Mr Occam, "and I have to hurt you, you'll be suffering for another man who cares nothing for you. A man who denies that you are even capable of thinking and feeling."

"But he'd be wrong there wouldn't he?" said Mr Thomas. "You *do* think, don't you Heinz? You *do* feel. Mr Occam and I, we know that and, like I said before, we aren't sadists, whatever you might think. We'd really rather not hurt a living thing who's done nothing wrong at all."

Heinz looked from one to the other of his two interrogators.

Help me God, he began to pray, but then stopped. How could he pray if he was a copy? What was he to God? God belonged to Karel Slade, laughing and joking in the restaurant with his pretty wife, not to this flimsy shadow, summoned out of nothingness by a machine.

"So what will happen to me? When this is done, I mean."

"Well if you stop to think about it, Heinz, I think you'll realise that we're going to have to terminate you," said Mr Thomas gently. "As you pointed out yourself, you can't legally exist. And copies don't last long anyway. A week or two at most. You'll have to go. But it can be peaceful if you want it to be, quiet and peaceful and soon."

"Yeah," said Mr Occam, "and think on this. If you act stubborn and we end up killing you the nasty way, well then we'll just take that blood-clot guy out of the inducer there and start hurting *him*. And if he doesn't play ball, well then we'll take out that cloudy guy – he should be good and solid by then – and start on *him*. And if he plays the hero, well then, we'll get a few more copies going that don't even exist yet, and bring *them* alive just so they can suffer like you. But if you talk, well then they're all on easy street. They can all stay in oblivion for good."

Mr Thomas touched a button on the Inducer and the lid slowly closed.

*

Back in the interrogation room, Heinz told them the codes and the names and the bank details. What were these things to him after all? He was no more responsible for them than a traveller at an airport was responsible for contraband slipped into his luggage when he was looking the other way.

When Heinz was finally done, Mr Thomas went and fetched three cups of coffee from a machine in some other part of the building that Heinz would never see. He brought the three cups in on a little plastic tray, along with some little packets of cookies, and used his remote controller to release Heinz's wrists from the shackles so he could hold his own cup and eat his own cookies. For a short time they all sipped peacefully in companionable, almost dreamy, silence, enjoying the warm surge of caffeine in their blood.

But after a few minutes, with the sigh of a man reluctantly picking up a burden, Mr Thomas placed his half-empty cup on the floor, reached into his jacket and took out an automatic pistol with a long white silencer.

Heinz felt no emotion. Less than twenty-four hours ago, after all, he'd been nothing but inanimate matter. He'd been a simple solution of minerals in a bath. Why fear a bullet that would simply return him to his natural state?

"Hey! He needs to know the truth first," Mr Occam said. "He needs to know the truth before he dies. He should know who he is and the price he's paid."

Mr Thomas sighed. Then, with a regretful grimace, he nodded.

"Listen Heinz," he said gently, lowering the gun. "Mr Occam is quite right. I'm afraid there's one more thing we haven't told you. One thing we haven't been straight with you about. You see, it *is* true that we copied Karel Slade. It really is true. But here's the thing. We lied to you when we said you were the copy."

"What do you mean?"

"He means," said Mr Occam, "that you really *are* Karel Slade. We knocked you out with chloroform in your hotel room and brought you here."

Heinz remembered the hospital smell and the dream of being held down.

"But... That can't be. I mean... what about the restaurant? I mean we saw Karel Slade in the..."

"He was a copy," said Mr Thomas. "Though *he* doesn't know that of course. He believes *he's* the real Karel Slade."

"But..." Heinz – or Karel – struggled to frame a coherent question. "But why swap us round then? Why not just leave me in the hotel?"

"Copies aren't perfect. They always die after a week or two. Sometimes it's a stroke or a heart attack. More often two or three body organs pack up all at once without warning. And copies have a way of just suddenly dying on us if we put too much pressure on them. Doing things this way round avoids that problem. And what's more it gives us a way of eliminating Karel Slade the terrorist without blowing our cover. It'll look as if he died of natural causes."

A small puzzle resolved itself in Karel's mind.

"Yes," he said slowly. "Yes I see. Just like with Leon Schultz."

"Exactly. We copied him too. He told us everything he knew. The rest of you took the copy for the real man and never suspected anything. Your copy will die soon just like his did."

"He might die tonight, of a heart attack, in bed with that lovely wife of yours," said Mr Occam, smiling coldly for the second time since Karel had met him.

"James!" reprimanded Mr Thomas.

Karel looked up. He'd barely been touched by Mr Occam's jibe, but he was rather startled to discover that his tormentor had a first name.

"What's *your* given name?" he asked Mr Thomas.

"Herbert," said Mr Thomas, a little uncomfortably. He quickly formalised things again by prefacing the name with a title. "Agent Herbert Thomas."

Then he caught Karel's eye and glanced down at the gun to remind Karel politely of their unfinished business. Karel nodded.

"Give me one minute," he said. "Just one minute."

"Of course," said Mr Thomas. "You need to sort out who you are again. I understand that. Just let me know when you're ready."

Transferring the gun to his left hand, he reached down for the remains of his cup of coffee.

"Ever had that thing when you wake up in the morning and, just for a moment, you can't think who you are?" he asked Mr Occam. "It's a mystery, this identity thing. I never cease to be amazed how quickly we can persuade a man to part with it. It's just..."

Then he remembered that these were Karel's final moments on Earth and he broke off, placing a finger on his lips with an apologetic glance at his prisoner.

In the silence Karel bent forward in his execution chair and tried to pray.

Dear God forgive me.

But there was no sense of a presence listening to him. *Well, of course not*, he thought. He couldn't really expect just to pick up the mantle of being Karel Slade again and expect to resume business as usual. Not after what he'd done. It didn't work like that.

Dear God forgive me, he tried again. *I just didn't know. I didn't know who I was.*

The Marriage of Sky and Sea

"They say," mused Clancy, looking down on a planet whose entire surface glittered with artificial light, "that Metropolis is the city on which the sun never sets. It's true in a literal sense because the city covers the whole planet. But it's true in another sense too. Sunset never happens in Metropolis because there is *no-one watching*. The city's inhabitants live inside absorbing worlds of their own construction. They have no attention to spare for that rather bare space under the sky which they call, dismissively, the *surface*."

Here he paused.

"Have we finished dictation for now?" enquired Com.

"Wait," said Clancy.

Com waited. Having no limbs, Com had no choice. Its smooth yellow egg-shape fitted comfortably into Clancy's hand.

"I am a writer and a traveller," continued Clancy, reclining on cushions in a small dome-shaped room, its ceiling a hemisphere of stars. "I am a typical Metropolitan soul in many ways, restless, unable to settle, hungry for experience, hungry to feed the gap where love and meaning should be."

He considered.

"No. Delete that last sentence. And I've had a change of heart about our destination. Instruct Sphere to head for the Aristotle Complex. There are several worlds out there which I've been meaning to check out."

Com gave Sphere its instructions in a three-microsecond burst of ultrasound.

"Message received and implemented," said Sphere to Com, in the same high-speed code. "Shall I send standard notification?"

"Did you wish to notify anyone in the city about your new destination?" Com asked Clancy.

"Hmm," said Clancy, with an odd smile, "that's an interesting question. And the answer, interestingly, is no. Take another note, Com, for the book."

He leant back with his hands behind his head.

"Ten thousand kilometres out," he dictated, "I changed my destination so that no one could find me if anything went wrong. I wanted to disappear. I wanted to dispense with the safety net, to get a sense of what it must have been like for those early settlers in the fourth millennium, setting out on their one-way journey into the unknown."

He considered, then shrugged.

"Right Com. At this point add a chapter about the Aristotle Complex. What we know of the early settlers, their motives, their desire to escape from decadence... and so on. Themes: finality, no turning back, taking risks, a complete break with the past."

"Neo romantic style?"

"Neo romantic with a small twist of hard-boiled. Oh and include three poetic sharp edge sentences. Just three. Low adjective count."

"Okay. Shall I read it through to you?" said Com, having composed a chapter of two thousand words without causing a gap in the conversation.

"Not now," said Clancy. "I'm not in the mood. Get me a dinner fixed will you, and something to watch on screen. How long will it be till we reach the Complex?"

"The distance is about five parsecs. It'll take three days."

*

It was not the first voyage of this kind that Clancy had made. This was his career. He travelled alone to the 'lost worlds', he got to know them – their way of life, their myths, their beliefs – and then he returned with a book.

Returning with the book was his particular trademark. The completed book went on sale, in electronic form, at the *exact* same moment that he stepped out of his sphere. It had become a publishing event. He sold a million within an hour and became for a while the city's most talked-about celebrity: the literary spaceman: brave, elegant, utterly alone. He attended all the most fashionable parties. He invariably embarked on a love affair with at least one beautiful and brilliant woman,

And when the love affair grew cold – as it always did, for there was a certain emptiness where his heart should be – and when he sensed that he had reached the end of the city's fickle concentration span, he would go off once more into space.

He had a fear of being trapped, of being tied down, of becoming ordinary.

*

"The first approach to a settled planet," said Clancy, "is a uniquely humbling experience. Here are human beings whose ancestors have gone about their lives without any reference to the universe outside for thirty generations. Invariably, in the absence of the vast pyramid of infrastructure on which modern society rests, their technology has become very basic. Invariably the story of their origins has been compacted into some legend. They have had more practical things to worry about for the last thousand years. My arrival, however it is managed, is inevitably a cultural bombshell. Their lives will never be the same again."

He considered. They had reached the Aristotle Complex an hour ago. Sphere was now using the shortcut of non-Euclidean space to leap from star to star and planet to planet, looking for inhabited worlds, very quickly but mechanically, like Com searching the Metropolitan Encyclopaedia for a single word.

"Some say that for this reason I should not disturb them. This is surely poppycock. On that argument no human being would ever visit another's home, no one would talk to another, let alone take the risk of love. Not that I ever *do* take that risk of course."

He frowned. "Delete that last sentence."

"Deleted. Sphere has found an inhabited planet."

*

A fisher king was fishing in his watery world when the sphere came
through the sky. Standing in the prow of his fine longboat, the tall,
bearded upright king watched a silver ball, like a tiny, immaculate
moon, descending towards his island home. And his household
warriors, sitting at their oars, groaned and muttered, watching the sphere
and then turning to look at him to see what he would do.

Aware of their gaze and never once faltering as he played his
hereditary role, he ordered them in a calm and confident voice to cut
away the nets and row at once for the shore.

*

When Clancy emerged, his sphere perched on its tripod legs on the top
of a tall headland, it was mainly women and children who were standing
round him. Most of the men were out at sea.

He smiled.

"I won't harm you," he said, "I want to be your friend."

The words didn't matter much of course. After all this time these
fisher-people had evolved a completely new language. It was salty as
seaweed, full of the sound of water.

"Iglop!" they said. "Waarsha sleesh!"

Clancy smiled again. They were pleasant looking people, healthy-
looking and well fed. Men and women alike went bare from the waist
up, and wore kilts made of some seal-like skin.

"Sky!" said Clancy pointing upwards.

"Sea!" (he pointed) "Man!"

It took them a while to grasp the game, but then they did so with
gusto, drawing closer to the strange man in his rainbow clothes, and to
his strange silvery globe.

"Eyes," said Clancy. "Nose. Mouth."

"Erlash," they called out. "Memaarsha. Vroom."

Hidden in Clancy's pocket, Com took all this in, comparing every
utterance with its database of the language of the settlers before they set
out a thousand years ago.

Com knew that there are regularities in the way that languages change. Sounds migrate together across the palate like flocks of birds. Meanings shift over the spectrum from particular to general, concrete to abstract, in orderly and measurable ways. Com formed fifty thousand hypotheses a second, tested each one, discarded most, elaborated a few. By the time the fisher king arrived with his warriors and his long robe, Com was already able to have a go at translating.

It was as the king approached that Clancy first became really aware of the massive presence of the moon.

*

"I was on a rocky promontory of the island. Beyond the excited faces, beyond the approaching king, was a glittering blue sea dotted with dozens of other islands. But all this was dwarfed by the immense pink cratered sphere above, filling up a tenth part of the entire sky.

"What is our moon in Metropolis? A faint smudge in the orange gloom above a ventilation shaft? A pale blotch behind the rooftop holograms? We glance up and notice it for a moment, briefly entertained perhaps by the thought that there is a world of sorts outside our own, and then turn our attention back to our more engrossing surroundings.

"But this was truly a celestial sphere, a gigantic ball of rock, hanging above us, dominating the sky. I had known of its size before I landed, of course, but nothing could have prepared me for the sight of it.

"I had yet to experience the titanic ocean tides, the palpable gravity shifts, the daily solar eclipses, but I knew this was a world ruled over by its moon."

Clancy paused and took a sip of red wine, seated comfortably in his impregnable sphere where he had retired, as was his custom, for the night. He had declined an invitation to dine with the King, saying that he would do the feast more justice the following evening. The truth was the first encounter was always extremely tiring and he needed rest. And alien food always played havoc with his digestion the first time round, guaranteeing a sleepless night.

"Com," he said, "prepare me a database of lunar myths."

He considered.

"And one on lunar poetry, and one on references to unusual moons round other inhabited worlds."

"Done. Do you want me to...?"

"No, carry on with dictation."

*

"The King is a genuinely impressive individual. His voice, his posture, his sharp grey eyes, everything about him speaks of his supreme self-assurance. He has absolutely no doubt at all about either his right or his ability to rule. And why should he? As he himself calmly told us, he is the descendant of an ancient union between sky and sea. He greeted me as a long-lost cousin..."

Clancy hesitated. A shadow crossed his mind.

"I pin them out like fucking butterflies!" he exclaimed. "I dissect them and pin them out! Why can't I let anything just *live*?"

Com was sensitive to emotional fluctuations and recognised this one, not from the *inside* of course but from the outside, as a pattern it had observed before.

"The first day is always extremely tiring," Com suggested gently. "In the past we've found that a cortical relaxant, a warm drink and sleep..."

"Yes, whatever we do, let's not face the emptiness," growled Clancy, but he seemed to acquiesce at first, collecting the pill and the drink dispensed by Sphere, and preparing to settle into the bed that unfolded from the floor...

Then "No!" he exclaimed, tossing the pill aside. "If I can't feel anything at least I can fucking think. Come on Com, let's do some work on the theme. Listen, I have an idea..."

*

Lying with two of his concubines in his bed of animal skins, the fisher king was also kept awake by a hectic stream of thoughts. His mind was no less quick than Clancy's but it worked in a very different way. Clancy thought like an acrobat, a tightrope walker, nimbly balancing above the void. But the king moved between large solid chunks of certainty. Annihilation was an external threat to be fought off, not an existential hole inside.

He thought of the power of the strange prince in his sphere. He thought about his own sacred bloodline and the kingdom which sustained it. All his life he had deftly managed threats from other island powers, defeating some in war, making allies of others through exchanges of gifts or slaves, or bonds of marriage. But how to play a visitor who came not from across the sea in the longboat but down from the sky in a kind of silver moon?

He woke one of the concubines. (He was a widower and had never remarried).

"Fetch me my chamberlain. I want to take his advice!"

*

"There are three kinds of knowledge," Clancy said, "let's call them Deep Knowledge, Slow Knowledge and Quick Knowledge. Deep Knowledge is the stuff which has been hardwired into our brains by evolution itself; the stuff we are born with, the stuff that animals have. It changes in the light of experience, like other knowledge, but only over millions of years. Slow Knowledge is the accumulation of traditions and traditional techniques passed down from generation to generation. It too changes, evolving gradually as some traditions fade and others are slowly elaborated. But, at the conscious level, those who transmit Slow Knowledge see themselves not as innovators but as preservers of wisdom from the past. Quick knowledge is the short cut we have latterly acquired in the form of science, a way of speeding up the trial and error process by making it systematic and self-conscious. It is a thousand, a million times quicker than Slow Knowledge, and a billion, billion times speedier than Deep Knowledge. But unlike them it works by objectivity, by stepping *outside* a thing.

"Deep, Slow and Quick: we could equate them to rock and sea and air. Rock doesn't move perceptibly at all. Sea moves but stays within its bounds…"

He laughed, "More wine, Com, this is *good*. Get this: Metropolitans are creatures of air, analytical, empirical, technological; lost worlders are typically creatures of the sea. They all are, but these guys here are literally so. So here's the book title: *The Meeting of Sky and Sea*. See? It ties in with the king's origin myth!'"

"That was a *marriage of sky and sea*," observed Com.

*

Clancy had retired for the night on a headland overlooking a wide bay, with a coastal village of wattle huts squatted near the water's edge. But when he woke in the morning there was no sea in sight. A plain of mud and rocks and pools stretched as far as the horizon and groups of tiny figures could be seen wandering all over it with baskets on their backs. The moon was on the far side of the planet, taking the ocean with it. The sky was open and blue. And when he climbed down the steps of Sphere (watched by a small crowd which had been waiting there since dawn) Clancy found that he was appreciably heavier than he had been the previous day.

Followed closely by the fascinated crowd – made up mainly of children and old people – Clancy went down from the headland to what had been the bay. A group of women were just coming off the mud flats with their baskets laden with shellfish. He smiled at them and started to walk out himself onto the mud.

Behind him came gasps and stifled incredulous laughs.

Clancy stopped.

"Is there a problem?" Clancy had Com ask. (Everyone was diverted for a while by the wondrous talking egg). "Is there some danger that I should be aware of?"

"No, no danger," they answered.

But why then the amazement? Why the laughter? They stared, incredulous.

"Because you are a *man!*" someone burst out at length.

Clancy was momentarily nonplussed, then he gave a little laugh of recognition.

"I've got it Com. Their reaction is *exactly* the one I would get if I headed into the women's toilets in some shopping mall and didn't seem to realise I was doing anything wrong."

He addressed the crowd.

"So men don't go on the mud when the tide is out?"

People laughed more easily now, certain that he was merely teasing them.

"These things are different where I come from," said Clancy. "You're telling me that only women here go out on the mud?"

A very old woman came forward.

"Only women of course. That is a woman's realm. Surely that is obvious?"

"And a man's realm is where?"

The woman was irritated, feeling he was making a fool of her.

"To men belongs the sea under the moon," she snapped, withdrawing back into the crowd.

"Sky and sea, sky and sea," muttered Clancy to Com, "it's coming together nicely."

The book was the thing for him. Reality was simply the raw material.

*

That night the king piled the choicest pieces of meat on Clancy's plate and filled his mug again and again with a thick brew of fermented seaweed. Clancy's stomach groaned in anticipation of a night struggling to unlock the unfamiliar proteins of an alien biological line, but he acted the appreciative guest, telling tales of Metropolis and other worlds, and listening politely as the king's poets sang in praise of their mighty lord, the 'moon-tall whale-slayer, gatherer of islands, favoured son of sky and sea.'

*

As he lay inside Sphere in the early hours, trying to get rest if not actual sleep, Clancy became aware of a new sound coming from outside – a creaking, snapping sound – and he got up to investigate.

He emerged to an astonishing sight. Over at the eastern horizon, the enormous moon was rising over a returning sea. Brilliant turbulent water, luminous with pink moonlight, was sweeping towards him across the vast dark space where the women had yesterday hunted for crabs.

But the creaking, snapping sound was much nearer to hand.

"What *is* that?" Clancy asked.

The king had posted a warrior as guard-of-honour to Clancy's sphere and the man was now sleepily scrambling to his feet.

"What is that sound?" Clancy asked him, holding out Com, his yellow egg.

The sound was so ordinary to the man that he could not immediately understand what it was that Clancy meant. Then he shrugged.

"It's the moon tugging at the rocks."

"Of *course*," exclaimed Clancy, "of course. With a moon that size, even the rocks have tides that can be felt."

He walked to the edge of the headland. He heard another creaking below him and a little stone dislodged itself and rattled down the precipice.

"Lunar erosion," he observed with a smile.

The warrior had come up beside him.

"It tugs at your soul too," he volunteered. "Makes you long for things which you don't even know what they are. No wonder the women stay indoors under the moon. It tugs and tugs at you and if you're not careful, it'll pull your soul right out of you and you'll be another ghost up there in that dead dry place and never again know the sea and the solid land."

Having made this speech, the young man nodded firmly and wandered back to his post at the foot of Clancy's steps.

"Wow," breathed Clancy, "good stuff! Did you record all that?"

Of course Com had.

The moon had nearly cleared the horizon now. It towered above the world. The wattle huts below were bathed in its soft pink light and the water once more filled up the bay.

"Take a note, Com. I said we in Metropolis had forgotten our moon, but actually I think our moon has gobbled us up. After so many centuries of asking for the moon, we have…"

"…we have…?"

"Forget it. I think I'm going to be sick."

*

"I visited a quarry," Clancy dictated, a week into his stay, "a little dry dusty hollow at the island's heart, where half a dozen men were facing and stacking stone. It was the middle of the day but quite dark, due to onc of the innumerable eclipses, so they were working by the light of whale-oil flares. The chief quarryman was a short, leathery fellow in a leather apron, his hands white with rock dust. I asked him why he worked there rather than on the sea like most of the other men. He had some difficulty understanding what I was asking him at first, then shrugged and said his father had worked there, and his grandfather and great-grandfather. It was his family's allotted role. (A *slow knowledge* approach to life, you see, a *sea knowledge* approach. Any Metropolitan would want to demonstrate that his job was chosen by himself.)

"But I realised that my question had left the man with some anxiety about how he was perceived. He stood there, this funny, leathery human mole, and stared intently at my face for a full minute as if there was writing there which he was trying to read.

"'It isn't on the sea,' he said at length, 'but it's real moon work! No women are ever allowed here.'

"And he told me that there were some rocks they only attempted to shift when the moon was overhead. The strain of the tide going through the rock made the strata more brittle. Hit the rock in the right place under the moon and it would suddenly snap. Hit it any other time and it remained stubbornly hard. With some rocks, he said, it was enough to heat the rocks with fire when the moon was up, and they flew apart into blocks. It was real moon work all right.

"So I told him that I had no doubts whatever about his manhood." Clancy paused.

"You know Com, I think we've got nearly enough material already. We just need one more episode, one more *event* to somehow bring the themes alive. Whatever 'alive' is."

He got up, paced around the tiny space of Sphere's leisure room.

"What is the point of all this? Back and forth across empty space, belonging nowhere, an outsider in the lost worlds, an outsider in Metropolis, no one for company but a plastic egg. What are my books anyway but mental wall-paper?"

Com conferred with Sphere by ultrasound, then suggested a glass of wine.

Clancy snorted. "You and Sphere always want to pour chemicals down me, don't you? Come on, back to work. Resume dictation."

*

Next day when the tide was out, Clancy got into conversation with a harpooneer, a sly, sinuous, thin-faced man, with two fingers missing from an encounter with one of the big whale-like creatures which he hunted under every moon.

As with the quarryman, Clancy asked the man why he did the work he did, and received exactly the same answer: his father, grandfather and great-grandfather had done the same. Then Clancy asked him would he not like to have a choice of profession?

When Com translated, the man did not seem to understand.

"I know the word for choice in the context, say, of selecting a fish from a pile," Com explained to Clancy, "But it does not seem to be meaningful to use this word in the context of a person's occupation."

"Okay," said Clancy, "ask him like this. Ask him does he prefer his ale salty or sweet? Ask him whether he prefers whale meat fresh or dried? Ask him does he prefer to fish when the sun is hot or when it is cloudy? Then ask him, how would it be if someone had said to him when he was a child, would he rather be a quarryman, a harpooneer or a fisherman with nets?"

Com tried this. The old man replied to each question until the last. Then he burst out laughing.

*

"They simply have no concept of choosing their own way in life," Clancy recorded later. "They follow the role allotted to them by birth and don't resent it because it has not occurred to any of them that anything else could be a possibility. How would they react if they could come to the city, and see people who have chosen even their own gender, changed their size, their skin, the colour of their eyes?"

He considered.

"There is something idyllic about their position. In some respects they are spared the burden of Free Will. Even marriage partners, I gather, are allocated according to complicated rules to do with clan and status, with no reference whatever to individual choice. I see no evidence that people here are less happy than in our city. In fact a certain kind of *fretfulness*, found everywhere in the city, is totally missing here, even though life is certainly not easy for those allocated the roles of slave, say, or concubine or witch…"

He considered this. Com waited.

"It is this idyll of an ordered, simple life (isn't it?) which the city pays me so well to seek out. Not that anyone wants it for themself. This life would bore any Metropolitan to death in a week. But they like to know it is there, like childhood...

"By the way, one new thing the harpooneer told me. He asked me when I would meet the king's daughters. I told him I didn't know the king *had* daughters and he laughed and said there were three, and no one could agree which was the most beautiful."

*

Clancy dined that evening on the high table in the hall of the king, with all the king's warriors ranged on benches below. In the middle of the room the carcass of an entire whale was being turned on a spit by household slaves. The whole space was full of the great beast's meaty, fatty heat.

"*Wahita wahiteh zloosh,*" chanted the king's poets on and on, "*wamineh weyopla droosh!....*"

Clancy leant towards the king.

"Your majesty, I am told that you have three very beautiful daughters. I hope I will have the pleasure of meeting them."

The effect of this on the king was unexpectedly electrifying. He jolted instantaneously into his most formal mode – and, seeing this, the entire hall full of warriors fell suddenly silent.

"Prince from the sky, I am most honoured that you should ask. They will be made ready at once."

He called to a servant, gave urgent orders and dismissed him with an imperious wave. The warriors began their talking and their shouting once again.

*

"An hour passed," Clancy dictated later, "and then a second. The warriors grew restless, wriggling on their benches like naughty children. The whale carcass, what was left of it, grew cold. The king and I, whose relationship consisted entirely of exchanging information, ran out of things to say to each other, and he eventually gave up all attempt at conversation, sinking into his thoughts, turning a gold ring round and round on his finger, and from time to time jolting himself awake and pressing more sea-weed ale on me.

"I began to wonder whether there had been some mistake. Surely it could not take that long for the princesses to be made ready? Had they been summoned from some other island? Had I perhaps completely misunderstood what was going on? But Com assured me that, yes, the king had said his daughters were being got ready.

"Another hour passed. I endured the king's poets repeating their repertoire for the third time. ('*Wahita wahiteh zloosh / wamineh weyopla droosh!...*' repeated after every one of twenty-three verses!)

"And then a door opened at the end of the dais, all the warriors lumbered to their feet, and the king's three daughters were led in."

At this point in his narration, Clancy asked for wine.

Sphere poured it for him.

"The harpooneer had not lied to me, all three princesses were indeed beautiful and it wasn't hard now to see why they had taken so long. Their hair was plaited, ribboned and piled in elaborate structures on their heads, their bodies, bare to the waist, had been freshly painted in the most intricate designs of entwined sea plants and sea creatures.

"They came round the table and knelt behind my seat, the youngest first, her sisters behind. Then, at a word from the king, the youngest daughter stood up, offered her hand to me briefly and went to stand behind him. The second daughter did the same. And then the third, the oldest…"

Clancy gulped down his wine and went across to the dispenser for more. He was agitated, scared.

"What the hell *is* that feeling?" he demanded. "It's not like lust at all, but you can't call it love, not when you don't know the person. It's like a buried longing for some kind of *sweetness*, which we try to stifle beneath worldliness and weariness and all the busy pointless tasks we lay upon ourselves. And suddenly a person touches it for some reason and it erupts, all focused on that one person, her lovely sad intelligent eyes, her unconscious grace…"

He checked himself.

"What a load of crap! What do I know about her except her face? What is it I want from that face? What can a face give me? What is a face except muscle and skin? Damn it, it means nothing, nothing! It's all just a trick played on us by biology!"

"Are we still doing dictation?" Com politely enquired.

"No of course we aren't, you plastic prat!"

Clancy swallowed the wine in one gulp and shoved the empty cup straight back into the dispenser for more.

"Okay, let's admit it. The oldest daughter, Wayeesha. When I met her eyes it felt as if something passed between us, some recognition, some hope that it might not always be necessary to be so... so terribly alone. It's all crap, of course: she's not much more than half my age, she's been brought up to marry some iron age warlord on some bleak little island. We don't even speak the same language."

He downed the third cup of wine in one, with a little shudder.

"All that we might possibly have in common is some kind of longing to *escape*..."

"Sometimes it helps to talk about what happened," said Com, after a ten-microsecond conference with Sphere. "Perhaps if you finished the story..."

"Oh for God's sake spare me your second-hand wisdom you sanctimonious *rattle!*" exclaimed Clancy.

But in spite of that he sat down again and carried on.

*

"So then when all three women were standing behind the king's chair, he smiled proudly at me and asked me whether or not they were indeed as beautiful as people had told me. Of course I said yes.

"'That's good,' he said, 'and now the choice is entirely yours.'

"I suppose I had been rather naïve, but until that point I hadn't understood that when I asked to see his daughters he had assumed that I wanted one of them for a wife."

Again Clancy jumped to his feet.

"Damn it Com, this is intolerable. One minute I was falling for a woman in a way that seemed scary and new to me, the very next minute I was being offered her hand in marriage. How could *anyone* deal with that? I played for time, of course. I said that in my own world a man sleeps on a decision like that... Delete that whole paragraph. You rewrite it. Leave out the nonsense about my personal feelings. Just describe her as very attractive and tempting. Generic rather than personal. Worldly rather than sentimental. Low adjective count."

"Done. Shall I read it back to you?"

"Later… It's maddening. This is *precisely* the event I needed to bring the book together. The marriage of sky and sea! The space traveller falls in love with the daughter of a fisher king. What could be better! *Damn! Damn!* Why has reality always got to be so awkward."

"Go on." said Com, who was a good listener.

"I mean it might make a good book, but if I marry her I can't just go back to the city with the book, can I? I have to go back with *her*. How would it look if I bring back some kid half my age who doesn't even know how to read or write? I'll look like a dirty old man."

"Don't forget," said Com, who had filed and indexed everything they'd learnt about the local culture, "that here it is the man who moves to live with the woman. Woman are not allowed to cross the sea."

"So I couldn't take her back with me? Yes, that's true. And if a marriage fails here a man returns to his own island doesn't he?"

Clancy sat down, picked up the yellow egg and turned it over in his hands.

"You may look like a kid's rattle, Com, but you have your uses. I could marry her here, and if things didn't work out, which of course they won't after a while, I can take off home. No harm done, a lovely honeymoon, and a nice sad end for the story. Sky and sea try to marry, but in the end they just don't mix. Spaceman has to be free, even at the price of loneliness and alienation. Ocean princess has to be with her people…"

Then he frowned. He was very cold and empty inside, but not wholly without scruples. He was concerned, at any rate, with how his actions might be *seen*.

"But that is just using her, isn't it? I can't do that. My readers wouldn't like it. They don't expect me to be an angel, but they do expect a certain… integrity. Damn."

He thought for a while.

"And anyway she is so beautiful, and so sad. I don't want to…"

A thought occurred to him.

"By the way, I meant to ask you. When she shook my hand she said something, very quietly, so no one else could hear. What was it?"

"*Eesha zhu moosha* – you have my heart. Do you want me to play it back as she said it?"

"*No!*"

Clancy jumped up as if he had been stung. He was shaking with fear.

"Oh alright," he whispered, shrinking back down, as if in anticipation of a blow, "go on, play it back."

When he had heard it, he wept: just two tears, but tears all the same, such as he hadn't shed for years.

"Damn it, Com, I'll do it. In this culture marriage is all *about* using people. It won't do her any harm to have been married to the sky man! I'm going to bloody do it. Do it and be damned for once."

He glared at the yellow egg as if it had questioned his action.

"Don't worry," he said, "I'll make the book come out right somehow."

*

Down in the wattle and daub settlement the fisher king had a lookout post beside his hall. It consisted of two tree-trunks fixed cleverly end to end, with a small crowsnest at the top. He invited Clancy up there on the night before the wedding to watch as the other grooms arrived from across the sea.

Weddings in the sea-world were communal affairs, taking place on a single day just once a year. Bonfires burned all along the beach. Under a huge half-moon that dwarfed the island and made the sea itself seem small, canoes appeared in the distance among the glittering waves, first of all as faint dark smudges and then gradually growing more distinct as they approached the land and the firelight. Each one was cheered as it approached and, as they drew close to the beach, the king's warriors waded out into the sea to greet the new arrivals and help to drag the boats ashore.

Clancy turned to the king and smiled. It was a magnificent spectacle.

The king laughed.

"And now," he said, "the burning of the boats."

He raised his arms and gave a signal to his followers on the beach, who at once set to, dragging the canoes one after another onto the fires. The grooms objected ritually and had to be ritually restrained, but there was a lot of laughter. It was clearly all in fun.

Clancy frowned.

"Why do you do that?"

"When a man marries, his wandering days should end, isn't that so?"

The king winked.

"That moon-boat of yours, it won't burn quite so easily!"

"What do you mean?"

Clancy looked over to the headland where Sphere was perched on its tripod legs. A fire was burning beneath it.

"Hey! What are they doing! Stop them!" he cried out, and then laughed at himself. How could mere fire harm a vessel designed to cope with space?

The king laughed good-naturedly with him, putting a friendly arm round the shoulders of his son-in-law to be.

"Those rocks are easily shattered under the moon," he observed, "and we have fires in the caves below as well."

When he heard Com translate this, it took Clancy a few seconds before he grasped the implications – and in that short time the first boulder had broken loose and crashed down into the sea.

"No!" Clancy shouted. "Make them stop! It's my only way back!"

The king roared with laughter.

"I'm not joking!" cried Clancy, looking around for the rope ladder to get down. "Have the fires put out at once!"

Over on the headland a second boulder crashed down, then a third. And then the sphere itself tipped over, its surfaces glinting in the pink moonlight as it rolled onto its back, its tripod legs sticking up in the air as if it was a stranded sheep. Some more rocks exploded. In agonising slow-motion, or so it seemed, Sphere went over the edge, crashing against the cliff – once... twice... – hitting the sea with a mighty splash, then slowly sinking beneath the waves.

With one foot on the rope ladder, Clancy watched, appalled. And the king, still laughing, his face wet with tears, reached down, helped him kindly back onto the platform and gave him a warm, fishy hug.

"The boats are burnt! So now you can go to Wayeesha."

Clancy walked over to the rough wooden rail at the edge of the platform, looked out at the bonfires, the glittering sea, the giant moon, and remembered Wayeesha waiting for him in the hall below.

As he had trained himself to do in even the most extreme situations, he examined his thoughts. What he found surprised him. He turned to the king with a smile.

"I'm going to regret this. And I fear that you, my friend, are going to be *seriously* disappointed. But right now, it's strange, I feel as if I've put down a burden. I don't think I've ever felt so *free!*"

*

"A good ending for the book!" Com observed.

"What book you idiot?" said Clancy. "Are we going to write it on seaweed, or carve it into the stones?"

Then he proffered the yellow egg to the king.

"Here," he said, "it's yours. I don't need it, and I feel you ought to get *something* from your alliance with the sky. No need to translate that last sentence, Com."

"Is this wise?" asked Com, as the king turned it over reverently in his large hands.

"No," said Clancy. "In a few months your battery will run out and you really *will* just be a plastic egg. Then what will the king think of my gift?"

He went to the rope ladder and began to lower himself, carefully avoiding looking down.

More quality fiction from Elastic Press

The Virtual Menagerie	Andrew Hook	SOLD OUT
Open The Box	Andrew Humphrey	SOLD OUT
Second Contact	Gary Couzens	SOLD OUT
Sleepwalkers	Marion Arnott	SOLD OUT
Milo & I	Antony Mann	SOLD OUT
The Alsiso Project	Edited by Andrew Hook	SOLD OUT
Jung's People	Kay Green	SOLD OUT
The Sound of White Ants	Brian Howell	SOLD OUT
Somnambulists	Allen Ashley	SOLD OUT
Angel Road	Steven Savile	SOLD OUT
Visits to the Flea Circus	Nick Jackson	SOLD OUT
The Elastic Book of Numbers	Edited by Allen Ashley	SOLD OUT
The Life To Come	Tim Lees	SOLD OUT
Trailer Park Fairy Tales	Matt Dinniman	SOLD OUT
The English Soil Society	Tim Nickels	£5.99
The Last Days of Johnny North	David Swann	SOLD OUT
The Ephemera	Neil Williamson	SOLD OUT
Unbecoming	Mike O'Driscoll	£6.99
Photocopies of Heaven	Maurice Suckling	SOLD OUT
Extended Play	Edited by Gary Couzens	£6.99
So Far, So Near	Mat Coward	£5.99
Going Back	Tony Richards	£5.99
That's Entertainment	Robert Neilson	£5.99
The Cusp of Something	Jai Clare	£5.99
Other Voices	Andrew Humphrey	£5.99
Another Santana Morning	Mike Dolan	£5.99
Binding Energy	Daniel Marcus	£5.99
The Last Reef	Gareth L Powell	£5.99
The Turing Test	Chris Beckett	£5.99

All these books are available at your local bookshop or can be ordered direct from the publisher. Indicate the number of copies required and fill in the form below.

Name_____

(Block letters please)

Address_____

Send to Elastic Press, 85 Gertrude Road, Norwich, Norfolk, NR3 4SG.
Please enclose remittance to the value of the cover price plus: £1.50 for the first book plus 50p per copy for each additional book ordered to cover postage and packing. Applicable in the UK only.

While every effort is made to keep prices low, it is sometimes necessary to increase prices at short notice. Elastic Press reserve the right to show on covers and charge new retail prices which may differ from those advertised in the text or elsewhere.

Want to be kept informed? Keep up to date with Elastic Press titles by writing to the above address, or by visiting www.elasticpress.com and adding your email details to our online mailing list.

Previously from Elastic Press

Another Santana Morning by Mike Dolan

This is a book about magic. It is also about love...and other emotions. But mainly it concerns those moments when suddenly we become aware of the magical aspects of the world, when we catch a glimpse of reality's other side, peering through ordinary barriers, past a split in the sky, into somewhere else, where we might find something wondrous.

...fresh and untried and interrogative... – Chaz Brenchley

Previously from Elastic Press

Binding Energy by Daniel Marcus

Marcus maps out possible futures and theoretical pasts, crisscrossing reality with fantasy, and weaving intricate storylines in the process. His characters are frightened and fragile, facing brave new worlds whilst retaining their humanity. If you want to know what the future really looks like, then look here.

This is Science Fiction of the highest level. The stores ring with authenticity. The language is sharp and funny and unflinching. The science crackles – Michael Blumlein, World Fantasy Award finalist

For further information visit:
www.elasticpress.com

Out Now from Elastic Press

The Last Reef by Gareth L Powell

Gareth L Powell's first collection of short stories is stuffed with mind-bending ideas and unforgettable characters. Ranging from the day after tomorrow to the far-flung future, these fifteen stories are perfect for anyone with a craving for intelligent and thought-provoking adventure. From noir-ish cops to disaffected space pilots, blind photographers and low-life hackers, everyone here is struggling to find a little peace amid the tumult of the future.

With an introduction from Interzone co-editor, Jetse De Vries.

Forthcoming from Elastic Press

Subtle Edens edited by Allen Ashley

In this anthology, award-winning editor Allen Ashley has collected 21 brand new Slipstream stories from across the globe from both established and up and coming writers. This is the fiction to thrill, puzzle, excite and disturb. You have nothing to lose but your preconceptions. Featuring stories by: Nina Allan, Neil Ayres, Daniel Bennett, Scott Brendel, Toiya Kristen Finley, Gary Fry, Jeff Gardiner, Ari Goelman, D. W. Green, S. J. Hirons, Joel Lane, Josh McDonald, Mike O'Driscoll, Marion Pitman, Kate Robinson, Ian Shoebridge, David Sutton, Steve Rasnic Tem, Richard Thieme, Douglas Thompson, Andrew Tisbert, and Aliya Whiteley.

For further information visit:
www.elasticpress.com